27/12/22 C1   £2.99

SNEGU

CH00920174

JUDITH HENEGHAN is a writer and editor. She
spent several years in Ukraine and Russia with her young
family in the 1990s and now teaches creative writing at the
University of Winchester. She has four grown up children.

SNEGUROCHKA

JUDITH HENEGHAN

To Madeline
Happy reading,
and good luck with
all your studies!
with lots of love,
Rudy xx

SALT

CROMER

PUBLISHED BY SALT PUBLISHING 2019

2 4 6 8 10 9 7 5 3 1

First published in Great Britain in 2019 by
Salt Publishing Ltd
International House, 24 Holborn Viaduct, London EC1A 2BN United Kingdom

www.saltpublishing.com

Salt Publishing Limited Reg. No. 5293401

A CIP catalogue record for this book is available from the British Library

ISBN 978 1 78463 174 1 (Paperback edition)
ISBN 978 1 78463 175 5 (Electronic edition)

Typeset in Neacademia by Salt Publishing

Salt Publishing Limited is committed to responsible forest management.
This book is made from Forest Stewardship Council™ certified paper.

For Rory, Nellie, Jeremy and Meriel

" 'I am talking about mercy,' Woland explained his words, not taking his fiery eye off Margarita. 'It sometimes creeps, quite unexpectedly and perfidiously, through the narrowest cracks.' "

from *The Master and Margarita*
by MIKHAIL BULGAKOV

SNEGUROCHKA

CHAPTER 1

KIEV, OCTOBER 1992

HIGH UP ON the fourteenth floor, a boy steps onto a balcony. He is twelve, maybe thirteen with slender limbs and shorn hair and he is naked apart from a pair of faded underpants. He scratches the bloom of eczema on his hip as he squints towards the neighbouring apartment block. No one is watching him. The steel hulk of the Motherland monument glints from her hillock across the valley, but she is a statue and her eyes are dead.

The boy moves to a pile of junk in the corner and yanks at a rusting bicycle until it breaks free from the chair leg that is jammed between its spokes. The bicycle's chain has snapped, so he props it against the waist-high wall and hoists himself onto the seat, side-saddle, with one foot on a pedal. Now, perched there with his narrow shoulders hunched forward, one arm hugging the ledge, he waits.

Below him, the air hangs still between the tower blocks and the strand of fractured tarmac that winds down towards the Dnieper. His pale eyes flick across the hazy crenellations of the industrial zone on the horizon. He ignores, to his left, the green and gold canopies of the monastery on the hilltop with those silent, rotting cottages like windfalls at its feet. Instead, lizard-like, he is watching for movement: the cadets playing basketball between crooked hoops on their rectangle of parade ground inside the military academy, the dogs gnawing their rumps in a corner of the car park, and the women spilling out of a tram like spores down on Staronavodnitska Street.

The spores work their way across the waste ground along concrete paths that intersect at sharp angles. Here comes Elena Vasilyevna, the caretaker for Building Number Four. When her dark form disappears between the dump bins far below, the boy shifts on the saddle, leans out and cups his free hand to his mouth. One deep breath, then his jaw juts forward and he makes a sound like a dog's bark from the back of his throat. For a moment the sound splits the emptiness before it drops down the side of the building. The old woman reappears, her face turning in the wrong direction. The boy smiles, pleased at the effect.

Then, just beneath him, he notices something else.

The balcony on the floor below is glazed, unlike his own, and the glazing abuts the base of his balcony, which forms a roof. One of the windows is open and the smell of a cigarette rises up towards him. Freshly lit – a Camel.

The boy stands up on the pedal and leans further over the edge. He can't see in through the glass below because the white sky is reflecting back at him, but a man's left forearm dangles out through the opening, fingers flicking ash.

Someone has moved in.

He studies the man's hand. The skin is pale with golden hairs. His shirt is unbuttoned at the wrist – white cotton with thin blue checks. His watch is analogue with a leather strap, not metal. This man is in his twenties, maybe thirty, western, but probably not German or American. He wears a

2

gold wedding band and when the arm withdraws a stream of smoke is blown out into the stillness.

The man says something, his voice muffled by the interior. Then a baby starts crying. Its mewls are a new sound, yet within seconds they seem to stake a claim on the building, seeping into the walls, travelling up through the concrete, the steel and the spaces in between.

This is the last day of summer. Tonight, the temperature will plummet and people will wake in the morning, sniff the wind and dig out their winter hats. For now, though, the boy remains balanced on the bicycle, a memory of warmth on his skin as the leaves drop silently from the rowans by the tramline, and the air cools, and the Englishman at the window below mutters to himself and lights another cigarette.

The foreign journalists say the city is holding its breath, but for Stepan it is one long exhalation.

❧

Lucas, the golden-haired Englishman, and Rachel, his wife, are standing in the kitchen of their flat in Building Four, Staronavodnitska Street. It is a narrow room with a small table at the far end, in front of the window. The floor is covered in shiny brown linoleum and the walls are papered with a pattern of orange swirls. The laminated chipboard cupboards look new and there's a small freestanding stove in one corner.

Lucas is holding a Geiger counter.

'The batteries *are* charged,' he says, frowning at a leaflet. 'The switch *is* on.' A pause. 'Nothing showing yet.' He waves the device in a circle through the air before pointing it at Rachel. 'So that must be good?'

3

Rachel stops biting the skin around her thumbnail and stares up at the ceiling, which is covered in the same swirling paper as the walls. There's a noise above her head, a faint squeaking sound that travels backwards and forwards from the window to the hallway like the wheels of a hospital gurney.

'Rach?'

Rachel turns her gaze to her husband. 'I thought they gave you some training,' she says.

'The training was for Pripyat and Chernobyl.' Lucas risks a smile. He has already spent five months in Ukraine, his first posting as a radio journalist on a retainer with the BBC World Service. Everyone agrees that it is perfectly safe for foreigners who weren't in the danger zone when the reactor exploded back in 1986. 'Trust me, Rach, I wouldn't have brought you and Ivan out here if there were hotspots in the city.'

Rachel stares at the gap beneath the stove. It is dark there, too dark to see underneath. This is her first day in Kiev. She arrived from London in the morning, frayed after the flight with their fifteen-week-old son. The airport felt hostile: people pressing all around, the threat of disease or some muttered sanction on their breath. The drive from Boryspil in a car with no seatbelts had done nothing to reassure her.

'What about seepage underground? Try pointing it at the tap. The water comes from somewhere else.' She leans across the stainless steel sink and raises the lever. Water gushes, then slows to a brown trickle. There's a clanking sound in the pipework under the counter. Rachel makes a noise through clamped lips and folds her arms beneath her swollen breasts; her eyes are rimmed red with tiredness and Lucas tries not to notice the dark patch that is spreading across her shirt. She's leaking again.

'Hey,' he murmurs, reaching for her hand. 'It'll be okay. I'll get Zoya to go through the instructions. I'll get the caretaker to sort out the taps. Until then we've plenty of bottled water.' He looks down at his wife, at her sad, soft face with its high forehead and crooked nose and gently receding chin and feels, not for the first time, a flutter of panic in his chest. They haven't seen each other for nine weeks because of doctors' appointments and immunisations. Now he wishes she'd tell him what she's really thinking: that she can't bathe their baby in brown water, even if it's not radioactive; that the cot in which little Ivan has finally fallen asleep won't pass any British standards of safety; that an amber-coloured cockroach scooted under the bath when she went for a wee; that the flat is on the thirteenth floor and he shouldn't leave her to go out with his journalist friends tonight so that he can catch up on what he's missed while he's been fetching her from the airport. Perhaps nine weeks was too long. Or not long enough. She's only been in Kiev for six hours and she's shutting down already. The thought makes him flap at the net curtains above the windowsill until he finds his cigarettes.

'Come out on to the balcony with me,' he says. 'You've not seen the view yet. Come out.'

Rachel remembers staring up at the block of flats when Zoya, Lucas's fixer, had driven them here earlier. The grey concrete balconies looked like something she'd once made for a school project, with matchboxes that fell off as soon as the glue dried.

'I need to change my shirt,' she mutters, pulling away.

Then the doorbell rings.

5

Once upon a time, Rachel told Lucas a story. She was a little drunk, a little careless and she told this handsome, suntanned student who looked like a famous cricketer or a polo player or maybe the Marlboro Man with his long limbs and blue sleep-with-me eyes that when she was eight, she thought she was having a baby.

Lucas tried to sit up, though the beanbag he was sprawled across made this difficult.

'What happened?' he asked, tipping sideways until he could fix the girl with the wonky nose and the large, slightly bulging eyes and the nice arse in his sights.

'Oh,' she said, surprising herself as the words came skipping out. 'I was in love with a boy at my primary school. His name was Charles. But my dad was an engineer and we moved to Swansea for a year for his job. So I had this old box of After Eights – you know, the chocolates with the little waxy envelopes? Well the chocolates were all gone, so I wrote 'I love Charles' on little bits of paper and folded them up and tucked them inside the envelopes. Then I took the box to Swansea and hid the notes all around our new house.'

Lucas held his wine glass up to his face and peered at her through its smeary double lens. 'Funny girl,' he said, wanting to touch her, but she hadn't finished.

'My bedroom was at the end the corridor, away from my parents. I used to lie in bed at night, listening to my stomach gurgling. And I knew that if you loved someone, you had a baby. So I thought I had a baby in my tummy.' She paused, her mind re-focusing on the soft green light she'd made when she closed her bedroom curtains and the silence she'd made when she held in her breath. 'I couldn't tell anyone, of course, because eight-year-old girls who weren't married weren't supposed to have babies, so I made a cot for it out of a shoe box and kept it under the sink. I thought it would come out of my belly button.'

'Oh deary me,' said Lucas, who hadn't expected to find her quite so entertaining. He leaned across and kissed her. The wine glass toppled over, spilling its dregs into the beanbag. Rachel felt a wet patch under her hip but it didn't matter; these things often happened at parties.

⁂

The doorbell keeps ringing and ringing.

Lucas is still fiddling with the locks at the far end of the hallway when Rachel emerges from the bedroom, yanking a clean top down over her bra.

'Quick!' she pleads. 'Before they wake Ivan!'

At last the bolt shoots back and the lever drops, but as Lucas pulls open the front door Rachel sways. She puts her hand against the wall as if it is the tower block that has shifted. Or maybe she's a little feverish.

'Oh, and here you both are!' says a woman's voice, in an accent that might be Canadian. Rachel sees two figures moving forward from the gloom of the landing. Lucas has mentioned his friends often: Vee, the Harvard-educated stringer for a Toronto daily who learned Ukrainian from her grandparents, and Teddy, the photographer from Michigan. Lucas hangs out with them a lot, he's told her. They have fun together. Now Rachel can, too.

Lucas moves aside and Vee steps in across the threshold.

She is tall, slender, with dark hair cropped short, red lip-stick, mannish glasses and a face more striking than beautiful. Rachel tries not to stare.

'Where's the baby, Lucas? Where's little Ivan? He's not sleeping, is he?' Vee pouts, clownishly. 'Dammit, I just *knew* he'd be sleeping . . .'

'Hey,' says Lucas. 'Rachel, this is Vee. And Teddy.'

'Hello – lovely to meet you.' Rachel tries to shake Vee's hand.

'Oh, I want a kiss!' says Vee, pushing her glasses to the top of her head and pulling Rachel towards her. 'Teddy wants one, too! I told him your witchy-faced caretaker downstairs needed a cuddle but he's too-too shy, aren't you, sweetie?'

This is clearly a joke, for Teddy isn't shy at all. He makes a great show of embracing Rachel, arms pretend-flapping like a penguin. When he stands back he's smiling, his brown eyes set close together, one hand rubbing the dark stubble on his jaw. He is wearing a faded Lou Reed t-shirt under a sheepskin jacket. Vee, too, has an air of not trying too hard and Rachel is aware of her own slack-waisted skirt, the hint of something sour-smelling on her shoulder, the thick, lumpy breastpad she's slipped inside her bra. Her vision blurs a little. Perhaps the tower block is swaying after all.

Vee is still talking. 'We've been desperate to get you out here!' she says, walking into the living room with its shiny parquet flooring and textured wallpaper that makes Rachel think of elbow skin. Pale October light filters through the net-curtained window and the glass door that leads out on to the balcony. 'We're sick of Lucas moping around, waiting for you to arrive. Jesus, this flat is amazing! It's so empty! Where's all the crap you had in that other place, Lu? Hey, a three-piece

8

suite! That couch must be hiding the cocktail bar . . .'

'Drinks!' says Lucas, ducking down the hallway to the narrow kitchen wedged in the corner between the living room and the bedroom. He raises his voice so that they can still hear him. 'It's more than we can afford, but I promised Rachel we'd have a bit of space, and Ivan will be crawling before we know it. My old flat was a death-trap.' He reappears, grinning and eager with three beers in one hand and a bottle opener poking out of his shirt pocket. Then he remembers what has changed. 'Hang on, there are four of us!'

'Not for me,' says Rachel, with a shake of her head.

Lucas slides an arm around her waist and gives her a squeeze. 'My beloved wife also demanded a lift. And a washing machine!'

'Well then,' declares Vee. 'That's it. You'll never see the back of me! I'll be camping out in the foyer with my bundles of dirty laundry . . .'

'We haven't got one yet.' Rachel's voice is flatter than she intends; her veneer of sociability is tissue-thin. 'I'll rinse things in the bath.'

Vee raises one of her finely arched eyebrows. 'That won't be easy – with a baby,' she says. 'Hey, you must let us see him – I bet he's adorable. Is he talking yet?'

'Are you kidding?' laughs Lucas, handing round the opened bottles. 'He's only three months old! Feeds, sleeps and leaks from every orifice. Now you *really* need to see this view . . .' He sweeps aside the net curtain, revealing the balcony beyond. For a moment, a shadow drifts downwards across Rachel's vision like a dust particle trapped on her cornea – tiny limbs, curling fingers, a floppy neck. She wants to shake her own head, erase the image of the falling child before it can take hold, but Vee's eyes are upon her, the tip of her tongue just visible through her teeth. Rachel extricates herself from Lucas's arm and sits down on the sofa.

'Oh – my – God!' exclaims Vee. She steps through the glass door with Teddy. 'The river, the monastery, that crazy Statue of Liberty looky-likey . . . Poor old maiden aunty Baba, they call her, Brezhnev's dildo, waving her sword for the Motherland. Always looks like surrender to me. I filed a colour piece for *The Economist* when I arrived. Assholes didn't run it.'

'They didn't have the right image,' remarks Teddy, his voice low, the base notes to Vee's contralto. 'Now, up here, at dawn, long exposure, the smog a little blue in the background . . .'

Lucas follows them out onto the balcony. 'Rachel used to be a picture researcher. Travel books, that kind of thing.'

'Is that right?' says Teddy, turning and smiling through the doorway. 'Who for?'

Rachel tries to relax. She smiles back. 'Gallon Press. Near the British Museum. No one's ever heard of it.'

'They use authors' own pics, mainly,' says Lucas. 'Tightwads. It's the same problem at the BBC. My lousy World Service retainer nails me to Bush House for all of three hundred pounds a month. I'm sick of peddling short bulletins that get knocked off the schedule by an old fart on the night desk. I need a story I can sink my teeth into – get a couple of solid half-hour features under my belt, something for Radio Four or a piece in the Sundays.' He takes a swig of his beer, then leans out through the open window and peers down so that Rachel can't see his head. 'Smells like burning plastic down there,' he declares, pulling his shoulders back inside and turning round to face Vee and Teddy. 'So, what are you two working on now?'

This, Rachel knows, is not the right question. Her husband seems jumpy, vulnerable in front of his Kiev friends. Here they are, Rachel and Lucas, saying things, stabbing at things, both, in different ways, out of their depth.

Vee, on the other hand, gives nothing away. 'Oh, you know,' she says, twisting the silver necklace she wears. 'Rule by decree. The World Bank's latest doom-mongerings. Those so-called re-formers whining about whether foreign films should be dubbed in Russian or Ukrainian – all talk and no action while the grandmas protest outside St Sophia's and war vets starve along the boulevards. There's a press conference tomorrow. They're printing bigger denominations.' She reaches into her handbag and pulls out a pack of Marlboro Lights. 'One hundred *kouponi*, these cost me – and they're counterfeit. See? The foil's too smooth. Now that's a story that won't end well for some hapless new kid who tries to follow the money.' She flips the lid with a glossy fingernail and holds the pack out to Lucas. He hesitates, until she turns and looks back apologetically at Rachel. 'Sorry. God, that's stupid of me. No smoking around the baby!'

'Don't worry about it,' says Lucas, quick with his lighter. 'It's fine out here. If we shut the door.' And Rachel sees now why he chose the flat with the glazed balcony where he and his fellow journalists can puff away all winter, guilt-free, even though he promised to give up when Ivan was born. This is his city, his job. These are his friends. Anyway, there are some things that only she knows. Ivan is stirring in his cot in the bedroom and immediately her breasts start to tingle as the let-down reflex floods the vessels behind her nipples. If she doesn't go quickly, the pads will leak.

Lucas twitches briefly as Ivan breaks into his high-pitched cry, though she's already on her feet.

'Can we see him? Will you bring him in here?' calls Vee.

'Sounds like an appetite!' adds Teddy.

'I have to feed him in the bedroom,' murmurs Rachel as she slips down the hall.

'We don't mind – truly!'

But Rachel is already closing the bedroom door.

⚜

Ivan's face is turned inside out. His eyes are squeezed shut and his mouth is a red cave with its glistening, quivering uvula and hard ridges of gum. When Rachel lifts him away from the urine-soaked cot sheet he stops crying, but his lips are searching and she must be quick. She sits on the bed with her back against the flimsy headboard and her fingers rummage for the clip on her bra. As soon as she peels off the sodden, sticky pad, milk spurts forward and hits Ivan's cheek. She hesitates only for a second, then bites down on her lip and brings his head towards her.

When Ivan clamps on, she catches her breath and resists the urge to scream. The cracks in her skin re-open and she can see by the dribbles at Ivan's mouth that the milk is blushed with blood. It's the pink of her mother's gelatinous salmon mousse that always made her want to gag. She closes her eyes, her head bent low over the baby as if this might ease the dragging, the burning. And it does ease, after a few minutes, as the pressure lessens and Ivan's saliva softens the fissures and the scabs.

Ivan is a big feeder and will drain her to the last drop.

When his sucking flattens out into a more contented rhythm she brings her knees up to cradle him and leans her head back once more. Milk from her other breast has pooled across her stomach. She doesn't wipe it away because she doesn't care, in here, in this private space. Besides, every second is precious now, when the pain is fading and she knows she has two or three hours before she must endure it again. Her own breathing settles. The voices outside are forgotten. Time to sleep, the midwife would say in her sensible, seen-it-all tone. This same midwife told her to put Ivan on the bottle; that she needed to heal before she took her baby to a place with no emergency numbers, no guarantee of antibiotics. But formula milk means using sodium-rich mineral water that might poison her child, or that brown stuff from the tap in the kitchen.

No, the midwife hadn't understood. Rachel is staying awake. She needs to do the inventory.

She starts with the bed. It is two singles pushed together; chipboard covered with a yellowish-brown veneer like every other piece of furniture in the flat. The mattress is hard and uneven. The blankets are heavy, boil-washed. Behind the bed, a large rug hangs on the wall. Not a traditional piece from Kazakhstan or the Caucasus but a factory-made brown rug with pink and red flowers. Opposite stands a wardrobe with her few clothes hanging neatly, not touching, where she placed them just two hours before. Lucas's shirts hang beside them, with underwear hidden in a drawer. Ivan's vests and babygros are folded on a shelf.

Now she turns her head to the two small bedside cabinets. The one nearest Rachel contains her evening primrose cream and her breast pads and contraceptive pills, neatly spaced on the shelf. On top sit two books: her copy of *Baby's First Year* full of words such as 'weaning', and a novel, *Jurassic Park*, which she found on the plane. She isn't in the habit of picking up other people's things, yet no one else seemed to want it. She will read ten pages a day, she's decided. This will take five and a half weeks. The calculation helps her relax.

Her eyes shift to the floor. The bedroom, the hallway and the living room are all coated in the same thick, uneven layer of varnish that reminds her of peanut brittle. Lucas says the landlord had it done so that he could raise the rent. The residue clogs up the gaps beneath the skirting.

The floor brings to mind things she cannot see. Under the bed is a pull-out drawer. If she leans over she can reach it, though you always save the best to last if you know what's good for you so she focuses instead on the large window. This window doesn't bother her, despite the fact that the glass is smeared, veiled with a sagging net curtain. There's no balcony on this side of the flat.

Rachel looks down, still bewildered by the sight of her white arms cradling her son with the small brown spot above his right ear that will one day be a mole, his eyelashes like tiny scratches and his pink, almost translucent nostrils. Earlier, in the living room, she had glimpsed Ivan falling. Such visions, she knows, must be dismissed with a sharp shake of her head before they can fix themselves like premonitions, like memories, but Vee had been watching her, so she hadn't moved. It's a long way down from the thirteenth floor. Five seconds, she thinks. Maybe six. As the calculation freefalls, the impulse to lean over the side of the bed is something she can no longer ignore.

Without detaching Ivan she stretches out her arm and gropes under the bed for the drawer. Out it slides, smooth on its castors and she is ready to weep with relief. The nappies sit exactly as she placed them: one hundred and twenty-six Pampers in twelve neat piles; four full packs she lugged over from England. Lucas has bought lots of cheap nappies, rigid and scratchy, imported from Latvia or Poland but they're not as white or as soft or as absorbent and their tapes don't stick and she suspects that, even now, a seepage of Ivan's runny yellow faeces is flowering up his back. She'll eke out the Pampers as she'll eke out her reading: one nappy per night. Lucas won't be allowed near them. He can change Ivan with the cheap ones.

From the hallway beyond the door she hears footsteps. With a swift tap she rolls the drawer back under the bed, then wipes the sticky milk from her stomach and pulls her shirt across her chest. A soft knock, and Lucas's face appears.

'Asleep?' he mouths. Rachel nods. Her husband slides into the room, closing the door behind him with exaggerated care. He is holding something in his hand. Dark green, rectangular, covered in shiny cellophane: a box of After Eights.

'Vee brought them,' he whispers, balancing the box on top of *Jurassic Park*. 'For you. Can they come in and have a look?'

Rachel eyes the chocolates with suspicion.

'You didn't tell them, did you?'

'Tell them what?' asks Lucas, staring her down, not blinking in the way he always does when he's guilty. Of course he's told them. He's always telling people how when she was eight she tucked love notes inside the little waxed envelopes and hid them all around her parents' house in Swansea before convincing herself that she was having a baby. He thinks it is funny, and charming; at their wedding reception he turned it into his story, the story of how he knew she was the one he wanted to marry. 'Christ, Rach! What's your problem? It's just a box of chocolates! People want to meet you, they want to get to know you!' He sighs, walks over to the window. 'Look, I know you've had a tough time – you're exhausted. But what else should I say? Just tell me what you want me to say.'

Rachel stares at Lucas's back, and strokes the plaster on Ivan's thigh that covers the site of the immunisations he had at the clinic near Clapham Junction only two days before. In those weeks alone after the birth, the fact of her husband had wavered. She would wake in the night when her son moved or murmured, unable to remember how she had arrived in that empty bed in the ground-floor flat with the trains rumbling and the wild, abandoned whoops of the sirens.

'You're still going out then?' she asks, removing Ivan from her breast with a scoop of her little finger. In her head the question seemed conciliatory, disinterested, but these aren't the sounds that come out of her mouth.

'Yes, I'm still going out. You could come too, bring Ivan – Zoya could give us a lift in the car. No one would mind.'

'Or you could stay in. I've only just arrived.'

'This is my job, Rach,' says Lucas, quietly. 'This is why we're here.'

'Right,' mutters Rachel. She doesn't look up until he's gone.

⚜

Once upon a time, Rachel and Lucas told each other a story.

'We are going to live in garret,' said Rachel, as the wind outside the tent whipped across the guy ropes and pummelled

16

the flysheet. 'In a crumbly old building with mice scratching in the eaves. I will make soup and sing at the window.'

'And I will pull on my felt boots and go out to bring the news to the people and come home with black bread and bacon. It will be hard,' said Lucas.

'We will be cold,' agreed Rachel, 'but I'll learn to knit. And we'll have a stove that I'll feed with kindling—'

'Kindling!' Lucas roared with laughter and pulled the sleeping bag up closer over their heads. 'What sort of a word is kindling?'

'Well,' said Rachel, undeterred. 'It's a fairytale word. It goes with woodcutters and forests and witches.'

'So I'm the woodcutter, hmm?' Lucas put his hand up her fleece. 'In that case, Princess Snow White, I happen to know you're nothing but a peasant underneath that prim exterior . . . a grubby little Cossack!'

'Oh yes,' said Rachel, as he rolled her over. 'A Cossack. That's *exactly* what I am.'

⁂

Rachel wakes a little after three a.m. and listens to the click as the front door closes. She doesn't move. Ivan is asleep in his new cot at the end of the bed; it took her two hours to settle him after his midnight feed. By the time her husband slides between the clingy nylon sheets her body is rigid with tension.

'Are you awake?' whispers Lucas. His hand brushes her shoulder. A nick of his dry skin catches on her t-shirt. 'Rach?'

Rachel says nothing, her thoughts pinning her down. If she responds, he'll want to have sex. They haven't made love properly since Ivan was born. She was too sore from the stitches, too tired. Then he flew back to Kiev. Anyway, sex might wake Ivan. This is what she tells herself. This is the story she'll tell him.

Lucas, however, is drunk and alcohol makes him persistent.

'You're all warm,' he murmurs, nuzzling his chin against her cheek, moving his hand down her breastbone towards her stretchmarked belly. At this she flinches, turns away from him, fingernails digging into her palms.

'I love you, Rach. I've missed you.' His moist lips wheedle. Soft words. She's got to decide. Her body is recoiling, yet her mind still toys with a different version of herself – a hazy, generous version, intent on pleasure, spreading her legs. Let go, Rachel. She knows it shouldn't feel like being someone else, turning around, unbending, letting his fingers circle her breasts. Maybe she can do this; it's what couples do and they are a couple. Outside, dogs are barking. It's only natural – don't overthink it. Or think yourself into it.

As Lucas pushes on she shuts her eyes and tries to relax, tries to block out the squeaking noise she hears, not from their bed but wheeling somewhere up above their heads. It's the same noise she heard earlier, in the kitchen. Back and forth it rolls. Up and down. Round and round and round.

CHAPTER 2

LUCAS AND RACHEL were supposed to conquer Eastern Europe. So said the best man at their New Forest wedding, the messages in the leaving cards from colleagues and the friends they'd accumulated along the way. Lucas's mother, a twice-divorced Reader in Renaissance studies at a northern university, teased her youngest son about his pale-faced bride who couldn't possibly imagine what she was getting herself into. Rachel's mother, on the other hand, accepted Lucas as a *fait accompli*, seemingly relieved that her secretive daughter with her silent, strangled rebellions was now off her hands.

Lucas, went the story, was a golden-haired adventurer in pursuit of the exotic, the Slavic, the surreal. Rachel, the soft-chinned picture researcher, was swept up in his wake. She wasn't a Romanian spymaster's daughter or a dissident-cum-catwalk model or an almond-eyed soloist from the St Petersburg conservatoire, though this was never discussed openly among the junior sub-editors and fledgling lawyers with whom the couple mingled back in London. She liked Cornwall, and expeditions to the National Portrait Gallery, and drinking frothy coffee in cafés along Northcote Road. No one considered that she might long for somewhere else. Running away was what her father had done, and he was a feckless deceitful bastard in anyone's eyes; most especially, Rachel's mother's.

Then one night, a little drunk, Rachel tried to catch a

pigeon in Old Compton Street, scooting along with her hands sweeping forward, swearing she'd pluck it and bake it in a pie. Lucas, who felt he was on the cusp of something and might otherwise, at some not-too-distant moment, have ditched her, made a mental note, along with the After Eights story and the Cossack in the sleeping bag and other minor adventures he'd committed to memory. He confessed to his debts, raised a glass to the future and eleven months later, they were married. When he told everyone his new wife was pregnant, eyebrows were raised, but not for long. She'd never made much of an impression.

Now, Rachel has a fever. She doesn't leave the apartment for a week – a week in which every day stretches out, each minute an hour. Instead she shuffles up and down the echoing hallway, waiting for the unfamiliar antibiotics that Vee has sent over to ease the infection in her milk ducts. When Ivan is feeding she lets out a little scream, because if she clamps her mouth shut she might bite off her tongue. When he is sleeping she bends over the yellowing bath to scrub the faeces off his clothes so that her breasts hang down, burning and engorged. Then when the chores are done, she lies on her back and reads *Jurassic Park* slowly, ten pages a day, measuring each word from the first deadly mauling to the infants bitten by strange lizards as she sucks on the wafer-thin chocolates by her bed. Luckily it is an extra-large box, the sort they sell in the airport Duty Free to shell-suited mafia men or liquor reps or the new apparatchiks or maybe foreign journalists with sick wives holed up in the flat on the thirteenth floor.

Lucas doesn't know how to help her, so he closes the front door behind him and strides about the city, looking for ways to make money, ways to make his name or career, anything to convince himself he's made the right decision and settle the panic in his chest. Radio bulletin after radio bulletin is filed down the wires, grey as President Kravchuk and just as unremarked-upon. The revolutions are over and in London there's no interest in the government sackings, the strikes and the price rises, the endless press conferences with their blank officialise and incomprehensible squabbles. Editors want colour, Lucas reckons, a nation's quirks and curiosities served up in ninety-second sound-bites, so he walks down blind alleys and files short fillers about girls in bright headscarves selling jars of *smetana* outside the monastery or the men in blue overalls who move along the boulevards stripping leaves off the trees. He'll have to be quick: autumn is a day's work in Kiev. Along the wide streets and beneath the market archways, women queue to buy bags of buckwheat flour. They lug them up dark stairwells and mix the flour with water to make a thick grey paste. Newspaper is stuffed into window frames then daubed with the paste, which dries into a tight, brittle seal. The city is sucking itself inwards.

Elena Vasilyevna, caretaker of Building Four on Staronavodnitska Street, awakes from her nap and watches to see if the foreign woman on the thirteenth floor will know what to do. She doesn't hold her breath, for the woman doesn't show herself for a week; she certainly doesn't go shopping for the right kind of flour. Instead, when she finally emerges from the lift with her fat little baby in that flimsy foreign buggy, off they dawdle past the kiosks on Kutuzova Street as if there's no such thing as winter. The baby isn't dressed properly and shouldn't be outside. Elena has tried telling her, but the woman just pulls an ugly face and leaves the lobby door wide open. The buggy makes marks on the floor.

Really, someone needs to put her straight and it's not going to be that lanky husband of hers. He carries a rucksack, for crying out loud. Elena knew a journalist once. He wore a blue serge jacket and a black leather cap. The cap made him look serious – someone who meant business. When they hanged him from the second-floor window of the post office it had fallen to the pavement like a fat drop of ink. No one dared touch it for a week.

❧

There are birds in the roof of the *universam*. Starlings or house martins, or maybe some middle-European species Rachel cannot identify. They don't chatter, though their sudden wing-beats startle her as she stands in the cavernous state-owned store less than half a mile from Staronavodnitska Street. She's not sure what's for sale at the counter, but a small crowd is milling and someone is pushing behind her and if she circles round to take a look she will lose her place. Some recent advice from Vee still echoes in her head. New deliveries don't stick around for long; never ignore a queue of more than five people.

It took her ages to find the shop or market or whatever she is supposed to call it. The antibiotics have muddled her. She felt the same when she left the hospital with Ivan. Everything beyond its shiny mint-green corridors seemed unfamiliar and unreal. This is a hairbrush, she would tell herself. This is a kettle. This is your front door and this is your newborn son.

The *universam* is a circular concrete bunker. Hexagonal grey and blue tiles tessellate its mushroom-shaped roof and rotting leaves pile up in its gutters. It squats in the middle of a courtyard off Kutuzova Street, half hidden by the surrounding horse chestnuts and bourgeois-era apartments with their iron balconies and the scrambling vines that characterise this part of the city. Inside, most of the shelves are bare. Rachel can see only a row of zinc watering cans and, further along, several pyramids of purplish sausage. Despite the lack of merchandise, women in nylon shop coats are leaning against the counters that surround the central foyer. Two of them bring out buckets and start to mop the floor. It must be quite a job, coping with all the bird droppings. The mopped area spreads like a stain.

Rachel squints at a one-word sign high up on the wall in front of her. The letters are orange, rounded. She sounds out the Cyrillic characters to herself – *dee-ay-tee* – and lessens her grip on Ivan's buggy handles as she realises this is a word she knows: 'children'. Perhaps they'll have some baby wipes. She has been using loo roll dampened with water since her two boxes of Johnson's ran out. It is making Ivan's bottom sore.

The man in front of Rachel is blocking her view. He is wearing a cheaply-finished blouson jacket and stiff, stone-washed jeans. His neck is red, almost raw, and dandruff speckles his shoulders. When he raises a hand to smooth his thinning hair she pulls Ivan's buggy back to avoid any falling flakes. Ivan kicks out his stubby little legs and waves an arm. He's cranking himself up for something. No one is talking. The air tastes fusty, as if spores of mould have settled on Rachel's tongue. The *universam* isn't a dollar shop, she reminds herself. Its empty symmetry and its silence leach the vapours of a stagnant collective past.

The queue is moving slowly; someone nudges her from behind. She looks over her shoulder and sees a young woman with blue eyeshadow and dyed black hair. The woman is about the same age as Rachel. She is licking a slab of white ice cream wrapped in a piece of paper.

'*Eezveneetyie*,' ventures Rachel. Excuse me. Her voice sounds louder than she intends and the words aren't the right ones; she remembers only a handful of phrases from the Russian classes she struggled to attend before Ivan was born. The woman, however, sees the buggy and leans around Rachel, offering her ice cream to Ivan.

'*Nyet!*' exclaims Rachel, putting a hand in front of his mouth. The woman straightens up and frowns as Ivan's arms reach out and he starts to whimper. The man with the dandruff turns round and finally the counter is revealed and Rachel can see that the items for sale are not baby wipes but plastic push-along toys, crudely moulded with gurning Donald Duck faces.

As she stares, the aproned clerk behind the counter sucks in her cheeks and waves her forward. It is Rachel's turn, apparently, despite the other queuers milling. She takes out her purse.

'*Skolko?*' How much?

Already she knows this is the wrong question. There's no till here, no cashbox. Where does she pay?

The clerk has no time for idiots. She rolls her eyes and beckons to the young woman behind Rachel to take her place. Only the man with the dandruff takes pity on her. He turns his head and says something to the clerk, who reaches for a pad of thin grey paper and a pen attached to the counter by a piece of string and scribbles down two words. She tears off the slip of paper and pushes it towards the man, who hands it to Rachel.

'*Spaseebo*,' she murmurs – thank you – still not sure what

24

to do next. The man nods gravely and points towards a counter a few yards away near the door. The sign above says *Kassa* – cash desk. She must take the chit and pay at the desk and return with a receipt for the goods. That's what everyone else has been doing.

Ten minutes later, Rachel emerges from the *universam* with a Donald Duck push-along toy dangling awkwardly from the handles of the buggy. She feels conspicuous, outlandish even, yet no one else seems to notice as she walks back to the apartment block. She passes an expensive-looking silver car in the car park, but its windows are tinted and she can't see if anyone is inside.

The old caretaker is absent from the foyer.

Lucas is in the kitchen when she struggles through the front door. 'Your first purchase!' he says, sticking his head into the hallway. 'Impressive! Shopping like a local! Tomorrow you should walk up through Tsarskoye Selo – the Tsar's Village. Visit the monastery. You'll love it.'

Rachel opens the cupboard next to the bathroom and pushes the toy inside. 'What do you mean, the Tsar's Village?'

Lucas shrugs. 'That's what the cottages on the hill are called. Zoya says they were built for Communist Party appa-ratchiks – a taste of suburbia for local flunkies of one sort or another. Most of them are wrecks now, mind you.'

Indeed, the houses of the Tsar's Village are wrecks. Rachel squints at them from the kitchen window. They cling to the slopes that lead up to the thick walls and golden domes of the monastery, little more than wooden shacks, one room upstairs and one room downstairs, a bit of land, broken fences, stray dogs and rusting dump bins. She wanders up there with Ivan the next afternoon, searching for shops as she maps out the neighbourhood. There's the *universam*, of course, echoing and empty apart from today's meagre display of household cleaning items such as wire wool and mops and bags of indeterminate powder that might be detergent or flour. There's the dollar store, called the *kashtan*, with its jars of out-dated baby food and packets of thick tan tights. Shiny loaves of white bread are baked and sold from a hole in the wall near the *universam*, or perhaps it is a part of the *universam* – Rachel isn't sure. Then there are the concrete kiosks where she can buy dusty yellow packets of Liptons tea, Tampax, stretchy hairbands and sugary drinks from someone with a midriff but no face; the darkened windows are always at the waist height of the vendors inside. Finally she stops by the old women squatting outside the peeling green doors of the monastery. Their wares are laid out on cloth squares: a trio of wrinkled lemons, a string of onions or pickled cucumbers floating in a jar like grey turds.

Rachel practises her Russian: *two, ten thousand, twenty thousand, how much, thank you.* The old women don't look up. They just stare at her shoes.

Elena Vasilyevna hobbles along Lavrska Street beneath the high white wall of the monastery. Her bowed legs ache; hoeing is easier than walking, but today is an anniversary so she must be here. She doesn't look over her shoulder, even though that boy from the fourteenth floor, Stepan, has been following her all the way from Staronavodnitska Street. He is up to something. She's seen him leaning in through the window of a fancy car parked outside the flats. Last week she found several handfuls of burning hair smouldering and stinking in the wastepaper bin in her cubicle.

He needs an occupation, she thinks. Like most boys.

As Elena passes the frescoed Gate Church of the Trinity, she glimpses the young Englishwoman, head uncovered, her baby on her hip. She is trying to drag that buggy of hers through the narrow wooden doorway. Well, if the gatekeepers don't send her packing then the pilgrims certainly will. They kneel and scrape as if the old faith has never stopped flowing through their dried-up veins. Elena sucks her teeth and spits. She has no interest in trinities or holy mothers. She won't cross herself when she passes, she won't mutter a prayer. Her faith fell out of her like a stillborn infant when she was barely grown.

This is Lavrska Street, where assassins creep.

She walks on.

❧

Lucas is out on the balcony. He is fixing his map of Ukraine to the side wall with pieces of chewed gum. It is taking him a long time to secure it; the gum won't stick to the tiles.

'Rach!' he calls. 'Rach!'

Rachel is sitting on the floor in the kitchen. She is giving her son his first taste of solids. Ivan is semi-upright in his bouncy chair in front of her, a bib under his chin and a panicky look in his eyes. Rachel is panicking, too. She has memorised the chapter on weaning in *Baby's First Year*, poring over the photographs of artfully messy kitchens and smiling, hippy-ish parents in high-ceilinged Victorian semis. She has sterilised the spoon, boiled the water, measured out the baby rice she brought with her from England and mixed it to the texture of sloppy wallpaper paste.

'Come out here, Rach! I want to take a photo of you and Ivan.'

Rachel wishes Lucas would go to his press conference. She nudges Ivan's chair a little further away from the open doorway with her foot.

'It's too cold,' she says over her shoulder.

'It's not cold!' shouts Lucas. 'January will be *cold*.' A pause. 'You haven't been out here at all yet.'

Rachel suspends the plastic spoon in mid-air, but she can't blink away the falling baby, the splayed limbs, the flopping head. 'The height makes me feel dizzy,' she murmurs, listening as the balcony door closes and her husband's footsteps approach along the hallway. 'I prefer going for walks.'

'I'm sorry you're not keen on the flat,' he says, leaning against the door frame. A rare memory stabs at him, swift and bright: Rachel, his new fiancée on a weekend away in Paris, stretching her arms up into the air from a viewing platform on the Eiffel Tower, flushed and teasing, pretending to fling his passport over the top of the safety barrier. She'd not been dizzy then, he thinks, though his head had been reeling. 'We can't move again. I've paid for the year up front. We wouldn't get the money back. Anyway, you should have seen the cockroaches in my last place, not to mention the lethal wiring. This place is brighter, and safer. In the spring we can put a table on the balcony, get some pots, grow some herbs like proper Ukrainians.'

Rachel nods, slowly, as if her husband has helped her to accept something she hasn't previously understood; as if this is the last time he needs to mention the subject. She waits for

Ivan to open his mouth, then slips the spoon between his lips.

'He doesn't like it much!' says Lucas, peering over Rachel's shoulder. 'He's just spitting it back out.'

'He's feeling it with his tongue,' she murmurs, leaning forward and using her little finger to scoop a dribble back into her son's mouth. 'He's not used to anything that doesn't come from me.' These are words she has memorised. They are easy to say. Easier than words about choking, turning blue, not breathing. She doesn't know where the nearest hospital is. Lucas can't tell her if there's an English-speaking doctor and she wouldn't be offering her son solids at all if he didn't scream for milk every two hours. Her body needs a chance to heal.

Lucas straightens up, goes to the window, sees the nearly empty box of After Eights on the windowsill.

'When did you eat these?'

Now Rachel really wants him to leave. She wipes Ivan's chin with his bib. Lucas opens the fridge and peers inside; fingers the packet of baby rice. Then he picks up her copy of *Jurassic Park* and flicks through the pages.

'Hey, you're not still reading this . . .' He doesn't know about her ten-pages-a-day habit. He doesn't know that six days ago she reached the part where the newborn's face is gnawed by baby raptors who climb in through the clinic window while its mother sleeps in the next room. Sometimes when she's finished her allotted words she goes back and reads that page again, three, four, five times, tapping each word with her finger, counting its beats to keep her own baby safe.

'Look,' Lucas says, turning towards Rachel, his tone softening as he tries to tackle her silent non-compliance. 'I know it's tough for you. You've been ill and you're knackered and you're doing everything for Ivan, washing his clothes, feeding him yourself, getting up in the night. I really think it would help if you went out more – I mean, come to the office sometimes, go into town. You've been here over two weeks. Which reminds me – you'll never guess who rang the office number this morning. Your mother!'

'Mum?' Rachel pulls the spoon away from Ivan's lips. 'Why didn't she call here?'

Lucas shrugs. 'She's never going to make it easy for herself, or you. I gave her the number for the apartment, but I think she just wanted to check the address. She said you'd left it on a piece of paper but she couldn't read your handwriting. Maybe she wants to send you a parcel.'

Rachel thinks about the last time she saw her mother. She had made a great fuss over the journey up to London, but the afternoon had been dismal, her mother tutting over the state of the little basement flat. She'd not offered to tidy up or cook; she sat upright in the only armchair and turned down her mouth when Rachel took her grandson into the bedroom to feed him.

'She can read my writing perfectly well,' she murmurs, letting Ivan suck on her finger. He judders slightly and his eyes half close, his whole body focused on satisfying this need. The familiar tingling starts up in her breasts. 'Did she ask about Ivan?'

'She went on about boiling stuff and and not giving him unpasteurised cheese,' replies Lucas. He looks at his watch. 'Anyway, next week I'll take some time off. We could go to a restaurant. Drive to a park. No – I tell you what – we'll all go out this afternoon – in the car, down to Khreschatyk. I've got some recording to do at the central market and we'll visit the dollar store near the office. We need to normalise things – find ways to make you more independent. Kiev is an incredible city once you start to scratch the surface. There's so much I want to show you.'

He stoops, rubs his hand across her shoulders. Rachel fixes her eyes on the curve of her son's cheek.

'It might help . . .' He falters, still searching for the right words to express an unfathomable doubt. Then the doorbell rings and they are both spared.

It is Zoya, his fixer. Zoya always likes to be at press conferences forty minutes early. She'd honed her English by listening to the World Service and identified herself as the BBC's eyes and ears in Kiev long before Lucas arrived. Now she is relegated to errands-runner, occasional translator, driver of the office car. She's a small, round-hipped woman of thirty-six whom Lucas assumes to be at least a decade older because of her bleached yellow hair and the nicotine-stained teeth she only shows when she's picking them. She pokes her head into the kitchen, her shiny forehead creased into a frown.

'The *dezhornaya* is angry,' she says, nodding at Rachel. 'Dirty nappies are coming down the rubbish chute. They make a bad smell. If you must use the disposables you will have to carry them down to the waste bins yourself. I am passing the message to you, however I am not your messenger. Now, please, the car is downstairs and we must not be late.'

Lucas smiles and rolls his eyes at Rachel, as if to reassure her that he's the one in charge. Then he and Zoya are gone, both lighting up before the front door shuts behind them.

Rachel doesn't notice, until she looks for it later, that Lucas has taken her book.

'How is your wife enjoying Kiev?' asks the Finance Ministry's press officer.

Lucas turns round. Zoya has ensured he is early for the press conference; the drab room with the usual nylon backdrop ruched in dusty folds behind the podium is still only a quarter full. Vee and Teddy are talking near the exit; their heads are angled towards each other. He pulls distractedly on his ear. They look as if they're discussing something interesting.

'Oh, it's all good, good . . .' he murmurs, wondering how the man with mousy flat hair and watery eyes knows about his wife. Maybe Vee's been talking. What's his name? Torin? Tarin? Zoya would know, but Lucas has sent Zoya off to buy more batteries for his audio recorder.

'The BBC is a fine broadcaster,' says the press officer, resting an arm on the back of the neighbouring chair. 'Reputable. We are glad to have you here.'

Now Lucas sits up a little, leans forward, drops his cigarette on the floor. He's heard this sort of thing before, reported by colleagues on recces to Belarus or stints in Moscow or Berlin. It's usually the preamble to some sort of threat. Empty, these days, but old habits die hard. It might make a good opening for a FOOC – *From Our Own Correspondent*. He needs an angle that'll interest Radio Four, not just the World Service.

'I see you like popular culture.'

'What?' Lucas frowns.

'*Jurassic Park*.' The man is pointing to the inside of Lucas's jacket. 'I know this book. Steven Spielberg is making a film.'

'Oh!' laughs Lucas, sheepish, loud enough for Vee to look

over. 'It's not mine. I don't read that stuff. It's my wife's, actually.'

The man nods, as if expecting Lucas to say as much.

'Well, my country has faced many difficult times. There is more bad news today. I, however, like to swim against this tide. *Ukraina* has a brighter future.' The man isn't looking at Lucas; he's looking at the back of his hand, his fingers flexed, as if admiring a new ring. 'We can work together. On a strong story. A story we are proud to show the world. There is someone I would like you to meet.' At these words the man leans in and though Vee is still watching, and might even be strolling over, Lucas doesn't move, doesn't catch her eye because already he is thinking he'll save this one for himself.

CHAPTER 3

ZOYA IS DRIVING down the broad, straight carriage-way of Lesi Ukrainky towards the city centre. Lucas lounges in the front passenger seat, one long arm slung around the base of Zoya's headrest. Rachel sits behind Zoya with Ivan on her knee. Her arms are clamped tightly about him.

Rachel looks out of the window at the spindly plane trees and the grey buildings and the shop signs that all use the same blocky orange Cyrillic letters. The words are in Russian, not Ukrainian. She spells out the sounds she recognises: *kee-no-tay-ah-ter* – cinema; *khleb* – bread; *kee-nee-gee* – books; *sok-ee* – she doesn't know that one. The beat of each word helps to distract her from the fact that Lucas has taken her book. She needs it back but must wait until they are alone.

'*Ffsh*,' whistles Zoya as they approach a large pothole. A broken-down trolleybus parked on the right means they cannot avoid it. As Zoya slows and eases the car across the ruptured tarmac, Rachel peers up and sees ten or twelve white faces all staring down at her from the stranded bus.

Zoya is sitting on a cushion to give herself some height. Today she wears a white pompom hat with a fake fur trim, even though it is only the middle of October and the heating is on full blast. The hat flattens her permed and peroxided hair and the pompom bounces against the headrest as the car bumps and sways. She drives carefully, with a frown of concentration, but Rachel cannot tell if this is because Zoya is concerned about the baby or because she fears for the beige Zhiguli's suspension. The car smells quite new, yet it has the character of something already past its prime, with its sagging ceiling, its friable plastic fittings and creaking underbelly.

Rachel doesn't care about the car. She can't stop thinking about her missing book.

'Re-stor-an,' she whispers into Ivan's soft ear. 'Too-flee.'

'Zoya,' says Lucas, shifting in his seat. 'I want you to do some research for a feature I'm working on. What do you know about Pavlo Polubotok? I need info on that legend about the Cossack leader's gold.'

Zoya checks the rear-view mirror, as she does every fifteen seconds or so, actually moving her head in the way that Rachel's driving instructor showed her before she took her test. Then she indicates and turns right. Only when the car is settled into its new course does she respond.

'Hetman,' she says. 'The hetman's gold. It is a fool's dream. In this country there are many fools.'

Lucas nods, undeterred. 'Well, okay, like I said, it's a legend, but it stands for something, doesn't it? I mean, it stems from some kind of historical fact. Polubotok was a real Ukrainian hetman, right? In 1723? And no one has managed to disprove the claim that he smuggled two barrels of gold across to London for safe keeping when he thought he was in trouble with the Tsar.' He pauses, as if to let his words sink in. 'So, what I'm interested in is the contemporary response. Polubotok promised that the gold would be returned to Kiev when Ukraine was finally free. I heard some nationalist poet took up the story and, after making a few calculations about compound interest on the back of an envelope, declared that it was now worth sixteen trillion pounds sterling and that this money belongs to all true Ukrainians.'

Rachel sees Zoya's eyes narrow momentarily in the rear-view mirror. Zoya catches her looking and, embarrassed, Rachel lowers her head.

'That madman has been discredited,' Zoya says, braking for a red light.

'Yes,' says Lucas. 'Obviously. But it's the *effect*. It's a metaphor for the state of the place, the way people are thinking. The dream of rightful ownership, denied for so long, a pot of gold, meddling from Moscow, reclaiming past glory, a nationalist resurgence . . .'

'There is nothing new to report. Just some hot-heads when your Mrs Thatcher visited.'

'All right.' Now Lucas is getting annoyed. He puts an unlit cigarette in his mouth, then takes it out and tries again. 'The point is there's going to be a film – some young director at the Dovzhenko studios. I've been given exclusive access.' He twists round and smiles deliberately at Rachel, looking for an ally, someone who will be as delighted as he is with the prospect of a scoop. 'It could be big, this story, Rach – the revival of Kiev's film industry, a national obsession, politics, propaganda – plenty of colour. I might even get one of the Sunday supplements interested, or syndicate it and start earning some proper money. Definitely a half hour feature for Radio Four.' He hesitates. 'We've got to be discreet, though, Zoya, okay? I don't want to share.'

Zoya, however, is rolling her eyes. 'Why do English people use this word *story?*' she grumbles, turning the wheel and pulling into a space amongst some haphazardly parked trucks. 'Stories are for children.'

'Unbelievable,' says Lucas. 'I thought you wanted to be a journalist.'

'*Kee-nee-gee*,' Rachel mouths, still clutching their son.

⚘

The covered market hunches beside a noisy interchange at the southern end of Khreschatyk, downwind of Independence Square. When Rachel climbs out of the Zhiguli the cacophony of cars and trucks and trolleybuses takes her by surprise; this is her first proper trip downtown and she needs a moment to remember how she has pitched up here. Then she sees a dirty white building with a domed glass roof like a railway station and MINOLTA in large Latin letters above the entrance. There are people everywhere, hustling for business through the exhaust fumes: boys washing cars with filthy pieces of rag; aproned women in a line selling jars full of every shade of honey along with bunches of wilting herbs; two khaki-coated men sitting down to beg – except she sees that they're not sitting, exactly. They don't have any legs.

Lucas slings his rucksack over his shoulder and starts un-folding the buggy. 'This is the Bessarabsky. It's unregulated, pricey, but they bring in fresh produce from Kazakhstan and the Caucasus – so no contamination problems. Fruit, meat, eggs, cheese . . .'

'*Ree-nok*,' murmurs Rachel, not moving. Before she goes inside, she needs to find out about her book. Then, just as she begins to frame the question, her husband starts waving at someone.

'Hey Lucas!' calls a female voice, assured, Canadian. Vee is emerging from an archway with Teddy in tow. 'And Rachel!

How are you? Did the drugs help? Look at this little fella! Hello beautiful boy . . . It's so nice to see you out and about! Now, Rachel, I've got to tell you, there's an English woman living in the block next to you. Actually, I think she's Scottish. Or should that be a Scot? You can be friends! I've got her number somewhere. Someone at the Finance Ministry passed it to me.'

'What are you two doing here?' asks Lucas.

'Ah,' says Teddy, smiling at Rachel and holding up a jar of lumpy soured cream. 'Vee always hunts down the best smetana.'

⁂

Rachel stands inside the entrance waiting for Lucas. She is watching a man arranging apples. First he takes one from a crate and spits on it. Then he rubs it with a rag until it gleams. The glossiest fruit is placed at the front of a pyramid he is building, alternating green with deep red. She doesn't want to watch him; she wants to knock his pyramid down because the red and green apples shouldn't touch each other, but Ivan's big grey eyes are staring from beneath his knitted balaclava. The fruit is keeping him quiet. Or maybe he's listening to the croaky tirade from an old man by the entrance, or the flapping of wings in the domed roof overhead. Rachel looks up and sees white dust drifting down from the skylight. It isn't feathers, though, or snow. It is tiny flakes of paint.

'Hey,' says Lucas, stepping up beside her. 'Shall we get some fruit?' He's still fiddling with his bulky audio recorder. The microphone is sticking out of his pocket.

Rachel looks over his shoulder. The tall woman in brown

overalls he was talking to is now loading jars of yellowish soured cream into a box. She bangs the box down on the back of a hand-cart and wipes her hands across her chest.

'I'm all done,' says Lucas. 'The women weren't very talkative. Vee got in first, it seems. I should have known she wasn't just shopping. Nice of her to remember about that Scottish woman though – great for you to start to make your own friends here.' He taps out a cigarette from the pack in his hand. 'At least I've got some audio ambience for my sound library. Background chatter. The domed roof makes for some interesting accoustics.'

The apple man is leaning across his display, offering Lucas a slice of green apple on the end of his knife. Lucas takes it.

'*Spaseebo*. You never know when you'll need stuff like that. When you're up against a deadline.'

Something swoops suddenly, almost skimming Lucas's shoulder. Rachel ducks her head, but it is only a bird.

'Where's my book?' she asks, her voice harsher than she intends.

'What book?'

'The book I was reading. The book in the kitchen this morning. You took it. *Jurassic Park*.'

Now Lucas remembers. His face is a picture of dissembling.

'Oh – you weren't still reading it, were you?'

'Where is it?'

The apple man extends a piece of fruit to Rachel. His arm is perilously close to one of his pyramids.

'Lady, Lady? You like? *Poprobye yablochko, moya khoroshaya . . .*'

Lucas waves the man away. 'I'm afraid I haven't got it. One of the press officers asked if he could read it. The one who

39

gave me the idea for my film feature, actually. Sorin, or Sarin . . . He's a fan of Spielberg. I could hardly say no.'

Rachel can taste something sour at the back of her throat; her palms prickle with sweat. She needs to stay calm, conceal the danger, yet all she can think about are the pages she hasn't read, the ten pages she must read before night comes.

She pushes her thumbnail into the tip of her ring finger. Hard. Harder.

'You – you *gave* it to him?'

'Well, yes. I thought you'd finished it. Come on, Rach, it's just some crappy airport novel!'

Lucas has no inkling. He doesn't know what he's done. Rachel needs to make good the ritual, a ritual that has been nudging, soundlessly, at the edge of her consciousness but which now snaps into focus.

The balcony is waiting. Ivan is not safe. She is going to have to compensate.

꩜

When Rachel was fourteen she answered an ad in the local paper. Babysitter wanted, it said. For a girl and a boy aged six and three. One pound an hour.

The house was an old rectory and Rachel thought it beautiful, despite the spiders. The garden was rambling, the wallpaper on the stairs was sprigged with yellow roses, the bathroom had actual beams in it. When the parents went out for the evening, for drinks or 'supper with friends', she moved through the rooms touching the comfortable furnishings and stroking the family's chocolate Labrador and all the while thinking how, one day, she would have a home like this one. The children had dark hair and blue eyes and she was bewitched by their fierce stares and quick fingers and high, mercurial voices.

'You're not the leader,' said Alice, the six-year-old, on Rachel's first visit. 'I am.'

Then one afternoon she was asked if she'd mind staying overnight. The parents were driving up to London and wouldn't return until two or three in the morning, too late really to run her back home. They'd pay her for her time, they said. They'd leave a telephone number. She jumped at the chance to sleep in the cosy little guest room. Her own mother didn't object.

That evening Rachel chased the children round the garden to tire them out. She fed them fish fingers, though they didn't put salad cream on theirs. She bathed them in the sloping bathroom, dried and dressed them in their brushed cotton pyjamas and gave the little boy, William, a piggyback to the bedroom their parents called 'the nursery'.

Then something bewildering happened. Rachel had left her watch in the bathroom and as she went back to fetch it, she heard the nursery door close behind her. When she returned, the door had been locked from within.

'Alice,' she called, her hand on the door knob. Now she could hear whispering and the sound of bed springs from the other side. 'Let me in.'

Alice didn't answer. Rachel knelt down and put her eye to the keyhole. She couldn't see anything – the key was still in the lock.

'Alice, please come to the door and turn the key. You've locked me out! You told me you wanted a story!'

'You're not my mummy or my daddy,' said Alice, as if

from far away. That was all Rachel could get out of her.

For the first hour or so she tried to reason with the siblings, bribing them with biscuits they weren't supposed to eat, but Alice wouldn't let William approach the door. Then, when William started crying and his wails of distress increased, Rachel banged on the old pine panels and pushed against them with her shoulder.

'Please, Alice. William is frightened. You're being mean. Please, Alice. You can both sleep in my bed. *Please . . .*'

Eventually William's cries faded to dry shudders. By about eleven, the sounds had stopped altogether and Rachel tried to block out images of him lying on the floor, slowly strangled by a sheet or stabbed through the eye with one of Alice's carefully sharpened colouring pencils. She was too scared to phone the children's parents because they were sixty miles away and a call would have repercussions that she didn't want to contemplate. She would have to manage on her own.

She sat down on the floor, leaned her head against the door and made a loud sobbing sound. It wasn't difficult; she was close to tears anyway. After some minutes, Alice turned the key. She opened the door and stared down at Rachel.

'Why are *you* crying?' she asked.

Rachel took the key and placed it on top of the fridge in the kitchen. When morning came, the father drove her home in silence. She was never asked to babysit at the old rectory again.

Zoya drops Lucas at the office and returns Rachel and Ivan to Staronavodnitska Street. All the way up Lesi Ukrainky, Rachel leans against the window and mutters syllables under her breath. *Kee-nee-gee, ree-nok, kee-no-tay-ah-ter, sok-ee* . . .

Back at the flats, the sky has darkened like a child's charcoal smudge. Rachel walks quickly up the steps with Ivan in her arms, willing herself not to look up towards the blank windows and the balconies. Inside, the foyer is gloomy; she can't see if the caretaker is sitting in her cubicle, though she feels the old woman's judgement upon her: her contempt for Rachel's presence and her baby's foul detritus.

As Rachel passes the pock-marked metal mail boxes she smells burning paper.

'*Adeen, dva, tree, chityrie, pyat*,' she counts as she waits for the lift.

Later, when Ivan is asleep, Rachel pulls the empty After Eights box out of the bin in the kitchen, sits down at the table and opens the lid. She removes the corrugated lining and stares at the dark waxy sleeves, lined up like gills, still smelling faintly of peppermint.

She plucks out one of the sleeves, rubs it between her fingers, then, gently, squeezes its sides. The opening gapes a little. She wants to put something inside.

Slowly, frowning, she picks up a biro and writes some words on a scrap of squared paper.

The tropical rain fell in great drenching sheets.

She knows these words. She read them in the book that Lucas lost. She puts down the biro and folds the piece of paper three times, scoring the edges with her thumbnail. Then she slots it into the little sleeve and tucks it between the others. There.

The note is well hidden, but all the same it bothers her.

After a few minutes she picks up the box and carries it into the hallway. Out on the shared landing, she shivers. Her reflection looms in the window by the rubbish chute. The iron handle is cold to touch and even before she pulls it towards her she can smell the sweet stench of rotting vegetables and the soiled nappies she threw away earlier. As the dark interior gapes, a rush of cold air blows up from below. The chute door clangs and she frowns as her deposit tumbles all the way down to the bin at ground level, to the caretaker who will no doubt finger it in the morning, sniff its strangeness, then toss it on the little fire she tends beside the cracked concrete path.

Back inside the flat, pipes grunt and cough. Girders stretch and creak and the squeaking, rolling sound like trolley wheels has started up again. Ivan murmurs in his cot, awake and round-eyed, but as Rachel bends to pick him up she sees her hands letting go of the After Eights box. This is what they do, she thinks. They let go. And because she must protect her child she carries him to the kitchen instead of the living room, then pulls up a chair and stares through the darkness down to Staronavodnitska Street where a shrieking, sparking tram makes its way towards the river and tail lights wink between the trees of Tsarskoye Selo. Across the valley, up on the hilltop, the floodlit steel bulk of the Motherland statue raises its sword to the heavens. Yes, thinks Rachel as she lifts her shirt and grits her teeth when her son's gums clamp on: that statue is another hollow thing in this black night.

'Dyed, kak tyi?'

Zoya's voice carries across the tiny hall and into the dimness beyond. Her grandfather doesn't answer. No one answers. For the past seventeen years it's been Zoya's name on the papers for this left bank apartment across the river on the outer edges of the industrial zone in Darnytsia, yet even now she cannot enter without calling out, as if asking for permission. She closes the door behind her and sniffs the sharp scent of the blackberry leaf tea her neighbour brews to disguise the smell of urine. As she unzips her boots by the coat stand and removes and hangs up her skirt, she considers making a cup for herself, but instead pushes open the door to her left. Beyond is the flat's only room, apart from the cramped cubby holes that serve as kitchen and bathroom. There is no sound from the bed that takes up most of the floor space, although the dull glow from the fringed lamp on the table shows a figure lying motionless beneath the covers.

'I'm home, Grandpa,' she says. 'I'll just wash my hands.'

In the bathroom, Zoya switches on the light and counts the sheets bunched up on the cracked tiles by the toilet. Two. It used to bother her that Tanya, her neighbour, wouldn't rinse them out. Now she doesn't think about it. Tanya might drink her tea and forage in her drawers, but without the woman's daily appearances Zoya wouldn't be able to go to work at all. She unhooks the shower head and turns on the tap. Water trickles out; at least it is warm this evening. She breathes in the chemical smell of the soap powder and stands there in her nylon slip, eyes closed, water pattering on the sheets as if they are a row of blackcurrant bushes outside a rural back door.

When the sheets are hung, dripping, over the bath, Zoya pulls on a faded floral housecoat and shuffles back to the kitchen in her slippers. She is too tired to cook, but there's cold soup on the stove and she eats some straight from the pan before decanting a little into a bowl, taking care to remove the soft lumps of cabbage. As she turns to look for a spoon, a note, scrawled on the back of an envelope and left underneath a bottle of yellow medicine on the windowsill catches her eye. 'Gone to my sister's,' it reads. 'Back Thursday.' So, Tanya is taking a break. Zoya can't go to work tomorrow. She'll have to call Lucas and tell him the car's got a problem. She'll say she's taking it to her cousin's to get it fixed and he'll grumble about how that's what happens when the BBC gives them a tin can in a city full of potholes.

She places the bowl of soup on a tray, along with a wedge of cured pig fat and a few slices of pickled cucumber she finds in the ancient refrigerator. Then she takes two glasses and pours water in one before filling the other with vodka from a bottle she keeps tucked behind the stove.

'Here we are, Grandpa,' she murmurs, carrying the tray into the bedroom.

The air above the bed smells of old skin and stale breath and when Zoya sits down on the only chair, the figure beneath the bedclothes releases a feeble stream of wind. 'Grandpa,' she whispers, bending down to kiss the top of his bony head. She tends to him then, cajoling him into raising his head, easing him up onto the bolster, bringing a spoonful of soup to his mouth, wiping his chin with the bib that Tanya has left there. Her grandfather's facial muscles strain and his tongue feels for the shapes of the words he can no longer find.

'I saw someone else doing that today,' she tells him. 'The English woman, trying to speak words in Russian. Not as

46

beautifully as you, though, my darling.' And when the soup is finished and she has eaten the cold *salo* and the pickle and drunk some of the vodka, she dips her little finger into the glass and pokes it, so gently, between his lips.

CHAPTER 4

ELENA VASILYEVNA IS pickling beetroot. Her arthritis has flared up now that the weather is colder and her shoulder joints grind, bone on bone, so she has enlisted the help of the boy Stepan. She can keep an eye on him in her lean-to kitchen on the hill in Tsarskoye Selo. He won't come to any good idling in the car park at the apartment block or leering at her beneath the monastery walls. The so-called uncle he lives with is a slob.

Stepan's job is to hold each jar steady while she stands on a stool and ladles in the soft purple heads. When the lids are secured and the jars wiped clean she will store them beneath the stairs with the bottled pears and tomatoes, the trays of chitting potatoes and the onion seeds in their twists of yellowed newspaper. If he likes, decides Elena, he could help her in the spring. She could start him on some digging.

Stepan screws up his face as the steam rises in vinegary clouds. He'll want payment, that's obvious, and he has a taste for preserved cherries so for now she will give him half a jar. Elena knows about hunger. She knows how starved limbs swell, how skin becomes shiny, almost see-through, before it splits open and the body's fluids leak out.

Famine eats you from the inside. When winter comes, hold on to what you've got.

CHAPTER 5

RACHEL IS STANDING in a stranger's apartment. She shifts Ivan on to her hip and turns her head slowly, eyes skimming from one object to another as her brain realigns itself to the changes in tone, texture, scale.

'It's so white,' she murmurs. 'Everything is so white.' The tasteful shades of pale envelop her within their seductive, muffling depths. She wants to sniff the cream leather armchair, sink her toes into the sheepskin rug, run her fingers across the Egyptian cotton tablecloth and even slip into the white blouse her host is wearing as she pours coffee into milk-smooth porcelain cups. The silky fabric reminds Rachel of her mother's face cream. Visibly Different, by Elizabeth Arden. For years she had watched her mother apply soft white dabs every night, frowning at the mirror, massaging her cheeks in slow, careful circles. Yet when Rachel, aged ten, had tried it for herself, twisting off the lid, sliding a fingerful under her vest and rubbing it across her stomach and chest, her mother had been furious. The pot was snapped inside her handbag after that. Such pleasures were only for grown ups.

Suzie, the Scottish woman Vee told her to call, straightens up and pushes her long ash-blonde hair back over her shoulder.

'White is so easy, don't you think?'

Rachel has been staring too long, but she can't help it. The only white things in the flat on the thirteenth floor are the Pampers, though her stock is depleting daily. Even Ivan's once-white vests and cot sheets are stained a greyish yellow. She can't quite believe the existence of this pure, untainted space on the eighth floor of the neighbouring building.

'It's beautiful,' she says, to Suzie.

'Well, it's easy for us. Rob just brings it all in through Finland.'

'What does he do?' asks Rachel.

'Do?' Suzie rolls her carefully mascaraed eyes. 'Pisses about, mainly. Don't they all? He's got lorries. Leases them for cross border imports. Sofas, freezers, all that stuff. You can't get anything decent down on Khreschatyk. A few folksy linens; painted trays and lacquered boxes – nothing you want to *keep*. If you're planning to stay, you'll have to bring in your own furniture. Our things here are mainly Swedish, though I made him bring out a few pieces from our house back at home.' She walks over to a lime-washed bureau, picks up a photograph in a plain silver frame and hands it to Rachel. The photograph shows a beautiful clap-board cottage with green wooden shutters and the sea, blue and hazy, in the background. 'That's us. Suffolk, near Aldeburgh. Where they have the music festival.'

Rachel blinks. This woman Suzie makes it all seem so ef-fortless. Of course her *real* home is a cottage in Suffolk. There are other pictures, too: a bridal couple in a village churchyard, soft focused, all daisies and cow parsley; a broad-chested man in a wetsuit, the top half peeled off, drinking a beer on a beach. This is how people live back in England, she thinks. Where things are nice.

Ivan bumps his head crossly against her shoulder blade. She remembers that her back is aching. 'Do you mind if I put Ivan down?' she asks. 'I've brought a change mat in case he leaks.'

Suzie is slicing into some freshly baked apple cake. 'Go ahead.' She puts a plate beside Rachel and sits down, her right hand encircling her left wrist. 'Sometimes I think I'd like a baby. Rob's adamant though. Not happening.'

'Oh . . .' Now Rachel doesn't know what to say. She lays Ivan down on his vinyl sheet and glances again towards the photograph of the man in the wetsuit.

Suzie laughs. 'It's okay. Hard to imagine a child in this flat. It can't be easy. For you, I mean. With a baby . . .'

Ivan is kicking his legs on the mat, staring up at the recessed lights in the ceiling. Here in this apartment where Rachel feels like she's floating, even though it's on a lower floor than her own, her son looks just like any other baby: all the babies she ever saw before she had one herself. Her head is full of the words she might speak: it's fine, everything's fine, nothing is fine; millions of women have done it before her and in markedly more difficult circumstances; the health visitor told her it wasn't safe to come though she had to come, had to escape her own mother with her bitter jibes and injunctions; she's lucky to be here at all; sometimes she wishes she'd never had a baby, never met Lucas. The balcony crumbles, the baby falls, she raises her arms above her head and flings her son into the void, but it won't happen if she remembers that her sole task is to keep him away from the edge . . .

'Lucas says I get a bit obsessive,' she responds, surprising herself. 'I do worry, though. I keep getting infections, and I don't know any doctors. What if he gets sick?'

'Oh, there are nurses at most of the embassies, and I've heard there's a British doctor coming soon. Rob says I'm not to go near a local hospital. You can always fly back to London. What about your mum?' Suzie pauses, waiting, but when

Rachel remains silent she breezes on. 'God, if I had a baby, my mother would be on the first plane out. And then Rob would leave me!' She laughs again, a throaty laugh like the laugh of a smoker and Rachel notices a little loose skin beneath her chin. She's probably nearly forty, though her body is toned and her limbs are slender.

'Look,' says Suzie, turning up the sleeve of her blouse to reveal a thin elastic band around her wrist. 'My shrink told me to do it. Every time I feel stressed about something I give this a ping.' She pulls it away with her other hand, then lets it go so that it snaps back against her blue-veined skin. 'It stopped me craving carbs, stopped me getting lazy. Maybe it'll stop me wanting kids.'

When they have finished their coffee, Suzie shows Rachel around the rest of the flat. There are two bedrooms, one with a rowing machine set up on the floor. The main bedroom contains an ornate limed oak sleigh bed with a mound of white bedlinen piled up in the middle. Rachel admires the way Suzie doesn't care about her seeing the unmade bed. She notices the expensive toiletries, the soft sweaters and pressed shirts revealed by the half-open wardrobe. There are white towels in the bathroom; a gleaming white Kenwood Chef sits on the counter in the kitchen.

'We should do dinner,' says Suzie, when it's time to slide Ivan back into his snowsuit. 'Sometime next week. Rob would love to meet you both. He's keen on some new restaurant near Andriyevsky Spusk. The food is terrible, but it's fun.'

'Okay,' says Rachel, thinking this is how it's done – you have coffee with someone, you introduce your husbands and then you are friends. Maybe things can be smoothed, made white and safe with pings from an elastic band.

Lucas will be pleased.

❧

When Lucas returns that evening Rachel is reading her copy of *Baby's First Year*. She has reached page sixteen. No skim-reading; she'll have to start again if she fails to enunciate every single word in her head. This book, she knows, will never carry the compensatory power of the novel Lucas took, yet it offers some distraction. Reading out loud is permitted, though only if Ivan is awake. Right now he is dozing in his bouncy chair, which she taps with each new syllable.

'The line's out in the office,' says Lucas, walking into the kitchen before Rachel can turn her page. 'Just when I'm ready to file. I'm going to have to do it here.'

Rachel closes the book and places it on the table. She hasn't worked out what to do if a page cannot be completed, but the memory of Suzie's elastic band still pricks sharp and bright. Just a pinch for now, then. Her finger and thumbnail pluck at the pale skin on the inside of her wrist.

'In here – you mean the living room?' She pushes the book against the wall behind the fruit bowl and places the salt cellar on top of it.

'No, in *here*. The acoustics are cleaner – less echo – and the phone cable is long enough to reach from the hall.' Lucas squats down and squeezes Ivan's stubby foot. 'If the quality's okay then London doesn't care where I file from and I could spend a bit more time with you two, maybe. It's all coming together now, Rach – there's an Interior Ministry day trip to Poltava next week and the news pieces are coming in, so I can't avoid the press pack, but I can do most of the background for the film feature from home.'

He looks so convincing in his button-down shirt with his pen in his breast pocket. Rachel's visit to Suzie's has made her feel like someone else and so, for a few minutes with her book tucked away and while her husband sets the kettle on the stove, then untangles wires and fetches a black metal box from the hall with plastic knobs and little dials before withdrawing for a cigarette and a read-through of his notes, she believes him. She believes he is a good journalist, a serious journalist who thinks on his feet and understands what is required and how to get it done. This is his profession and she is his wife and the mother of his child, the woman to whom he comes home and for whom he makes coffee and smokes out on the treacherous balcony.

She watches him set up his microphone and adjust the levels. She even feels a little guilty that she won't let him light up in the kitchen while he works. Maybe tonight it will be all right, if he is gentle, if his piece is well-received and they can play at being this straightforward couple a little longer. Crisp white sheets. Photos on the side table.

'I went over to Suzie's today,' she says. 'You know, the woman who lives in the other block. Vee put me in touch with her. She's invited us for dinner next week. To a restaurant.'

'Great!' says Lucas, but he is absorbed now, pressing one side of a set of bulky headphones against his ear and dialling the global filing number for Bush House. This feels okay, too, so she retrieves her book, picks up Ivan in his bouncy chair and decamps to the bedroom.

'You won't make a noise, will you?' she whispers as she sits on the bed, opens her shirt and puts Ivan to her breast. 'Daddy's busy.' She shuts her eyes, bites her lip until the pain subsides, then listens to the low, modulated sounds from the kitchen and drifts off for a few minutes to the rhythmic squeaking that comes from somewhere above the ceiling. Daddy's busy Daddy's busy Daddy's busy Daddy's busy.

The mantra doesn't work.

She opens her eyes. Lucas is shouting in the kitchen.

'What's the matter?' she calls, leaving Ivan asleep on the bed.

'Bush House won't use my piece! They say they can't strip out that noise from upstairs! That squeaking! I'm going up there. Some randy wanker . . . how am I supposed to get anything done in this place?' He marches down the hall and slams the front door behind him.

Now Rachel doesn't know what to do. She ought to go after him, she thinks. She ought to call him back, so after a few seconds she leaves the apartment, too, stepping on to the stale grey landing, past the rubbish chute and through the heavy door to the concrete stairs. She won't take the lift.

The fourteenth floor feels strange. There are three doorways, the usual locks and quilted sound-proofing and spyholes, but one door has a rubber doormat outside, while another has a complicated bell. Lucas is already knocking. Rachel stands a little way behind him, not sure now that she wants the squeaking noise to stop.

'Lucas . . .'

They hear a low muttering. Lucas knocks again. This time a cough, then suddenly the door swings open and an older man with a large belly steps out.

'*Shto?*' he says, aggressively. What?

Rachel doesn't catch her husband's reply. In the rectangle of electric light behind the man's sagging outline she looks down a hallway that is exactly like their own. The floors are uncarpeted, with the same over-varnished parquet and she can tell that all the doors in the flat are open because more light spills out from them and into that light swings a boy on rollerblades. He is tall, with a child's narrow chest, and he is naked apart from some old cotton pants that don't quite cover a flaky red patch of skin on his hip. He looks twelve, maybe thirteen, and she realises she's seen him before, perhaps in the lift or loitering near the kiosks by the Eternal Flame. The boy glides towards the old man's back and just when she thinks he is going to crash into him he executes a sharp, squeaking turn and stumbles a little before pressing his hand against the wall and pushing off back down towards the bedroom.

The old man heaves up his trousers with his thumbs. '*Koleni!*' he shouts over his shoulder, before turning back to Lucas. Rachel catches his eye, though she doesn't mean to, and at that precise moment she realises her arms are unencumbered – she has left her son on the bed downstairs instead of in his cot and she cannot recall if she closed the door behind her. Her chest constricts, she imagines him falling, down through the parquet and the concrete and the joists, down like the nappies in the rubbish chute, crumpling and flopping and broken.

She utters a soft cry, turns and clatters down the stairs.

The boy, Stepan, sees two faces like pale moons in the darkness of the landing. The man is angry, affronted. The woman flees, but first she looks. He spins on his toe and pushes off from the wall with his hand. The rollerblades squeak on the parquet as he glides back to the bedroom. That woman, he

56

decides, is being beaten by the man. Some days he hears her crying and, once, a muffled scream.

Mykola will want to know. Mykola wants to know everything.

CHAPTER 6

RESTORAN AMADEUS DOESN'T have a sign – not one that Rachel can see. She steps back across the pavement of the little side street that runs northwest from Khreschatyk and stares up at the stone facade. It looks like all the other downtown apartment buildings in the darkness: everything a little larger than it needs to be with its chunky corner blocks, chiselled grooves and deep, frowning doorways. Like the sets from Batman, she thinks: the mocked-up Gotham of a Saturday night TV show, except this stone is solid, and cold.

'The new restaurants like a bit of mystery. Gives them an air of exclusivity,' says Lucas, flicking away his cigarette and pointing down some narrow steps. Rachel leans forward and sees a blue neon treble clef glowing above what must be the entrance. She wants to get Ivan into the warmth. Her husband grasps the front of the pushchair while she grips the handles. The temperature has dropped to minus two or three and a feathering of hoar frost makes the steps dangerously slippery. She is concentrating so hard on conveying her son to safety that she doesn't see the figure loitering at the bottom until Lucas backs into him.

A short burst of Russian ensues, with some protest from Lucas, who can't set the pushchair down while the man, hands in the pockets of his bulging leather jacket, bars the way.

'For crying out loud. He says we can't take the buggy inside!'

Rachel hauls the pushchair back up the steps. She has already half-imagined a scene of some kind. When she was changing her clothes in the bedroom, tugging her pre-pregnancy silk shell top over her head, adding her blue lambswool cardigan with its slight pilling under her breasts and digging out a pair of dangly earrings that she hadn't worn since the night she left her job with the travel publisher, it was easy to believe she would never pass muster. Anyway, she knows Ukrainians don't like mothers. She's witnessed it herself dozens of times – the stares, the refusal to make way, the casual acceleration of approaching cars when she crosses the road with her son. The men are as bad as the old women. It's no wonder the population is in freefall.

'He says the baby is okay, but not the buggy,' translates Lucas, clouds of breath rising from the stairwell as he huffs his exasperation. 'How does he think that's going to work? Fucking ridiculous.'

'I'm not leaving it outside,' says Rachel.

'Absolutely not,' says a low, lilting voice. Rachel turns to see Suzie looking down into the darkness. 'It's all right,' continues Suzie. 'Rob will sort it.'

As she speaks, a stocky, square-headed man in a black padded jacket moves past her. At the bottom of the steps he murmurs quietly to the doorman. Nothing concrete is exchanged. Just words. Then they are all waved inside as though the problem has never existed.

'Nicely done,' says Lucas, as the four of them introduce themselves in the narrow foyer. The men shake hands. 'You've been here before?'

Rob smiles as he helps Rachel and Suzie off with their coats. He has disconcertingly round blue eyes, freshly barbered hair and thick, short arms. 'BBC, eh?' he says, so that Lucas and Rachel both know this is his night and he is in charge of everything that may or may not unfold.

Ten minutes later, the four of them plus Vee, who has persuaded Lucas to invite her, are seated at a central table next to a brick pillar. Rachel had asked Rob if she could tuck Ivan and his pushchair somewhere unobtrusive, but Ivan was having none of it and started crying, so now he is propped up in her lap.

'Where's Teddy tonight?' Lucas asks.

'Oh, Teddy,' says Vee, with her faux-mournful, teasing voice. 'Doing his thing, night-stalking, looking for sleaze . . .'

Rob laughs. 'I hope he can afford it.'

'You should see him!' exclaims Vee. 'He never pays.'

The restaurant is stuffy, overheated, and the tablecloths are an unappealing shade of brown. A couple of brash abstract canvases adorn the walls. Electric light is supplied by several opaque glass pendants that hang at different heights from the ceiling, making the room feel both too bright and oddly dull. A dark-suited man sits in the corner opposite them and near the door a couple of heavily made-up young women are sipping cokes.

Rob quickly arranges for the lights to be switched off and some candles lit instead. Three half-bottles of Stolichnaya are delivered to the table by a silent young waitress in a tight black dress, along with some imported beer and plates of cured *salo* and sliced pickle. Rachel sits facing the pillar, Lucas on one side, Vee on the other. Suzie, opposite, rests her hands on the table and smiles. Rob is on her right. Her cheekbones glimmer with powder and her hair is scooped up into a soft pile. She looks beautiful in the low light, thinks Rachel. She can't see Suzie's elastic band; her wrists are covered by her creamy angora sweater. She keeps glancing around, first at Rob, then back to Lucas and again across to Rachel. Suzie seems happy to have them all here together.

'Right,' says Rob, leaning across and pouring the chilled, oily vodka into five glasses. He is wearing a navy polo shirt with the collar raised up at the back. 'There's no menu, but the mushrooms are excellent and they slow cook the pork.'

'Hey, and welcome to the cuteist baby in town!' says Vee, laughing each time Ivan clutches at Rachel's wrist and smiles with his mouth open, his soft chin shiny with drool. 'This little guy's got to get out more often!'

As the young waitress brings iron pans of mushrooms in garlicky melted cheese and the others talk about what it is like to work in this city with its excise restrictions and corruption and the petty vendettas in parliament and the catastrophic inflation that is screwing the population to the floor, Rachel sips her vodka and feels the liquid burn her throat. While Vee entertains Ivan, she wonders at how all this might actually be real – restaurants, meeting people, talking and eating and drinking. Why shouldn't it be real? She smiles across at Suzie and nods and composes her face as if she belongs here, at least for a while.

Lucas and Vee are describing their latest visit to Chernobyl.

'It's a kind of hyper-reality,' says Lucas, stabbing at a mushroom. 'Pripyat more so than the reactor itself. I'm not saying it's surreal, because we're all tired of that cliché, but it's weird to walk through those buildings and look out over the old playgrounds, the schools with everything either shattered or

61

looted. Silence and stillness aren't great for radio, mind you. I recorded some footsteps walking through one old *gastronom*, through snow, then broken glass, then stopping and talking so you get this great echo in the old Hall of Sport and Culture.'

'What about safety?' asks Suzie in her soft Edinburgh voice. 'Was it safe?'

Lucas shrugs. 'We had all the gear on. Overalls and slip-on shoes and disposable caps. I took the Geiger counter and they keep tracking the hot spots. One Russian guy – some kind of scientist – told me he wore a lead undergarment. I didn't ask to see it, but maybe I should have – must've chafed!'

'You've got to change vehicles when you reach the restricted zone,' says Vee. 'That's the funny part. We all totter off the rusting press bus and get allocated seats in the limos that haven't been allowed to leave the area. So I'm being driven through Pripyat in this crazy fucking Zil – the only time I'll ever get a ride in one of those.'

Rob is wiping his mouth with his napkin.

'That restricted zone is a waste of time,' he says. 'They can't agree on its boundaries but it's arbitrary, out of date and it's holding back my trucks. There's a good road cuts round to the east from Belarus and then straight down to Kiev, but because of some Ministry knee-jerker they set up a new layer of checkpoints and now we have to live with it.'

Rachel pushes away her mushrooms, worried suddenly about where they were grown. Has Lucas been careful? Has he brought back any radioactive dust to their flat? Don't be selfish, she tells herself, as the vodka washes through her. The damage is done already – those children in bleak hospitals, those sick little babies being born, those recent spikes in thyroid cancer that Lucas tells her people have been protesting about. Their mothers had been trapped in that monstrous toxic cloud.

'Well, I'm not sure I'll go back,' says Lucas, as the dishes are cleared and the pork cutlets are delivered, each bearing a garnish of limp dill. 'Not unless I get a commission. Anyway, interest will most likely die down now until the tenth anniversary, unless there's another fuck-up. That's the trouble with this place. Everyone looks backwards – to Chernobyl, to the Soviets, to the Great Patriotic War. There's a line between real news and digging over old bones dressed up as analysis that frankly, sometimes, feels gratuitous.'

Vee rolls her eyes, comically. 'It's your job, you dick. You love it, so stop pontificating.'

Lucas leans forward. He won't be put off. He's out to impress one of the new breed, thinks Rachel. He is making it up as he goes along.

'I'm after a story that looks to the future,' he continues. 'Something to develop, get my teeth into, something that's not already being recycled by every junior anchor on the ten-day tour of former satellite states.'

He stops to pour himself another vodka. Vee flicks her hand. 'Hey,' she teases. 'Mister Loo-cas! Forget Bosnia! Forget the Middle East! Dontcha geddit? History's all we got!'

'That's not what I meant,' says Lucas. There's a hint of petulance about him, as if he has been caught trying out different versions of himself. 'I'm looking ahead. I've got some leads.'

'Great!' says Vee. Then, widening her eyes for Ivan and raising her voice to a cartoonish pitch: 'Whaddya know, little buddy – your daddy's gonna scoop us all!'

Half an hour later, once the vodka has numbed their nerve-endings and the plates have been cleared, the two men are telling stories. Rob recounts some trouble with the Hungarian border police over a shipment of chrome bar stools he had to dole out as bribes. Lucas makes everyone laugh with a tale about an angry old man shouting 'knees!' in his underpants. It takes a minute or two for Rachel to realise he is talking about the encounter with the boy and the man from the flat on the fourteenth floor. The old man had been wearing trousers, remembers Rachel, but when Lucas tells the story, it sounds like something else – a story about an idiot or a pimp. He makes it sound funny.

Vee has moved her chair over to the top end of the table so that she can smoke away from the baby. Rachel, meanwhile, is trying to nurse Ivan. She has draped a shawl around her shoulders in an attempt to be discreet, but he keeps waving his arm and pushing it away. It doesn't seem to matter. The women by the door have been joined by a trio of pasty-faced young men dressed in shiny nylon shell suits and branded trainers. They order a bottle of Chivas Regal and drink it with frowning intensity.

'So,' murmurs Suzie, leaning forward to catch Ivan's flailing hand. She pats it a little. 'I'm dying to know. What is it like to have a baby?'

Rachel looks up, pulled out of her reverie. Rob, she remembers, won't let Suzie have a child.

'Oh,' she says, warily, 'you know. Pretty amazing. Tiring. And amazing.'

Suzie smiles, frowning at the same time, as if she's puzzling over something. 'Yes. But how does it *feel*? What did you feel when you first held him in your arms?'

Right now, Rachel is starting to feel dizzy. The brick pillar has split into two, the sides moving in and crossing over like a Venn diagram. She focuses instead on Suzie, at a tiny white scar just below her left eyebrow. Something in Suzie's earnest, searching gaze makes her want to speak honestly, to reach for something true. Or maybe it is the vodka.

'It was a shock,' she says. 'I had a shock, the night Ivan was born.' She bends her neck and brushes her lips against Ivan's downy head. 'It wasn't the pain, or the mess, or caring about what Lucas might think, seeing me that way. The shock came afterwards, when I'd stopped shaking and the stitches were in and the blood was washed off.' Rachel pauses. She remembers the bright light above her head; the midwife lifting her feet out of the stirrups and pressing down on her uterus to expel the afterbirth. 'Lucas had gone home to our flat, and the ward was as quiet as it was going to get and the lights had been dimmed and the nurse had finished her checks or obs or whatever they call them. Ivan looked so peaceful in his cot beside my bed, and I didn't love him yet, but the antenatal classes had been very reassuring about all of that and I suppose I felt happy and proud and ready to learn. There was just one more thing to do before I could sleep and that was to go and brush my teeth.'

Suzie nods, as though all of this is as she expected.

'And you got up and went to the bathroom?'

Rachel thinks back, trying and trying to catch hold of what it was she had done.

'No. I pulled my gown around me, and checked that I wasn't – you know – leaking, then swung my legs over the side of the bed. I felt a bit wobbly, I suppose, but I decided I'd be all right. Then, just as I stood up, Ivan made a squeaking sound and moved his head so that his nose was pressed against the mattress. I didn't know how to turn him over without hurting him, so I picked him up and held him across my stomach, which felt all spongy and strange. The nurses were busy at their station, you see, and I didn't think I could walk without dropping him so I leaned there against the bed, until my arms were stiff and aching. Tears were falling down my cheeks and on to Ivan's head and I remember they pooled in that little hollow that new babies have – where their skulls haven't fused.'

She stops, the sickly scent of baby powder and her own sweat returning, washed up on a tide of fear.

'And?' presses Suzie.

'Then a midwife came by. I think she took the baby. She kept asking me what I was trying to do.'

'What did you tell her?'

Rachel falters again; she tries to pin down the formless things that waver in her mind's eye.

'I don't know. I . . . I didn't know.'

She raises her head and sees that Vee and Lucas and Rob are listening. Lucas is looking down, tracing the curve of a plate very slowly with his finger. Rob has his hand under the table. The little green Lacoste crocodile on the front of his shirt inches back and forth as he kneads his wife's thigh.

'Excuse me,' murmurs Rachel, standing up. She hands Ivan to Lucas, who, she knows, longs for her to tell a funny story like everyone else, something that might make her seem a little kooky and unpredictable and desirable and so explain her presence here, with him, in this restaurant, in this city. 'I just . . .' She searches for the words that keep floating out of her reach. 'I'll be back in a minute.' With her shawl pulled tight across her chest, she weaves her way between the tables and chairs towards the bathroom. A man in a dark suit sits at a table in her path. He has to uncross his legs to let her through, and as she passes he turns his head with a small frown that might express concern or irritation. Rachel assumes it is the latter. She pushes her way into the cubicle and locks the flimsy door.

Ten minutes later, after her racing heartbeat has slowed and she has dried her tears on a sheet of grey toilet paper, she returns to the restaurant. The man in the suit has gone and Lucas is jiggling Ivan ineffectually against his shoulder. She slides back into her seat beside her husband. Vee is saying something to Suzie and Rob, more vodka has been poured and there is a stiffness now, a new wariness around the table.

'. . . It pays quite well,' finishes Vee. 'So, how about it?'

Rob's head is moving up and down in a series of tiny nods, as if he's thinking about what Vee has just said. 'Thanks, but Suzie doesn't need a job,' he replies, carefully.

Vee raises an eyebrow. 'It's only three days' work.'

Now Rob exhales. 'Hair, nails, all that stuff – they're full time, aren't they baby?' He takes his wife's hand in his own and rests it between her legs.

Vee blows cigarette smoke over her shoulder. 'And how is that for you, Suzie?' she asks. Her voice sounds cool, neutral. She picks an invisible speck off her lip.

'Oh, this takes work,' says Suzie, pulling her hand away from Rob and holding it up to reveal her immaculately man-icured nails. 'I do my aerobics for ninety minutes a day. Besides, I'm still sourcing things for the apartment. I'm not looking for a job.'

Lucas shifts in his seat. Ivan starts to grizzle: warning signs. Rachel takes the baby from him, hoping someone has asked for the bill, but Rob, it seems, still has things he wants to say.

'My wife,' he says, raising his glass. 'She has everything

she needs. She likes to look good. But do you know the best thing about her? No? Well I'll tell you. It's that gap between her thighs.'

'That what?' Vee narrows her eyes.

'That gap – you know, between a woman's legs! Her triangle of light. I couldn't be with a woman who doesn't have one.'

'Oh *please* . . .'

'That's just it,' says Rob, leaning his elbow on the table and pointing a finger at Vee. 'You think I'm making some kind of sick joke because I don't talk a lot of righteous crap like you lot. But I know what I want and that's the deal and Suzie understands that. See?' He tugs on Suzie's arm. Instead of pulling away again, Suzie rises jerkily to her feet, turns round and thrusts out her backside. She is wearing a pair of white jeans that stretch across her buttocks and pull tight between her thighs.

'You bastard,' Vee says. 'Time to go.'

'I'll get the bill,' says Lucas, thickly. He waves to the waitress, but she is staring at the wall.

Rachel looks at Suzie and fear fills her throat, because Suzie's face has changed; it is closed and brittle now as she turns back towards her husband.

'It's sorted,' says Rob, and he takes the remaining bottle of vodka, pushes back his chair and heads over to the shell-suited young men. 'Jesus,' he mutters over his shoulder. 'You journalists should fuck off to Sarajevo.'

'You could do it,' says Vee, who seems remarkably cheerful after their sudden departure from the restaurant. She is sitting next to Rachel and Ivan on the back seat of the fume-filled Volga she flagged down to take them home.

'Do what?' asks Lucas, trying to turn round in the front passenger seat. He gives up and slumps back. The driver, a young man in a Dynamo Kyiv bobble hat, is hunched behind the wheel, eating sunflower seeds from a bag on the dashboard. His gearstick is sporting a jaunty crocheted cover and Rachel wonders if his grandmother, or maybe his girlfriend, made it for him.

Vee yanks on Lucas's scarf.

'The cost of living survey! For the UN! The job I was telling Suzie about. I thought she was going to say yes until that prick gave us the benefit of his misogyny. I should have thought of Rachel first.'

'What?' Rachel raises her head from where she was resting it against the freezing window. The night outside is dark and mysterious beyond the steady repetition of the streetlamps. They remind her of a zoetrope she once saw as part of a touring exhibition that came to the library in Lyndhurst. You were supposed to focus on the flickering pictures, yet all she saw were the shadows in between.

'You're a mom!' persists Vee. 'You're going to need that stuff in the survey, and they'll pay you five hundred bucks. Just visit a few stores and write down the ticket prices.'

'Oh. The survey. Yes, I suppose so.'

'Great.' Vee sits back. 'I'll tell the woman at the mission to call you. They've been trying for a while to find a third party. You're what they call an impartial expatriate.'

'Okay,' murmurs Rachel, but she's not thinking about the survey. She can't get Suzie out of her head. Suzie who bakes apple cake and wears white angora and speaks with a gentle

Edinburgh accent. Refined Suzie. Except she isn't those things at all. Or at least, she wasn't tonight.

The apartment block is quiet when she and Lucas return. The lift appears when summoned and there's no sign of the caretaker. Back on the thirteenth floor, Lucas retreats to the balcony for a smoke while Rachel feeds Ivan and settles him into his cot. In the bedroom, the full moon slides through the gap in the curtains and across the shiny parquet. Rachel undresses slowly; she hasn't drunk as much as the others, but two modest shots of vodka leave her reeling a little. Her skin is white in the moonlight. She pulls open the wardrobe door and stands in front of the mirror in her knickers. Her stomach rolls over the top of the elastic and stretchmarks gleam their silvery trails across her hips. She turns, looks over her shoulder, twisting her neck, but all she sees is the drooping shadow in the overhang of her buttocks. There's no thigh gap. No triangle of light.

'Hey,' Lucas says, stumbling in from the hallway as she climbs into bed. 'We should do that again.'

'I don't think so,' says Rachel, wondering if her husband had even registered what Rob had said.

'I don't mean see *them*. I mean just – go out. Meet people. Have fun. I worry about you, Rach. You need friends, especially when I'm away.'

'What?' Rachel raises her head, twisting round. Lucas has his back to her as he peels off his socks.

'Ah – didn't I tell you? I meant to tell you before dinner,' he says. 'The Ukrainian Service editor called – she wants voices from the regions. I couldn't say no. It's only a week – commissions guaranteed. Looks like I'm going on a trip.'

CHAPTER 7

THE FIRST PROPER snow falls on the morning of Lucas's departure. While he packs, then shaves, stooping in front of the small mirror in the bathroom, Rachel pulls back the nets and stands at the bedroom window with Ivan in her arms. She watches as the shapes below her soften, the concrete paths become white ribbons and a small lorry fan-tails across the tramlines. When snowflakes drift out of the greyness they don't always fall, she thinks. Sometimes, they rise. When you are already high in the sky, the air currents lift you and push you up against the building and out and round again. Perhaps you never reach the ground.

'Lviv tonight and tomorrow,' calls Lucas, above the whirring of his electric razor. 'Zoya has the phone numbers. Then three days in the Donbas and a couple in Crimea. More if she can get me a permit for Sevastopol. The Russians are still rattling their sabres.'

Ivan is in the shuddering phase after a prolonged bout of screaming. His eyelids droop, his damp head lolls from the exhaustion of his assault upon himself, yet every time Rachel turns towards his cot the crying begins again. So she flicks off the lamp and rocks him in the strange blank snow light, swaying from one hip to the other in a movement that sometimes she continues even when she isn't holding him; when her body, no longer weighted, tries to float up into the air.

'Once upon a time,' she whispers, 'once upon a time there

lived a little old man and a little old woman in a hut in the middle of the forest.' She pauses, brushing Ivan's ear with her lips. There's a story about the snow buried deep in her childhood. If she thinks too hard she won't remember, but if she speaks it, she might. 'They had enough to eat and plenty of kindling for the fire and they had each other, yet still this wasn't enough. They longed for a child.'

The whirring sound stops in the bathroom.

'Then one winter,' she continues, pressing her forehead against the cold glass, 'when the snow lay deep and thick on the ground, the old couple went outside and made a child out of snow.'

'I know this story,' says Lucas from somewhere behind her. 'Snegurochka, the little snow maiden. She melts in the spring. Mind you, these days poor Snegurochka has Ded Moroz for a sugar daddy. She's morphed into some busty blond with plaited hair extensions handing out free samples of coke in a spangly cape down in Independence Square.' He pulls open a drawer. 'The nationalists hate those Russian folktales, but as long as Snegurochka dispenses gifts, she's a keeper.'

Rachel stops swaying. She thinks she can see a figure far below – a smudge, really, sweeping the path that leads away from the flats towards the road. Is it the caretaker? She looks like a small grey crab, jabbing and flailing.

'Sometimes the caretaker comes up in the lift and leaves Ivan's dirty nappies on the doormat,' she says.

'What? Oh Jesus, that old witch is such a communist. I'll get Zoya to put her straight.'

'Zoya says it's not her job,' Rachel reminds him. 'Anyway, she says the caretaker hates nappies because they can't be re-used. Plastic, cardboard, food waste is all good. But not dirty nappies.' She touches the bridge of her nose, comforted by the familiar contours of cartilage and bone. 'Do you think we could buy a washing machine soon?'

Lucas packs his aftershave into his holdall and steps over to the window. Small words can open deep chasms, he finds. He never knows what might set his wife off these days, or cause her to retreat into the dull silence that made him put that call in to his editor at Bush House. It's just a short trip he's taking, so he can clear his head.

'Maybe,' he answers, cautiously. 'We've maxed out on Visa, but I'll be earning while I'm away. Then in the new year I'll focus on my film project.' Another pause. 'Vee says she'll call you. But if you're worried, I mean, worried about anything – the snow, Ivan – you could use the emergency office dollars. Zoya can always book you a flight. You could go back to the UK and spend Christmas with your mum. I bet she's missing you, even if she's crap at showing it.'

Rachel has been waiting for this. She knows it would be the sensible thing to do – the midwife, her GP, the few acquaintances she can call on in London would all agree. The prospect cannot be allowed to distract her. Fear, ever-present, makes Rachel grip Ivan more tightly. Instead she recalls her parents' fifties bungalow: her old bedroom with the stained hand basin in the corner and the pyrocanthus scratching at the window; the cramped porch where her father used to smoke before he took himself on a golfing holiday to Singapore and never came back. Her mother blamed Rachel, the child who had made her tedious. Rachel pictures her now, slicing carrots in the kitchen, fist gripping the knife, hammering it down on the red formica worktop, never looking her daughter in the eye, never asking the right question.

'I like the snow,' she says, counting Ivan's ten toes with her fingers, the ten days that Lucas will be away, each with its five separate parts: sleeping, feeding, washing, shopping, reading. Truly, when she parcels it up like that it's not so bad. 'And anyway, we can't afford the flights. Though if you see any Pampers in Lviv . . . the sixteen to twenty-four pound size?'

'I know!' Lucas says, with a look that might be relief, or disappointment. 'I know! Top of my list!'

Once Lucas has left and the tail lights of his taxi have vanished into the weather, Rachel attends to her routines. First she steps into the living room and shunts the sofa up against the balcony door. Then she moves the telephone out to the hallway, setting it up on the cheaply laminated bureau with the three-sided vanity mirror next to the front door. As she closes the living room door she wedges a kitchen chair beneath the handle.

'*The tropical rain fell in great drenching sheets*,' she murmurs, as if an incantation from her lost book might set a seal on her actions.

At midday she mashes a little stewed carrot into Ivan's flaked rice. She washes all the bedlinen in the bath and hangs it to dry on a clothes rack in the bedroom, then realigns the depleted pile of Pampers in the drawer beneath the bed, despite her nagging awareness that Ivan has outgrown the size she brought with her from London. In the afternoon she takes her son outside in the pushchair, piling on the blankets to protect him from the caretaker's disapproval as much as the cold. She learns to dislodge the build-up of slush around the

74

wheels with a quick jab of her boot, and counts the strange, floating balls of mistletoe in the tops of the bare trees. At night, she re-reads chapters from *Baby's First Year*, staring at the photographs of cluttered British homes, their chaos carefully constructed and cropped to put new mothers at their ease. Sometimes, when the squeaking starts up, she thinks about the rollerblading boy and the old man in the flat above her head, but she never meets anyone on the landing.

Then, one day, as she stoops to remove the dirty nappy that, yet again, the caretaker has deposited on the mat outside the front door, she finds a note tucked underneath it, written on a piece of thin squared paper that looks as if it has been torn from an exercise book. The note consists of two words:

Close windows!

It seems the caretaker knows a little English, but Rachel doesn't understand. Is this a warning, or an admonition? The windows aren't open. She picks up the nappy, places it back inside the rubbish chute and slams the steel door shut with a clang that makes her teeth rattle.

Later that afternoon, as she draws the curtains in the bedroom against the creeping dark, the telephone rings. Its harsh vibrations repeat along the parquet. Rachel scoops up Ivan, who is trying to pull himself along, knees beneath his hips, ready to crawl. His head bobs against her collarbone as she hurries from the bedroom. His grubby fingers clutch her shirt, but he is quiet. As Rachel bends down to lift the receiver from its cradle on the bureau, she sees her reflection in the three-sided mirror – a triptych of mother and child, strangely familiar, like a painting in a church.

'*Allo?*' she says, as Lucas has taught her. It can only be one of four people, she thinks.

'*Adeen, dva, tree* . . .' she counts.

The silence presses against her ear.

⚜

When Rachel was nine, her mother caught her thinking. Rachel was sitting on the swing in the narrow garden behind the bungalow. Her legs were a little too long already for the height of the seat so she'd tucked them under as she rocked back and forth, gently scuffing the toes of her sandals on the paving slab her father had placed there.

'Rachel?' shouted her mother from the kitchen window, hidden from view behind ragged stems of buddleia. Rachel didn't know what her mother wanted, but she knew it would be a chore of some sort, so she slid off the swing and lay down on her side by the hedge, hoping no one would find her. She was just beginning to relax, enjoying the sensation of looking at the swing from a new angle while her lips formed the shape of the swear word she'd gleaned from the older children next door when her mother shouted again.

'Don't think I don't know what you're up to, trying to hide. Come inside now!'

At any other time, her mother's words might have washed over her and meant nothing, but instead they came at that particular moment; at the exact moment to spark a new thought in Rachel's mind.

At teatime that evening, as her mother piled spoonfuls of mince and onions onto three plates and then drained the peas, Rachel stared at the back of her head and tried to enter her thoughts. *If you can read my mind then that's a horrible thing to do and you had better stop it because it's not fair and thoughts are* PRIVATE *and* I HATE *you.*

'Is the salt on the table?' asked her mother, without turning round.

Yes.

'Rachel – did you hear me?'

YES.

Now her mother looked over her shoulder.

'Oh, for heaven's sake – what's got into you? It's right under your nose!'

Stop pretending you can't read my thoughts. I know you can and you should STOP IT RIGHT NOW.

Her mother put her plate of food down in front of her and turned back to the counter. Rachel would have to be careful. Her mother was very sneaky.

The phone isn't dead – Rachel can hear a sort of fizzing on the line. Lucas has told her all about phone taps. He says they are still in place all over the city, though no one listens in any more. Rachel ought to replace the receiver, but she hesitates. That woman downstairs, the caretaker, the *dezhornaya* – isn't it her job to spy on them all? She sifts through their rubbish with her dirty fingers. What if she is listening? What if she's been trained, and what if she can hear Rachel breathing and Ivan snuffling through a headset clamped to her ears in her little cubbyhole downstairs? It's possible – so why not?

'*Gavareetyi po'angliski?*' she tries. 'Do you speak English?'

More fizzing.

'All right, then,' she says, feeling bolder. 'Here is a message for you. Pass it up to Sorin or Sarin or whoever it is who stole my book. Tell President Kravchuk if you like. People should be allowed to have private thoughts and private conversations. Maybe you've been spying for so long you've forgotten to stop, down there with your earpiece in and your nasty prying eyes. What exactly would you do if I said I had a really big secret – a secret about the Russians or nuclear missiles or NATO or an awful terrible thing I might do, up here where you can't stop me?'

She pauses to catch her breath and stares at her thighs and stomach mirrored three-fold in the glass, along with Ivan's dangling leg, which is all she can see of him at this angle. Her heart is thumping beneath his downy head. Perhaps it is her reflection that is speaking, another version of herself. The one with no face.

'I bet you'd do nothing, because you are pointless and no one would care about what you said.'

Silence. Of course, silence. Rachel breathes in the waxy smell of Ivan's scalp and brushes his forehead with her lips. She is just about to replace the receiver when she hears another click.

'Allo?' says a voice.

She freezes.

'Allo. Good afternoon. Am I speaking to Mrs Porter?' The words, faint at first, emphasise the P as if it is being punched out of a Dymo machine.

'Yes . . .' whispers Rachel. 'Who is this?'

'Good afternoon,' repeats the voice, a woman, her articulation too precise to be British. 'My name is Lizbette Solwein and I am deputy director of human resources at the UN mission in Kiev. Mrs Porter, I have been given your name as someone who might be willing to undertake an independent consumer survey on behalf of our international staff. May I ask, do you hold a British passport and is this something that might interest you?'

Rachel breathes, in and out, in and out. This stranger can't have heard; she *can't* have heard . . .

'Mrs Porter? Can you hear me? Mrs Porter?'

'Yes,' she manages. 'Thank you. I see.'

❧

The survey is delivered three days later by a man driving a silver Volvo. It is a fat slab of computer paper in a black ring binder. Eight hundred and seventy items, neatly tabulated, each row requiring her to insert the price charged by three different stores. Rachel tries not to be deterred by the impossibility of 'Brie, French, 400g' or 'Sandwich toaster, Breville, model A530, silver'. Instead she resolves to start with things she knows how to find: tea and onions.

'Come on, Ivan,' she says as she packs her son into his snowsuit and his mittens and balaclava and belts him into his pushchair. 'Let's go shopping.'

Down in the foyer, she hurries past the caretaker's booth without looking in. They set off for the kiosks and she hauls the pushchair over the tramlines, then up the lane past the decaying wooden houses with their skeletal cats and their arthritic trees to the ancient Kiev Pechersk monastery, at the top of the hill.

CHAPTER 8

TODAY THERE ARE no onions for sale at the road-side. Fortunately, however, the concrete kiosks with their barred windows stuffed with cigarettes and lighters and plastic combs have plenty of Liptons tea bags; they oblige Rachel with three different prices. She also finds bananas, or rather, one banana, lying next to some frost-blackened carrots and a trio of cabbages on a sheet of newspaper outside the Gate Church of the Trinity. The banana and the vegetables are crusted with snow. So is the old woman with sunken cheeks who squats on a crate beside them. Her head is swathed in several thick scarves. Her hands are wrapped in strips of dirty cloth.

'*Dobrey dyen. Skolko?*' asks Rachel. She points at the single piece of fruit, remembering too late that she needs a kilo price.

As the woman looks up, Rachel hears a click from some-where to her left. She turns and there is Teddy, Vee and Lucas's photographer friend, lowering his camera.

'Don't worry,' he tells her. 'You're not in the shot.'

'Oh, hello!' she says, dismayed. She would rather not be watched by this grinning American as she tries to purchase a solitary banana from a babushka with bandages for gloves. Teddy is wearing an oversized hat made of rabbit fur, with the ear flaps dangling round his jaw. The fur is patchy and matted, as if the hat is diseased.

'Shopping?' he asks, tilting his head to one side.

'Not really,' Rachel says, as she realises she is being teased. 'But I need bananas. Onions, too.'

Teddy smiles and exchanges a few words in Ukrainian with the woman.

'She says your baby looks strong. And the banana is yours for twenty-five *kouponi*. You might find onions inside the monastery. Shall we take a look?'

Rachel finds her purse and pulls out a dollar. The woman takes it without demur and Rachel considers handing over her thick thermal gloves as well, but Teddy's presence makes her hesitate.

'They don't like the pushchair,' she says, sliding the banana into her pocket. 'I've tried it before. Lucas says they think the wheels will damage the floors.'

'Ah,' says Teddy, with an exaggerated frown. He turns towards the entrance. 'The Baba Yagas.'

'Pardon?'

'The Baba Yagas. The old witches. They sit in dark nooks in churches and museums, waiting to pounce on unsuspecting mothers, but any child will tell you the story of the *real* Baba Yaga, the witch who lives in an old house that struts about on chicken legs. She rides around the woods in a mortar, with a pestle for crunching babies' bones.' He sucks his cheeks in, comically, and Rachel glances back at the old woman hunched over her vegetables as Teddy lifts the pushchair through the narrow door. When he guides her beneath an archway with its flaking plasterwork and slippery paving, no one protests.

The monastery is starkly beautiful in the snow. Rachel has managed glimpses of it on previous walks, and Lucas has told her about its miracles and shrines, its concussion-inducing catacombs crammed with the remains of dead saints preserved in their coffins, fingers exposed at the hems of their shrouds like thin, shrivelled dates. She lets go of Ivan's push-chair and turns round, taking it all in. The whiteness blankets the narrow flowerbeds and scrappy verges and draws her eye upwards to the green roof tiles, the gold domes and the small cross at the top of the tiered bell tower. Even the stark remains of the ruined church directly in front of her seem picturesque. Two pairs of black-robed monks process from one doorway to another, their skin bluish beneath their dark beards. Women in tight headscarves scrape the paths with ancient spades, and crows congregate in silence around a neat pyre of rubbish, each playing their part as if directed by an unseen hand.

Teddy finishes putting away his camera.

'Don't you want to photograph this?' asks Rachel. 'I feel like I'm in a painting.'

Teddy grins. 'Nope. Already got what I want.'

'What about over there? It looks like it was bombed.'

'Not bombed. The main church was blown up. In 1941. The retreating NKVD laid explosives in the cellars. Two years ago UNESCO made it a world heritage site. The pilgrims and the tourists are returning now. Orthodoxy's back.'

Teddy seems at ease here, she thinks. He leans over a table a few yards from the entrance. The table is laid out with wooden stacking dolls – *matryoshki* – each curved body split in half with five or seven or even ten smaller dolls lined up in descending order. Traditional models in brightly painted folk dress pout their red lips, the brushstrokes a little rough in places, but cheerful enough. The old man behind the table tries to tempt Rachel with what is clearly his most expensive item, a fancy ten-piecer with licks of gold paint. Teddy, however, is more interested in a series of Russian leaders. He counts them down for her: Yeltsin, Gorbachev, Chernenko, Andropov, Brezhnev, Khrushchev, Stalin, Lenin, Tsar Nicholas II and a tiny little figure no bigger than her finger nail with a black moustache and fierce, slanting eyes.

Teddy picks it up and shows it solemnly to Ivan.

'Your namesake, The Terrible!' he says, laughing as the old man flaps a mittened hand and scolds him for touching.

Rachel watches with an unexpected flush. She finds herself noticing how Teddy is not the same as Lucas. His eyes are brown. His hands are smaller, broader. His voice has a wider register, at ease with the notes at its disposal. She wants to count these differences, sort them and hoard them.

'Look, there are your onions,' he says, pointing to a basket in the snow beside the table. Then, once he has asked the price per kilo, and the old man has stuck up four fingers and Rachel has added what she hopes are the right number of zeros, Teddy wanders off.

When she has completed her purchase Rachel turns to see him standing a dozen yards away in the lee of the bell tower. He is talking to someone else – a young man, slightly built – Ukrainian, by the look of his bleach-spattered denim jacket and his sharp eastern cheekbones. Teddy brushes a snowflake from the man's arm. They seem close, almost lovers. Their heads tilt together and their breath mingles in clouds about their heads.

Oh, she thinks, they *are* lovers.

Teddy beckons her over.

'Meet Karl,' he says, smiling. 'Karl, this is Rachel, Lucas's wife. And this is their baby, Ivan!'

Karl nods and smiles down quickly at Ivan, but he seems more serious, more reserved than Teddy.

'Nice to meet you,' says Rachel. 'I must be getting back. Ivan is getting cold.'

'This is not a good place to buy vegetables,' says Karl, speaking with a strong Kiev accent and pointing to the bunch of onions she has hooked over the pushchair handles.

'No.' Rachel recalls the banana seller's bandaged fingers and tells herself that next time, when she is alone, she'll definitely give away her gloves. 'But I am doing a survey, you see. A consumer survey. And I have to find three prices for everything.'

'Ah, the UN!' exclaims Teddy. 'Vee put you on to this, didn't she? You'll be the most popular expat in town if you hike up the dollar prices. Everyone's been waiting. The diplomats, the execs from the internationals – you're setting the hardship allowance for the next three years. Just imagine the bribes . . .' He stops, sees Rachel staring, round-eyed. 'Hey, I'm joking. Three prices? That won't be easy.'

'I have to find dishwashers,' she says. 'Max Factor lipstick. One hundred per cent Arabica coffee beans.' Suddenly, the enormity of the task overwhelms her. She shivers, and wishes she is back in the flat. She needs her rituals, her pages.

'You're freezing. Come with us,' says Teddy. 'We know a warm café.'

Karl looks up, contemplates the grey sky. 'And Max Factor,' he says.

⁂

The café is in a cellar in Podil, so Karl flags down a Lada saloon to take them there. The driver, a middle-aged man in khaki fatigues, glares at the pushchair with its dirty wheels and

Ivan with his runny nose and his bright red cheeks, but Teddy feeds a dollar bill through the half-open window and soon they are bumping along the cobbles in the old part of the city, past the small huddle of protesters waving their placards near Independence Square, past the ragged line of schoolchildren at the top of the funicular and through narrow lanes that have wound their way down to the river between the merchants' wooden warehouses since the days of old Kiev Rus.

'Welcome to my gallery,' says Teddy, once the three of them are seated on stools in a low-ceilinged back room with a stove blasting out heat in the corner. A young woman wearing an oversized purple sweater places three black coffees in front of them. The coffee is thick with grounds that leave a residue around the inside of Rachel's cup. She takes a sip and stares at the photos that cover the smoke-stained walls; some are in clip-frames, most are just tacked up with tape. The images are of people, mainly, in washed out greys and greens, captured so that only part of each face is showing, unsmiling, a single eye staring away from the lens as if there is something far more important happening outside the frame.

Teddy seems pleased with the attention Rachel gives them. 'So, I believe Ivan is the first baby to come here. He's definitely the first *English* baby.'

Rachel hugs her son protectively on her knee. He gazes upwards, eyes bright, absorbed by the macramé lampshade that dangles from the ceiling. She wipes his nose with a paper napkin and rubs his cool hands in hers.

'Most people in Kiev don't like babies,' she murmurs.

'We love babies,' says Karl.

'I'm sorry. I didn't mean . . .'

'We love babies, but there are problems, and the cancers.

85

Many cancers. Also diphtheria. Everywhere there is sickness and no one is paying the doctors. People are afraid for any little ones. You are a foreigner, protected from danger. So they watch to see what you do.'

'Oh.' Rachel frowns as she processes this logic.

'Vee says *you've* been unwell,' says Teddy, stirring his coffee with his finger. 'But here you are, out and about, no Lucas in tow, doing your thing, getting a job . . .'

'It's not a proper job,' says Rachel. 'Only collecting prices. It seems a bit pointless, really. They'll have changed again by tomorrow.'

'Dear Rachel,' says Teddy, mock sighing, rolling his eyes. 'You're already infected.'

'What do you mean?' asks Rachel.

'I mean you've picked up Expat Disease. It's the wall we all hit. And then you have to decide. You can sink into the system, tie yourself up in red tape and grow cynical and sticky with all the misery and corruption, even when you tell yourself you're above it all.'

'Or?'

'You say fuck it, and have a good time!'

Rachel is silent for a moment. 'I just meant the price rises,' she says.

'Ha!' Teddy smiles. 'So – this survey. You ought to be careful. If I were you I'd just make it all up, because the kiosks have always been compromised, but now the gangsters are deep in every fancy import store. You've seen them – the thugs in their shell suits, the money men in fancy tailoring and cashmere coats. No price tags or bar codes. I mean,' he glances at Karl with just the hint of a wink – 'take a Max Factor lipstick. Eight bucks back home in Kalamazoo. Here, fifteen? Twenty? And it's still fake.'

'I'm supposed to give a store name, or at least a location,' says Rachel.

Now Teddy is leaning back and reaching into a drawer behind them. He rummages a little, then extracts a shiny black cylinder of lipstick and places it on the table in front of her. The Max Factor brand name is embossed in gold on the lid.

'Special for you, ten dollars, Café Karl!' says Teddy with an exaggerated salesman's drawl.

Ivan lurches forward and grabs hold of the lipstick, almost hitting his chin on the edge of the table. Rachel prises it from his hand before he can jam it in his mouth, then puts it down, out of reach.

'Shame it's not my shade!' she says, brightly, needing to know that Teddy is still joking.

Teddy nods, then smiles as he always does.

'Sure,' he says. 'Hey, that little tyrant looks hungry. Let me know when you're ready to go home.'

৵৻৻

By the time Rachel returns to Staronavodnitska Street, Ivan is howling. He's thirsty, and his nappy is bloated and sagging inside his snowsuit. She prays that the lift is working, that she won't have to climb the stairs. Her need to count the depleting pile of Pampers beneath her bed is making her heart race.

She navigates the double doors of the entrance by pushing backwards with her hip and rocking the buggy wheels over the metal grate. As they rattle into the foyer, she remembers she's forgotten to knock the snow off the wheels. Clumps of blackened ice drop in her wake as she hurries across the floor. She'll have to be quick so that the caretaker won't catch her. Ivan's wails echo around the walls, but the lift is ahead of her now, yawning open, its interior empty like the vertical box that the magician's assistant climbs into before the door is locked and trick swords are thrust through its sides. It's all right, she thinks, we'll make it. Then as she approaches the toneless bell pings and a weak light glows above her head. Someone on the ninth floor has just called the lift, so she shunts the pushchair quickly over the threshold. This is a mistake. The scuffed brown doors make a grinding noise and judder towards each other. Before she can pull back, they clamp against the metal frame. The pushchair is trapped.

Rachel tugs, so hard that an onion from the string dangling down from the handle breaks off and rolls out into the middle of the foyer. She stabs at the buttons on the control panel as her mind floods with visions of her son's head crushed beneath the lintel as the lift starts to rise. Then sense kicks in and she stoops forward, releases the straps and lifts Ivan out of his seat. Holding him against her shoulder, she yanks again at the pushchair. The frame is stuck tight. Ivan's feet scrabble for a purchase beneath her ribs. Perhaps she should simply abandon the pushchair and take the stairs. But what if someone else removes the pushchair? She can't manage without it. There is only one thing to do. She'll have to find the caretaker.

The caretaker - Teddy called her something. Baba Yaga. Well, Rachel doesn't believe in witches, though the old woman clearly sees herself as some kind of spy. In the old days, she thinks, the caretaker must have been paid to listen and watch and poke through the rubbish. If you spoke against the Party, she'd have heard it. If you hoarded fuel, she'd have smelled it and if you took a lover, well, she'd have sniffed that out, too. Now, Lucas says, no one is rewarded for whispering any more. But what if other people's business is all you know, and searching out weakness is what makes you feel strong? That old woman, she sits in her little hidey-hole across the foyer and purses her lips whenever Rachel walks by, wagging her finger like a stick to beat the bad wife who dares to leave her flat and flaunt her baby as if she's proud of him, proud of what she's produced. They're everywhere, these crones, barren with secrets, berating her on the trolleybus or in the bread shop or murmuring and crossing themselves outside the cathedrals and the churches, tugging at her hair when she doesn't cover her head and kicking the pushchair when she wheels it across the painted floor to show Ivan the candles at the back of those dark, cloying shrines....

Ivan has stopped crying. The only sound is her breathing, shallow and rapid. Rachel turns towards the caretaker's cubicle. It has a glass front. A curtain strung on a length of drooping wire is drawn across the window.

'Allo?' she calls, her own voice unfamiliar in the empty, echoing space. 'Dobry dyen?' There is no reply. Shifting Ivan round to her hip, her forearm slotted under his shoulder, she walks over to the cubicle. The door is partly open. She steps closer, sees a chair with a worn, flattened cushion. It appears empty; all the same, she thinks she must knock, so she taps her fingers lightly on the glass. At her touch, the door swings wide and now she can see further inside – a cheap desk, a black telephone and some yellowing notices stuck to the window frame and pinned along the back wall.

The smell from Ivan's nappy is sharp and sour. Rachel knows she needs to get him upstairs, that the ammonia that is forming will burn into his flesh. She ought to abandon the pushchair or exit the building and go outside to the steps that she thinks must lead down to the basement, but instead she's distracted by the brown and white patterned tea cup and saucer placed to one side of a stained ink blotter. Above the tea cup hangs a calendar with an image of a teenage girl in folk dress, and there, pushed into a corner, lies a small pink plastic hairbrush with its nest of grey hairs. The muteness of these objects repels and moves her and she holds herself in for several seconds or even a minute until, finally, her eyes register something else. On the shelf behind the chair is a slim cardboard carton, rectangular, dark green, a little crushed. The gold clock is still visible on the side.

A box of After Eights. Her box – the one she threw down the rubbish chute.

Carefully, she lies Ivan down on his back across the desk and stretches over the chair to reach it. She raises the dented lid, runs her forefinger across the waxy sleeves. There's no folded slip of paper, no hidden note; just a soft rustle like shifting sand and a fusty smell that mingles with a trace of peppermint.

'*Shto?*'

The harsh voice behind her makes Rachel jump. In the same moment she sees two arthritic hands in fingerless gloves reaching forward. The hands pick up her son, who grabs hold of the teacup, and when Rachel turns round the caretaker is clutching Ivan to her chest and Ivan is opening his mouth to bawl, so she lets go of the box and all three of them look down to where dark squares are fluttering and thousands upon thousands of tiny black seeds are spilling and spinning across the cold floor.

Rachel needs her baby back, but the old woman is holding

him tight. Her wrinkled face is no longer a mesh of disapproval. Instead, her mouth is open and her eyes are aghast. Something terrible is happening here. Something terrible has already happened.

⚜

Dreams bleed into memory and memory sinks into dream. Later that night, dogs bark as Elena Vasilyevna moans in her sleep. The old caretaker sees dark water; bodies glistening in the reeds. She is fishing, or trying to, for she has no lines or nets.

Her sister is crying. That English baby is crying while his mother makes strange noises, opening then shutting her mouth.

Elena should have told her. The river cannot feed them. The fish are all gone.

CHAPTER 9

Lucas WAKES ON the morning of the twenty-fifth of December to find his legs trapped in a tangle of bedsheets. When he rolls over he pushes a solid object with his foot. It lands on the floor with a dull thump. His head is hurting, his mouth tastes of sick and something that feels like a strand of hair is caught at the back of his throat. He buries his face into the pillow. He wants to hide from the cold light that is seeping under the fringed curtain but a question nags him back into consciousness. What has he knocked off the bed?

He levers himself up, sees that he is alone and peers over the side of the mattress. On the floor is a dark shape, like a lumpy forearm or a badly packed Christmas stocking. With a grunt he reaches out and scoops it up. There's a label attached with an elastic band. 'To Daddy,' it reads. 'From Santa xx.' It *is* a Christmas stocking.

'Rach?' he croaks. His voice isn't working so he puts his hand into the top of the sock – not a thick sock, just one of his black work socks with a small hole in the heel. The contents, as he pulls them out, seem rather apt, in the circumstances – a bottle of imported Heineken, a six-pack of Bic lighters, a handful of walnuts in their shells and, in the toe, a shiny pair of nail clippers. The lighters make him want a cigarette and he contemplates an illicit one in bed until the fact that he is now a father breaks over him once again. Instead he leans back, opens the beer on edge of the headboard and tries to reassemble the events of the night before. He didn't get back from Crimea until eleven and he hadn't been through the door for more than three minutes before it all kicked off.

They'd had sex, him and Rachel – he is almost certain of this. The details are hazy – he remembers worrying that the two mattresses pushed together might suddenly separate and land them both on the floor. He takes a swig of his beer and then he feels guilty. They'd argued for a long time beforehand, Rachel weeping because he'd not brought any Pampers, then because he'd lost that stupid novel she'd picked up from somewhere and she might even have cried something about a Baba Yaga, though he'd probably dreamt that part. Anyway, he'd been too busy insisting that it was impossible to buy what wasn't for sale and that this was a crap homecoming.

The problem, nevertheless, was that while the crap might be true, it was also true that he'd had a great time away from Kiev. What was it Sorin had said when the omnipresent press secretary had popped up at that junket vodka reception in Dnepropetrovsk? 'A man must know when to be with his wife, and when to stay away.' Straight out of the dark ages, and just the sort of Slavic macho anachronism Lucas could riff with in a slot on *From Our Own Correspondent*. All the same, he knew what Sorin meant. He'd smoked in the hotel bathroom, jacked off when the mood took him and, most important of all, he'd felt like a journalist again, wandering around, asking questions, observing and speculating without worrying about how to justify his actions.

Lucas tries to crack a walnut with the nail clippers but the shell is a bugger.

Things start to look up when he smells coffee and French toast.

'Hey, Rachie, Merry Christmas!' he says, strolling into the kitchen and kissing her on the mouth with the smell of beer on his breath. He produces an over-priced store-wrapped silk scarf, a box of German *lebkuchen* and, finally, an enormous plastic binliner with a Russian-made baby carrier inside. 'Don't read anything sinister into it,' he pleads. 'I just want to make life a little easier for *both* of us.' The baby carrier is rigid, square, with thick shoulder straps, an aluminium frame and a simple canvas hammock for Ivan to sit in. Lucas had to leave it outside the front door the night before so that Rachel wouldn't find it.

'Thank you,' she says, knowing she has been unreasonable about the Pampers. Lucas would have bought some if he could.

Rachel's gift to Lucas is a set of mugs she found in a craft shop in Podil. They are rough to the touch, like sandpaper, with an unusual dark grey glaze lining the insides. One of them shatters as soon as she pours hot water into it.

There is a parcel, too, from Lucas's mother that she'd sent to the office. Socks for Lucas, gloves for Rachel and a hat and mittens set for Ivan. 'Cashmere! Hand wash only!' says the scrawl in the card. Rachel strokes the gloves along her cheek and drinks in the pale amethyst colour.

Nothing has arrived from her own mother.

'Why don't you give her a call?' suggests Lucas. 'You can't stay incommunicado for ever.'

'Maybe,' murmurs Rachel, vaguely. All she had sent her mother was a postcard with a bland greeting in Russian she bought at a kiosk near the monastery. She had tried to please her the previous Christmas when she and Lucas had visited the bungalow. It hadn't gone well. This year she hadn't expected a present – not really. But ignoring Ivan was deliberate, and mean.

At midday Lucas nips out to the office. He needs to check in with Zoya, who isn't answering the phone.

'Odd,' he says. 'She told me she wouldn't take time off in December. I thought she was saving it for the new year holiday next week. Hey, do you want to come too? You could give that baby carrier its first outing.'

Rachel shakes her head. 'Ivan's coming down with a cold,' she says. 'I'll practise indoors.'

Lucas's hand is on the door catch.

'You are okay, aren't you?' he asks. 'After last night?'

'I'm fine,' she says, with a quick smile. 'I'm glad you're home. I'm fine.'

⚜

In the evening, Vee comes for dinner. She brings a festive litre of Stolichnaya with a red ribbon tied round its neck, and a knitted toy with stuck-on googly eyes for Ivan that he'll chew and choke on if Rachel doesn't remove them first. Lucas fusses over the chicken he picked up in the Bessarabsky market, while Rachel slips the toy into a drawer and looks after the rest of the meal – carrots, red cabbage, onion stuffing, bread sauce made with UHT milk and some last-minute spaghetti. The potatoes she'd left under the sink have gone rotten in the middle.

Lucas jokes that Vee has turned up because she wants to fleece him for stories. Vee jokes that she's come to see Rachel and Ivan, not him.

'So, have you started the survey yet?' she asks Rachel, to prove her point.

'Sort of,' says Rachel, draining the spaghetti by tipping the saucepan and holding it back with a knife. A few pale strands slip over the top and threaten to take the rest with them in a slimy cascade. 'I've done the basic fruit and veg and some dried stuff like this pasta . . . toothpaste and shampoo were easy, but electrical goods and furnishings – I don't know where to start.'

'A new place has just opened down off Khreschatyk,' suggests Vee. 'A basement store, plenty of stock, German brands.'

Rachel turns to the kitchen table and starts plating up.

'Teddy says those places are all run by gangsters.'

'You've seen Teddy? God, I thought he'd vanished to some love nest with that new boyfriend of his. Well, he's right, but honestly, don't let it worry you. Those mafia guys aren't threatened by an expat consumer survey. Just get Zoya to run you there, check a few tickets and say you're looking for the washing machine that your husband has so far failed to provide!'

'Shut up,' says Lucas, grumpily, as Vee picks at a tail of spaghetti that has stuck to the pan, then dangles it above her mouth and drops it in. 'Anyway, Zoya, it appears, went A.W.O.L. while I was away. I couldn't get hold of her today, and London aren't happy because we missed a technical inventory, so she won't be running Rachel around any time soon.'

'Oh dear.' Vee smiles at Rachel as she is handed a plate. 'Then why don't you fire her?'

'I can't fire her. When she's on form, she's the best. Trouble is she knows it and takes the piss. She'll be moonlighting somewhere, probably translating for one of the Nordic embassies . . .' Lucas takes a sharp swig of his beer. 'Anyway, when she is around she's always so disapproving, questioning my story ideas. She's ambitious. Probably wants a Ukrainian

Service job and a stint in London, but if she expects a good word from me she's going to have to start providing some proper support.'

'So,' says Vee. 'If I take Zoya out and get her drunk, will she tell me what you've been plotting with Sorin? I know you're working on something!'

Lucas pulls a face of mock pity.

'Good luck with that. I don't think she drinks. Or if she does, she'll drink you under the table. Anyway, I had a great time on my travels, thanks very much for asking.'

'So what did you discover? Did you go down a coalmine in Donbas?'

'I did, as it happens. The lift was terrifying – you leave your stomach behind and it's so fucking *deep* and black – though, as you'd expect, everything else was stage-managed as usual and I didn't need to go all that way to hear them deny the stats about stillborn births, unpaid wages and the rest. The whole of eastern Ukraine is an environmental disaster zone, but the old guard aren't about to roll over and die. Crimea was more fun. I got some ranting vox pops from ethnic Russians and several bottles of sticky Massandra wine, as well as a few bulletins about the Black Sea fleet. It's a weird mix – shifty, militarised with a seaside café culture. We should fly down there for a weekend, Rach – maybe in the summer. The coastline is to die for. We could stay in one of the state sanatoria, take Ivan for a paddle.'

'Nice diversion, Lulu,' says Vee, waving her fork, notching up a stroke on an invisible tally. 'I've not forgotten there's something you're not telling me. You've got a story you're keeping secret!' She turns to Rachel. 'Hey, you okay? You're not eating! I hope you're not on a diet. Have you seen how skinny that Suzie woman is getting? I bumped into her husband at the Interior Ministry, knee deep in shit, I bet. What a creep.'

Rachel remembers something about Rob and his trucks coming in from Finland. Suzie had told her he could get hold of anything. Perhaps he could find some Pampers.

'I'm not hungry,' she says. 'Have some more chicken.'

'Did you call your mum?' asks Lucas.

Rachel pinches the skin on the inside of her wrist. 'I forgot.'

⚜

'Off to Russia. *Pregnant.*' Rachel's mother had expelled her daughter's news like a pip or a piece of eggshell.

Rachel gazed out of the kitchen window, across her mother's grey December garden to the bare, diminished shrubs and the bonfire patch with its tide of sticky ash where her father used to burn hedge trimmings and leaves. Lucas was out there having a smoke by the compost bin, flicking his butts into a pile of vegetable peelings.

'It's not Russia,' she said. 'It's the Ukraine.'

'How far gone?'

She shifted her weight so that her still-flat abdomen brushed against the edge of the sink. 'Thirteen weeks.'

'Well you can't take a baby out there, whatever they're calling it. Your husband has to concentrate on his job. You'll have to stay here.'

Rachel hated the way her mother said 'your husband'. She kept her hands in the washing up bowl, pushing them down so that her palms pressed flat against the base, the warm water

98

her only comfort as its soapy meniscus clung to her forearms. Her mother's irritation would expand, she knew, in the silence.

'I'm going to have the baby in London,' she said. 'St Thomas's. I've already had two scans. Lucas will come back for the birth. It won't be a problem. Then we can fly out together.'

Her mother hadn't moved, despite the fact that the dining table was still only half-cleared and the turkey carcass was waiting to be stripped and the Christmas place mats needed wiping.

'But you're not being sensible or responsible. You'll be nursing the baby. You won't get any sleep. The baby will need immunisations – polio, whooping cough, all of that. I'll have to clear out your old bedroom. Honestly, Rachel! You've no idea about what you put me through. You never have.'

'Mum,' said Rachel, suddenly angry. 'I'm going to Kiev and I'm going to love this baby. I'm not like you or Dad.' She took a quick breath, then half turned as if to snatch the words back, but it was too late for that.

Her mother stepped up close.

'I can't help you, out there,' she said, gripping the gravy boat with its residue of whitish fat.

Rachel took her time with the last plate. 'Don't worry,' she muttered. 'I won't ask you.'

❧

While Vee and Lucas go through to the living room and out on to the balcony to smoke, Rachel stays in the kitchen to give Ivan his night-time feed. Breastfeeding is more efficient, now – automatic even, and almost pain-free. Ivan pushes his shoulder up against her ribs with his dense, solid warmth.

His hand rests proprietorially. His eyes roll back and his lids droop.

As she holds him, her eyes drift to the Christmas card from Lucas's mother. The picture is a painting by one of those old Dutch masters – Brueghel or Van something – a skating scene.

Ivan doesn't know about Christmas, thinks Rachel. She looks down at the baby who came out of her, who is now so completely and utterly separate in his difference, in his vision of the world and everything he will ever experience or feel or understand. When she was a teenager, she used to lie on her bed beneath the window and look up at the sky through a frame she made with her fingers. Sometimes the sky was grey. Sometimes it was blue, or black. But she didn't think you could tell, just by looking, whether it was ice cold and freezing, or hot and burning. You might be a girl in Eastleigh or a penguin in Antarctica or her dad with a new wife in Singapore, or maybe the sky wasn't blue at all in someone else's head, but red, or yellow or some other colour she couldn't even imagine. No one could be sure. No one could see what she saw.

Now her baby must live in his own version of the world, just as she does. The thought is unbearable to her, and she wants to share something with him, help him feel less alone, even if it is the tired tropes of Christmas trees and carol singers and glowing log fires in pictures on cards, so she starts to sing, hesitantly, rocking him in her arms.

Silent night, holy night
All is calm, all is bright . . .

She can't remember the next line, so she tries something else.

Oh come, all ye faithful . . .

Again the words are swallowed by the louder voice in her head, or maybe she never really knew the words at all, but instead sang them without thinking from a dog-eared hymn book in the school hall, rocking back on her heels, cheeks flushed red as she bellowed the last two lines.

Oh come let us adore him,
Chri-ist the lord.

⚜

Rachel and Ivan are both dozing off when the doorbell rings. The sound makes Ivan's arms fly out and his newly erupted tooth bites into her breast. She hears Lucas open the door and say goodbye to Vee, then other voices murmur. Perhaps it is Zoya, she thinks, bringing news of a resignation or a scandal with that fierce pout of hers. However, next she hears some rapid Russian, and a boy's voice speaking in halting English.

After a minute or two the front door closes and Lucas walks down the hallway.

'Hey,' he says, as he sits down and peels off the fingerless gloves he wears for smoking on the balcony. 'It's cold out there. Vee asked me to say goodbye – she didn't want to wake Ivan. Happy Christmas.'

'Who was at the door?' asks Rachel.

'The *dezhornaya*,' says Lucas. 'She doesn't seem to realise that it's past midnight, or that it's Christmas in some parts of the world, or that I speak Russian. She brought that sulky-looking boy from upstairs with her to translate.'

Rachel cradles Ivan's head with one hand as she rummages under her shirt for the clip on her bra strap. 'I met her – the other day. We had a bit of a confrontation.'

Lucas looks alarmed.

'Were you okay?'

Rachel doesn't know how to answer this question. The old woman caught her trespassing in her cubicle. Rachel spilled her seeds all over the floor. The old woman cried, Rachel ran up the stairs with Ivan, then later the abandoned pushchair had appeared by the front door, a little dented, but otherwise still serviceable.

She nods.

'Well, anyway,' says Lucas. 'She says she needs to come in next week to do something with the windows. The boy didn't explain it very well – apparently it's a condition of our rental.'

Rachel remembers the note left outside on the mat, under the dirty nappy. *Close windows!*

'I might be out. The survey . . .'

'She said she'd only come up when you are in.' Lucas peers over the table piled with dishes, sees Rachel's exposed breast, Ivan's saliva still glistening and a milky dribble on his lips. 'Come on, Rach, I'm knackered. You're knackered. Let's both go to bed.'

※

Zoya sits on the back seat of the Zhiguli. Ice is forming on the windows in two-dimensional fronds, strange pinnae unfurling across the glass. It is cold outside, colder than usual, a bitter, frozen, silent cold that will kill the homeless and the drunks caught out tonight, but her own breath swirls warmly around her face; she's been cleaning vigorously for the past half hour.

She finishes her scrubbing and rests for a moment. This is where Lucas's wife sits, she thinks. Rachel sits here with her baby on her knee and stares at the back of her head. Zoya breathes in through her nose, and sighs. The interior still stinks of fecal matter, layered now with the astringency of the lemon Jif she has used on the plastic seats. She wonders if she should leave the windows open, just a crack, to air it overnight, but car thieves are everywhere and while they'd steal the Zhiguli without such assistance, she doesn't want to make their job easier. Besides, she thinks, the windows will have frozen solid by now. She ought to get out before the door freezes, too, but she lingers, despite the smell. It is a space she knows intimately, like any driver, yet without the engine running its silence seems to wrap her in something like comfort. Outside, the road is empty, inhospitable; a street light flickers weakly as the cold descends.

Up in Zoya's apartment, her grandfather is sleeping at last. If she hadn't brought the car home with her the previous week she would never have been able to drive him to the clinic when his temperature started raging, when his lips turned black and when, stretched out on the back seat of the Zhiguli with his thin legs folded up and his head against the door, his insides had started pouring out in a hot, steaming torrent.

Zoya had only been to the clinic once before. It is a private practice near the Dynamo stadium, with a receptionist and a waiting area and nurses in white rubber clogs. If she'd taken him to the public hospital near the bridge, he would almost certainly have died. When she arrived at the clinic with her grandfather they took samples and put him on a drip, but as soon as the diaorrhea slowed and his temperature dropped she signed his discharge slip and brought him back to the apartment. When Tanya came out to help carry him upstairs she told Zoya she ought to have left him there. Tanya thinks Zoya's made of money because she works for a foreigner, but the daily rate at the clinic is a whole week's wages. The new pills in the box with the German brand-name cost even more. In the end, though, it's not about the money. This is the man who made her pancakes with cherries when she came home from school; the man who made up stories about a mysterious underwater world and who washed her knitted tights when she started menstruating. He tried to hide her grade papers when she told him she wanted to study English at the university, because English meant American and those people were lascivious, not to mention dishonest and duplicitous with their claims about who won the war. He had fought with the Red Army at Zaporozhye in the autumn offensive of '43. No one leaves a man like that with a nurse in white clogs. He belongs with his granddaughter at home.

The car door has already frozen tight. Zoya rams it with her elbow until it flies open and she almost falls out. She collects her cleaning materials and kicks out the bag with the soiled nylon seat covers so that it lands in the snow at some distance from the car. If the car smells in the morning, there's nothing more she can do. She can always blame it on Lucas's baby. He should never have brought his child to this place.

CHAPTER 10

R ACHEL LEANS HER head against the cold kitchen
window and looks down towards the car park. The sun
is bright for early January, glancing off the broken glass in one
of the dump bins and burnishing the snowbanks. She has been
standing like this for the past hour, waiting for the caretaker
to leave the building and make her midday pilgrimage across
the tramlines, then up the lane that rises between the cottages
of Tsarskoye Selo. Only then can Rachel go out without being
intercepted. This is how spies operate. You watch, you are
patient, you learn your mark's routines. Then you do what you
must. The new year has brought new resolve. She will source
a supply of Pampers via Suzie, she will finish the survey and
she will recover her copy of *Jurassic Park*.

The problem, of course, is that no one with a baby could
ever be a spy. When the caretaker finally leaves the building,
Rachel lowers Ivan into the new baby carrier. She almost tips
sideways as she swings it across her shoulders and picks up
her gloves, but already she is learning to bend her knees and
take the weight across her hips. Outside, as her breath con-
denses in pale clouds and she picks her way past the empty
bottles of new year vodka strewn like curling stones between
the vehicles, her son's legs find the ledge of her hips and he
bobs up and down in his padded snowsuit, murmuring his
appreciation.

All the same, when Rachel spots the boy from upstairs she

wavers a little. He is loitering on the steps to Suzie's apartment block. He stares at her, his hands in his jeans pockets, shoulders hunched inside a hooded nylon anorak. Then, suddenly, he leaps in the air and executes a kind of pirouette, before sliding away from her like a figure skater on a rink. He's just a child, she tells herself. He's bunking school, vulnerable and adrift. Lucas thinks the old man is his pimp. The thought horrifies her, yet the boy still gives her the creeps.

Rachel takes the lift up to Suzie's. When she knocks, the door opens almost straight away.

'Hello, Suzie—'

'God, I thought you weren't talking to me.'

Suzie is wearing a dove grey suede skirt and a pale silky blouse. Her eyes are accented with mascara and her hair is arranged in a perfect French plait that reminds Rachel of the souvenir snow maidens with their doe eyes and New Year pouts in shop windows along Khreschatyk. Suzie pulls Rachel inside and shuts the door.

'Don't worry,' she says. 'Rob's out. By which I mean to say, he didn't come home.'

All at once, Rachel is sorry she hasn't followed through with Suzie. She abandoned her after that night at the restaurant; she'd been frightened, but Suzie on her own is a different person: open, self-deprecating. Suddenly Rachel wants to sit down on her soft leather sofa, drink her coffee, chat and laugh about how stupid things are and how they might be.

'I'm sorry I've not been in touch,' she says. 'Lucas went away, and I've had this survey to do and then it was Christmas—'

Her excuses sound hollow, though Suzie doesn't seem to notice. She is busy helping Rachel with the baby carrier and then taking her coat. Rachel kicks off her snowboots and pads after Suzie into the living room, carrying Ivan in her arms.

'Shall I get a blanket for Ivan to lie on?' asks Suzie.

'Oh, no thank you.' Rachel sets Ivan down on the rug. 'Look, he's sitting now. If I just put a couple of cushions behind him . . .'

'He's growing up so fast!' exclaims Suzie. 'Look at you, wee man!' Ivan is leaning forward, clutching at the long fibres of the rug, tugging them towards his mouth. Suzie goes into the kitchen to put the kettle on and while she's gone Rachel wipes the drool off his chin.

'Wee man!' she whispers, trying to make the words fit.

When Suzie returns she sits down on the sofa and smiles. 'Rob can be a prick sometimes, but I don't want that to stop us being friends.'

Rachel takes a deep breath. 'He goes to Finland quite a bit, doesn't he?'

'Yes, though I hope you don't feel we can only see each other when he's out of the country!'

'No, no, what I meant was, do you think he could do something for me?'

Now Suzie is surprised.

'Like what?'

'I – well, I really need some Pampers – Ivan needs them. A dozen packs would be great. I brought some with me but they're too small now, and the local brands . . .'

'What size?' asks Suzie, quickly.

'Oh, well, the large ones – one size below Junior. I'll pay whatever it costs, plus the shipping . . .'

Suzie smiles and nods. For the next half an hour the two women moan about the snow and the shopping and Rachel tells Suzie about the white goods shop she's on her way to visit and Suzie tells her how to find a pharmacy in Lipki where they sell Nivea hand cream and Tylenol. Yet when Rachel gets up to leave, she knows they have both been play-acting. She came because of nappies, and Suzie is nobody's fool.

⁂

The white goods shop is in a basement down a side street on the west flank of Khreschatyk. There's no sign, but the new-looking steel shutters are raised and Rachel can see Hotpoint and Bosch stickers in the large picture window that rises up to the level of the street. The familiar names startle her with their confidence, their branded superiority. This is the place Vee told her about. She shunts Ivan's carrier higher across her shoulders and reaches up to check that his mouth is clear of her scarf.

'Washing machines!' she whispers over her shoulder, as if they are about to enter Santa's grotto or the frost cave of Ded Moroz.

The steps down to the doorway have been swept clear of snow, but there's a shiny grey mass of impacted ice on the pavement at the top. Rachel treads carefully in her thick-soled boots, still adjusting to the weight of the baby she is carrying on her back. The doorway is lit from above and there is a security alarm instead of the usual dented sheet metal. She hesitates again. In this shop they'll speak the smooth, sleek language of microwaves and spin cycles. The queuing, the spitting, the grit on the floor and the women saying *nyet* – she won't find those things here.

Imposter Syndrome – that's what Lucas calls it. He thinks it's a joke.

A buzzer sounds as Rachel pushes open the door. Ivan starts to grizzle beneath his balaclava, but she is already distracted. The shop is full of machines. Some are encased in shrink-wrap plastic. A few are still boxed, while others are stacked up to the ceiling in twos and threes. Recessed lighting spreads its soft sheen over the ceramic plates of an electric hob, the curved glass door of a tumble dryer. No harsh fluorescent strips here. Rachel pulls off a glove, ready to touch.

'*Dobry dyen!*' A young woman, skinny in a tight blue dress with black hair and pale, pearlescent lipstick, appears from behind a row of air conditioning units. Rachel hides her hand in her pocket.

'*Dobry dyen . . .*' she says, her nerves returning. 'Do you speak English?'

The young woman frowns. 'Mykola!' she calls, not looking away.

'You see I'm doing a survey, a consumer survey. It's for the UN and I wonder if you'd mind . . .'

The woman has disappeared; Rachel is now talking to herself. She peers round a box with 'INDESIT' printed on the side. A door is ajar, but she cannot see anything through the gap. It must lead to a back office, because there's no desk in this part of the shop, no telephone, no paperwork; just the appliances, some packaging and a bentwood stand in the corner from which hangs a man's dark overcoat and a lozenge-shaped hat. The hat is made of a black fur that undulates in silky soft waves like the coat of a newborn lamb. Astrakhan, or something like that. If he could reach it, Ivan would clutch it in his fingers, bring it to his mouth. She moves away, stifling the urge to run her forefinger along its rippled crown.

A man's voice exclaims from close behind her.

'A baby? Yes! A nice good little baby!'

She tries to turn round, but someone is scooping Ivan out of his carrier and the sudden loss of his weight makes her lose her balance.

'Such beautiful cheeks – like apples! A boy, no? So strong . . . and it is so cold this afternoon!'

With a sharp shrug, Rachel shucks off the baby carrier and twists round to see Ivan in the arms of a man who is perhaps in his early forties – slim, balding, not tall, with a thick moustache and dark eyes fringed with full lashes. His face seems familiar, though this might be because there are many men with moustaches in Kiev. He's wearing a suit, an expensive one, and Ivan is already crushing its lapel in his chubby little fist.

'Please,' she says, aware that this is not the first time she's had to ask a stranger to stop touching her baby. However, this man isn't like the caretaker. His eyes register her distress and he passes Ivan back to her straight away.

'A baby needs his mother,' he says. His voice is deep and accented, with an emphasis that suggests his delight in speaking English. He nods at the baby carrier. 'It is good to visit places together. So,' he stands formally, heels touching, 'in what way may I help you?'

'Oh.' Rachel frowns. 'Do you have a price list you can show me? I'm doing – I am conducting a survey.' She fumbles with the flap of her bag, tugs her other glove off with her teeth and produces the thick file of paper. 'It's for the UN. A consumer survey to help them establish the cost of living for their staff in Kiev. I have to find three prices for everything. Food items, services, soft furnishings, electrical goods . . .'

The man doesn't move. He is smiling at Ivan, who is

wriggling, straining away from her as if he wants to be put down. Rachel forgets the rest of her carefully prepared speech.

'You work for the UN?' he asks, holding out his finger so that Ivan can grasp it.

'No,' she says, hoping Ivan won't pull it towards his mouth. 'I'm –' there is an official phrase but the words veer away from her – 'a third party. The UN always asks a third party to do the survey.' She feels embarrassed now, just as she knew she would. It sounds so ridiculous, saying words like 'the UN' as if she's their spokesperson or something. She isn't remotely credible, standing here with a baby, feigning competence and importance in her snow boots. This man, this Mykola will see right through her and send her straight back out on to the street. 'My husband works for the BBC,' she adds, knowing before the words come out of her mouth that this sounds even more ridiculous.

Mykola takes her seriously, even so.

'Ah,' he says, nodding. 'BBC. World Service. Very good. Good to have you here in *Ukraina*. And the United Nations. Also very good. Kiev, London, New York. You respect us and we respect you – joint enterprise, START treaty – this is how it is now. But a survey . . .' He reaches out and takes the file from Rachel's hand. 'A survey is a special thing. Prices are a delicate matter. With inflation, with our *kouponi* – as a wife, as a mother you know how it is. Viktoria!'

With a flick of her hair the young woman returns. Mykola hands her the survey and nods, murmuring something in Russian.

'She will make a copy. One for you, and one for me. Okay?'

Rachel stares helplessly as the woman retreats behind the door. She hears a beep, then a wheezing sound as a machine warms up.

'So,' he says. 'In a few minutes we can talk about this survey. First, some coffee? No? I can see you are interested in appliances. You are new here. You have apartment, a baby. You need things! What do you like? Bosch? You like German I think?'

Rachel tries to concentrate on what the man is saying, but now she is aware of another difficulty. A sweetish smell, cloying and rancid, rises up from her son. Ivan is filling his nappy. The odour is spreading fast and because he has nappy rash he will soon start to scream. She will have to get him out of here. She must find somewhere she can change him, though there's nowhere but the snow.

'The survey . . .' she says. 'I'm sorry, I have to go – my son . . .'

Mykola's dark eyes look concerned, sympathetic.

'Your son needs some attention, I think. Please, there is no need for you to leave. Viktoria will help you. Here.' He doesn't touch her; instead he guides her towards the door behind which Viktoria disappeared and pushes it open. 'Take your time.'

Rachel sees a new-looking photocopier. The survey whirs through its innards. Viktoria, holding the empty ring-binder, glances at the man and there's only the faintest flicker of disgust before she steps aside. There's a desk on which sits the grey bulk of a computer, but the beige carpeted floor is clean and Rachel is grateful, absurdly grateful as she kneels down, lays Ivan on the floor and unzips his snowsuit. Viktoria retreats, and the man speaks to her softly. They both stay in the shop, which is just as well, because Ivan's bottom is as ghastly as Rachel fears. Pale faeces are already leaking out of the soaked nappy, caking his skin and soiling his clothes.

When she lifts away his vest, the stench fills the airless room. She finds some baby wipes and a spare nappy in her bag, but the sores are like craters, glistening and inflamed. Ivan whimpers as she cleans him; he twists his head and arcs his back. Quickly she secures the straps of the new nappy, removes the stained vest and returns him to his clothes. If she was back in the apartment she'd feed him now, but she can't do that here so instead she licks her little finger and inserts it into his mouth for him to suck. He accepts it greedily, his grey eyes fixed on hers.

'I will take that.'

'Oh . . .' Rachel looks up. Mykola has picked up the soiled nappy. She should have hidden it straight away. Now he has touched it and she feels dizzy with panic, even though he is smiling. He opens a plastic bag and the nappy disappears. She struggles to her feet. 'I'm so sorry . . .'

Mykola watches her for a moment. His dark eyes are like a weight upon her, but he has Ivan's dirty things in his hands and she cannot hold his gaze.

'A mother with a baby should never apologise,' he says. 'Nevertheless, you are worried. This survey – the UN are paying you well, I hope, because I think you do not have a washing machine.'

Rachel is startled.

'How do you know that?' she asks.

Mykola points to her right hand – the one that is supporting Ivan.

'Your hands are rough. Your son's vest has many stains. This is bad and it must change. I want to give you something.'

Rachel covers her right hand with her left. The room is very quiet. She realises that the soft hum and shush from the photocopier has ceased. The newly duplicated survey sits silently in the tray. What was it Teddy had told her? Something about imports and the mafia.

'I must go,' she says.

'Yes, you must go. First, however, I want you to have something every mother needs. A gift. Not one of these,' he waves towards the shop, 'but good, nevertheless. I have machines that are a little older, maybe a dent or two, guarantees expired. I cannot sell them – my customers want everything to be perfect; it is natural. You see, I can help you with this.'

'I have no money,' says Rachel, slowly. Her head is spinning again. She knows she ought to take the survey, both copies, and leave, but the sense of unreality overwhelms her.

'I do not ask for money,' continues Mykola. 'Journalists – they are never paid enough! I know these things. Your little boy – so sweet. Let us agree it is a gift for him.'

'I couldn't possibly . . .' murmurs Rachel.

'Tell me where you live,' says Mykola.

Rachel stares blankly for a moment.

'For the delivery! I will send someone to install it.'

'Oh,' she says, again. And then, even though something is ringing, a kind of warning tinnitus, the words come tripping out. 'Staronavodnitska Street. Building Four.'

Mykola has turned his head. She can see a mole above his left temple. His mother must have stared at that when he was a baby, she thinks, when she held him to her breast.

'Apartment?' he asks as he picks up the baby carrier and holds it while she slides Ivan's legs inside. He lifts it carefully onto her shoulders and opens the street door.

The bitter chill almost steals her voice. 'Thank you,' she whispers as he offers her the survey, now in an opaque plastic folder. She tries to take it, but he doesn't quite let go.

'I understand your caution,' he says. 'You are a mother. It is difficult.'

Rachel knows she'll start to cry if she stands there any longer. Let him be a good man, she thinks. Why can't he be a good man?

He releases the folder. It is enough.

'Apartment thirty-four,' she says. 'But the lift is sometimes broken.'

Later that afternoon, behind the thick walls of the monastery, a man removes his lozenge-shaped hat and stoops beneath a doorway. The space inside is dim, the air heavy with the grease and smoke from burning tapers and the smell of bodies sweating beneath thick layers of clothing. The man knows that with a flick of his hand he could have the little Church of the Nativity of the Holy Mother of God to himself. Two monks stand ready to shoo away other worshippers, but the crowd, he believes, is his penance, so he moves to an alcove to cross himself, then kneels down on the cold tiles and mutters his prayers. Two young monks in their black robes wait behind him. Only when he raises his palm do they step forward, bearing a wooden icon between them. It is a triptych, though it is small enough to be carried in one hand.

The icon itself is dull and faded – its colours worn almost away. There are hints of red, brown, some blue and a suggestion of gold in the halo around the Holy Mother's head and along the edge of the veil that she holds out as she shields the man-baby who sits upright in her lap. The saints and martyrs are ranged like tiny dolls on either side of her, their faces upturned.

The man bows low over the icon. His lips touch the edge of the wood, then he shuffles backwards on his knees and prostrates himself before it, lying face down on the floor while the grey forms of his fellow-worshippers murmur and step over his legs.

Twenty minutes later, when the man has reemerged into the twilight and replaced his hat a skinny boy with close-cropped hair wearing jeans and a nylon anorak sidles up to meet him.

The man in the hat does not like to see a boy with his fingers tucked inside his trouser pockets in this holy place. The boy, however, whispers quickly, and the man is placated, pulling out his wallet and rewarding him with two ten-dollar bills. Satisfied, the boy slides away, pushing his feet across the snowy cobbles as if he is wearing ice skates or cross-country skis. He doesn't look back until he reaches the corner, at which point he spins full circle on his toes and makes a sign of the cross, touching his forehead, breast and each shoulder with his first two fingers, then pointing them at the man as if to say *I see you, Mykola Sirko*.

The man in the hat turns away. *Perhaps*, he shrugs, *we see each other*.

CHAPTER 11

T HE DAY AFTER Rachel's trip to the white goods shop someone hammers loudly on the front door of the flat. Rachel has convinced herself that the washing machine was a ruse and she wishes she hadn't divulged her address. You fool, she thinks, grimly, as she puts her eye to the spyhole. She'll have to pretend she's gone out.

Instead she recognises the boy from upstairs. He is with the old woman again, and this time he shouts.

'*Dezhornaya* is here!' he announces. 'Open door. It is condition of lease!'

Rachel hesitates, then pushes down on the handle. 'Yes?' she asks, hoping she sounds annoyed.

The caretaker is standing on the doormat with two bulky string bags in her hands. The boy is behind her, clutching a bucketful of old newspapers. He is wearing the nylon anorak that is too small for him, and a pair of plastic trainers.

'*Dezhornaya*,' he repeats. 'Elena Vasilyevna. She come to do windows.'

Elena. This is the name of the midwife in *Jurassic Park*, the one who leaves the nursery window open on page twenty-seven. Her mistake allows the baby raptors to climb in. Rachel frowns as she tries to re-focus. There'd been that note on the doormat. It said 'Close windows!' in blue writing.

'Doesn't she speak any English?' she asks.

'No.'

'Will it take long? I am very busy . . .'

The boy shrugs. 'Now I go.'

'Wait!' says Rachel, panicking. She's not sure which is worse, being alone with the caretaker or inviting the boy to stay too. 'What if I can't understand her?'

The boy stares for a moment, then steps into the flat, brushing past Rachel. Elena Vasilyevna follows. He opens the living room door and marches straight across to the window that looks out onto the balcony, pushing away the sofa that Rachel still heaves in front of it whenever Lucas goes to work.

'She will do here and here,' he says, pointing. 'All rooms. Leave for spring.' He looks around at the bookshelves and the furniture, sees a pack of Lucas's chewing gum on the side table and picks it up. 'I take?'

'Yes, thank you, please go,' says Rachel, quite clear now that she does not want this boy in her flat.

'Ciao!' he says, as he saunters out.

Rachel's palms are sweating. When she shuts the front door behind him, the caretaker Elena is already shuffling down the hallway towards the kitchen. By the time Rachel has secured the lock and caught up with her the newspapers are on the table and Elena is emptying a kilogram bag of rough brown flour into the bucket which is sitting in the sink.

'Pazhalsta . . .' begins Rachel, wanting to ask her how long it will take and why she needs flour, but Elena turns and holds out a green overall she has brought with her. She waggles her fingers, motioning Rachel to put it on. Then she opens a kitchen cupboard, rummages until she finds a suitable saucepan and passes this, too, to Rachel.

'Seychas,' she says, 'davai rabotat.' Now, work.

Rachel's job, it seems, is to sit on the red chair in the living room and tear sheets of newspaper into rectangles the size of a small matchbox. The first pieces are too small, so Elena takes the newspaper from her with a tutting noise and demonstrates the desired proportions. The rectangles go into the saucepan, while Elena turns her attention to her bucket of flour and water. She mixes it with immense concentration, testing it on her tongue and squeezing it between her fingers before pressing the mixture into the gaps between the window and its frame. As soon as she finishes one side, she wipes her hands on her pinafore and begins to layer the newspaper pieces neatly over the paste to create a seal.

Rachel finds the work strangely calming, despite the presence of the old woman in the apartment. Ivan chews on a bread ring in his bouncy chair, perfectly content as long as she rocks him regularly. There is no need to speak. The television news hums softly from the set in the corner. Pictures of a forest somewhere in the Balkans. Two truckloads of skinny soldiers. A square-headed commander in a peaked green cap striding across a hillside. She notices that when the old woman frowns her twisting black eyebrow hairs tangle above her nose. Her misshapen hands shake a little as she works, but there is no point in signalling for her to stop. Elena, she can tell, will complete this task, even to her last breath. If Rachel were to try to prevent her she would never have the courage to cross the foyer downstairs again. So she doesn't intervene when Elena moves across to the balcony door and seals that up, too. On the contrary, the glued door offers immediate relief from her struggles with the building's outer fabric. Rachel doesn't care what Lucas will say. He promised to stop smoking and he hasn't. She jogs the bouncy chair with her foot and leans forward to smile down at her son.

'Smatri!' says Elena, loudly. She is pointing at the television. 'Simplemente Maria.'

Rachel doesn't understand.

'Simplemente Maria!' Elena moves over to the television and mimes the action of turning up the volume with sharp flicks of her wrist.

'Oh.' Rachel rises to her feet and does as she is instructed. She's noticed *Simplemente Maria* before, bemused by the Russian dubbing of what appears to be a Mexican soap from the early eighties. The station airs it at least three times a day, in between the aerobics workouts with young women in uncomfortably tiny leotards, so perhaps it is popular: after all, it isn't hard to follow. Maria the maid gets seduced by the polo player. His shirt is very white against the straw. His long black boots stay on. She still gets pregnant, though. They always show the birth in the closing credits.

This time, however, the plot seems quite complicated; it involves a young girl who is either Maria's child or Maria as a child or the child of her employers. In the next scene Maria seems older, still with long raven plaits. She is dispensing sugary *churros* as the cameras linger on her tear-filled eyes and brave half-smile.

As the episode unfolds, Rachel looks over at Elena. The caretaker has finished working at the window and is now leaning against the wall. She has pushed her hands deep into the front pockets of her overall, as if cradling her belly. Her face bears the same expression of deep concentration she wore as she tasted the flour paste; narrow lips pushed out, eyes flicking from one character to another. Rachel turns her attention back to the screen, curious about what so enthrals her. Soon she herself is equally absorbed, puzzling over whether Maria has been penetrated by the family patriarch as well as his playboy son.

When the doorbell rings, both women jump.

Elena straightens up, muttering, disconcerted perhaps to be caught so far from her cubicle downstairs. Rachel responds more slowly. Maybe it is Zoya, who will most likely sneer at both the nature of the drama unfolding on the television and Rachel's latitude with the caretaker. She crosses to the front door and puts her eye to the spyhole. Something is blocking the light. Then the view clears and she pulls her head back sharply.

The little fish eye lens has shown her the face of a madman.

'*Zdravstvuyte!*' shouts a voice. A fist bangs twice against the door. '*Steeralnuyu mashinu zakazyvali?*'

Elena comes hurrying.

'*Shto? Steeralnaya mashina?*' She glares at Rachel suspiciously, then takes hold of the little stool that sits by the phone and hauls it over to the door so that she, too, can peer through the spyhole. A stream of Russian invective ensues, mainly from Elena, with one or two muffled words from the madman. The caretaker keeps glancing over her shoulder with a look of increasing fury until Rachel understands that it isn't the madman she is appalled by so much as Rachel's own ineptitude in causing him to appear. Then Elena climbs down from the stool with a huffing noise and begins working both locks with fingers like gristly chicken bones.

'Don't!' implores Rachel. It is too late. The door is open and the madman isn't a madman at all, but a man with a horribly damaged eye, the eyelid so bruised and swollen she cannot see his eyeball. Next to him sits a huge cardboard box that reaches up to his waist. She sees the picture before she forms the words. A square with a circle inside it. A washing machine.

'Mykola!' the man says, helplessly, at which point Elena falls silent.

Mykola. Rachel recognises that name, but before her emotions have time to rearrange themselves, the man shrieks and puts his hand up to his face.

Elena has spat at his black eye.

๕๛

Rachel knows all about consequences. As a child, these consequences had a physical presence; they bore down upon her like giant transport lorries, loads strapped tight beneath flapping tarpaulin. Her friends didn't seem to share her fears; she faced this nightmare alone.

When she was six or seven her parents went away. She wasn't sure where, exactly; to a funeral or on a holiday or perhaps they simply disappeared, walking out of her existence for a week. They left her in the care of some friends, a middle-aged couple with five children of their own, all of them older than Rachel. The family lived in Portsmouth, one street back from the sea, and while the two oldest boys were told not to let Rachel swim out of her depth, other restrictions were few.

The sun was hot the week she stayed there. It must have been the summer holidays, as the narrow beach was teeming with families and every day she and the others were given ten pence for a Ninety-Nine from the ice cream van near the entrance to Billy Manning's. But the others didn't spend their money on Ninety-Nines. Instead they ran underneath the Ferris wheel and made a beeline for the long, low shack on the far side of the funfair. The shack was called Tam's Treasure Trove and when Rachel first stepped underneath the peeling sign she felt swallowed up by its darkness after the glare of the concrete and the bright, sharp shingle. The air smelled like a tidal cave and straight away she fell in love with the buzzes and bleeps, the flashing lights and the grown-ups huddled, intent, over the machines. They took no notice of her.

A sudden jangling crash to her right had made her jump, but the others just laughed and winked at each other.

One of the boys showed her how to hand over her precious ten pence piece to a man with purplish-green tattoos all over his forearms. The man sat up high on a stool in a narrow booth by the door. Neat towers of brown pennies had been lined up along the shelf in front of him, and when Rachel fed her coin under the window he pushed a stack of ten towards her without looking up. The older boy immediately took three of the pennies out of her hand and she followed him towards a long, brightly lit machine with revolving trays of money inside: thousands of pennies she could watch if she pressed her face against the sticky, curving glass.

The boy pushed one of her pennies into a slot. It rolled down a chute and spun on its axis for a second or two before the tray above it moved forward and knocked it flat. Rachel quickly understood that the penny needed to fall in just the right place, at just the right moment, if it was to be shunted onwards with any chance of toppling on to the tray below and perhaps starting a waterfall of pennies like the one she had witnessed when they first entered. All around her, people were scooping up coins from the dark holes underneath and pushing them back in. The jangling sound made her skin tingle and she wanted it to happen for herself. It wasn't her lucky day, though. One penny in particular seemed to defy the laws of gravity as it hung lop-sidedly over the edge. She longed to see it fall. It wasn't fair.

When her money was gone she wandered towards the back of the shack, where the smell of mould and vinegar made her want to pinch her nose and the machines only took five pence pieces. A woman in an orange dress leaned over a tall machine in the corner; it lit up her thin face and made her cheekbones stick out. The woman muttered something, then gripped the central rim with her fingers and rammed her hip against the glass. The machine tipped slightly and released its bonanza with a plashing cascade.

Rachel returned to her machine. She tried copying the woman, and when her child's weight couldn't shift it, she gave it a kick. The kick hurt her bare toe and still the coins wouldn't budge, yet the man in the booth had seen her and he started banging on his window and shouting that he'd call the police. As she fled the arcade, Rachel saw him climbing down from his stool. She didn't stop running until she got back to the house and though the others didn't tell on her, she spent the next four days in bed, fear pushing her down into the mattress and under the pillow while she cried about a stomach ache and listened for the policeman's knock at the front door. When no policemen came, she concluded that they hadn't known where to find her. They were probably still searching, house to house. Those were the consequences. There is no such thing as an empty threat.

Now things are complicated. Elena has pushed Mykola's black-eyed delivery man into the stairwell and sent him on his way. She strips the old green overalls off Rachel and picks up her bucket before disappearing downstairs herself. Rachel doesn't know what to make of any of this, but she does know she hasn't heard the last of it.

Lucas bumps into the machine when he comes home that night. He catches his hip on one corner and Rachel hears him cursing as he fumbles in the darkness by the front door.

'What the hell is that?' he asks, as she steps out of the bathroom, still brushing her teeth.

'It's a present, I think,' she mumbles, wiping her mouth. 'A washing machine. From Mykola, the man I met in the white goods shop. I don't know how they got it into the lift.'

Lucas is not feeling so open-minded.

'A present? If you didn't pay for it, and I hope to God you didn't as there's nothing left on the Visa card, then it's a bribe. Jesus, Rach, it's a fucking great bribe. He hasn't even tried to disguise it. Something for the wife – very clever. Well, it's going right back to wherever it came from. Just as well you didn't let him bring it in – then we'd be in receipt.'

Rachel lowers her toothbrush.

'It might not be a bribe,' she says. 'It's only a second. Some Russian make.' She thinks of Elena spitting at the delivery man, his black eye. And then she remembers how Mykola had looked at her, how he had put his hand on her son's head.

Lucas knows none of this. Alarm is twitching across his face. No one gives washing machines away for no reason. Not even a damaged one.

'What exactly did this Mykola guy say to you?' he asks. 'He doesn't expect us to pay him for it, does he? And how did he know where to bring it?'

Behind Rachel, the day's washing drips from the nylon line above the bath: Lucas's shirts, Ivan's yellowing vests and her own knickers and stained nursing bras. She wants the machine. She wants clean laundry, but she doesn't understand what Mykola wants.

'We don't have to keep it,' she says, following Lucas as far as the living room and flicking the light switch so that the view beyond the windows is obscured by bright reflections. 'I didn't pay anything. I didn't sign anything.'

'Okay,' says Lucas, taking out a pack of cigarettes. 'I'll get Zoya to call the shop. You've got to be careful, Rach. You don't know how these people operate – starting small, finding your weakness, inveigling their way in and then suddenly I'm expected to reciprocate in some way. What the hell is this?'

Lucas is peering at the balcony door and before Rachel remembers to stop him he grasps the handle and gives it a yank. The frame makes a sticky sound like an Elastoplast being pulled off a knee. He has broken Elena's freshly made seal.

The lorries start thundering towards Rachel as cold air rushes across the floor. There will be consequences, now, tomorrow, or sometime. She cannot shut out the balcony. The balcony will not be shut out.

CHAPTER 12

THE WINTER FREEZE deepens throughout January. As an Arctic front sinks down from Siberia dead crows drop out of the sky. On the afternoons when it snows, when the apartment blocks are shrouded and tiny flakes like splinters whip across the road, muffling the shrieks of the trams and swirling in dim halos around the streetlights, Rachel and her son stay indoors. Ivan pulls at her skirt hem and practises his rolling on the bedroom floor. When his erupting gums make him whimper, or his nappy rash flares up and he howls for three hours at a stretch, she rocks him on her hip in front of the mirror by the front door, or distracts him with a mobile made from bottle caps, but she never takes him into the living room. On days when the skies clear and the thermometer won't nudge over minus ten, Rachel dresses him in five or six layers, with little zip-up bootees she bought near the football stadium and a pom-pommed balaclava on his head. Then she bumps him down the steps in his pushchair with the see-through rain cover pulled around him to keep out the worst of the cold that burns her nostrils and makes her eyes sting, and they walk around the car park or take a trolleybus to the ramshackle BBC office, where Zoya frowns her disapproval and Lucas lets him play with his keys.

The washing machine is still out there on the thirteenth floor landing. At first Lucas tries to get Zoya to have it returned, but she tells him she won't do his dirty work and besides, everyone knows about Mykola Sirko's dealings with the new racketeers. His shop is almost certainly used to launder their money.

'Exactly!' says Lucas, exasperated. 'Why do you think I want it out of my hallway?'

Elena Vasilyevna, on the other hand, cannot leave the washing machine alone. She climbs the stairs almost daily, arriving after Ivan's nap to watch the next episode of *Simplemente Maria* on Lucas's TV. She'll skip it if Lucas is at home, though most of the time he's out and when Rachel opens the door to let her in, Elena bangs on the washing machine with her fist and mutters some curse in Russian.

The TV sits in a corner of the kitchen now – it is too big for the narrow space, but Rachel has balanced it on a box opposite the stove, telling Lucas it is too cold in the living room. This is true, but also she doesn't want Elena to notice the broken seal on the balcony door. She is still wary of Elena and assumes the old woman wants to nose around the apartment and peer at her private things. Nevertheless, she is learning that Elena's visits offer a crucial, if temporary, reprieve from the fear that on some days makes Rachel lock herself in the bathroom while Ivan naps. When Elena is around, her son is safe from harm – safe from treacherous hands that might pluck him from his cot, carry him to the open balcony window, dangle him out and let go. Soon Rachel finds herself anticipating Elena's impatient rattle of the door handle. They cannot speak to each other and Elena wants the volume turned up loud, which always wakes Ivan, but when he's fed and sitting in his bouncy chair or sliding around on the kitchen floor, the caretaker tickles him with the toe of her felt slipper. Ivan giggles, which sometimes makes him bring up his mashed potato or cough on his bread ring, though mostly the three of them settle down to a tolerable silence.

One afternoon Rachel finds herself offering Elena some coffee. The next day, she opens a packet of biscuits.

☙

Rachel wakes in the night to the sound of dogs barking. She can hear them thirteen floors down, despite the double glazing. They sound as if they are fighting, their yelps and snarls echoing between the buildings and across the valley. Lucas isn't home yet; he is filing late from the office and as Rachel stares into the darkness the sounds seem to get louder, until she imagines the dogs are on the balcony, though she knows this can't be true.

In the morning Lucas has returned. Rachel sees him from the hallway, looking tired and unshaven. He is smoking out on the balcony.

'Christ,' he says, peering down through the open window. 'Those dogs have murdered each other.'

'What dogs?' she asks, willing him to pull his head back inside.

Lucas straightens up and takes a long drag on his cigarette. His chest expands with the inhalation and he holds it in for three or four seconds before breathing it out.

'Two of them, down by the bins. They'd been tied together by their back legs. They must have attacked each other or died from exhaustion. Horrible. The caretaker is dealing with them.'

'Oh, that's awful.' So Rachel hasn't dreamt it. 'Did you see them last night? The dogs?'

'Yes, when Zoya dropped me off.' Lucas flicks his butt over the side of the balcony, shuts the window and steps back into the living room. 'I couldn't untie them, before you ask. They would have gone for me. They were half-crazy already. It's a mess down there. Don't look.'

Lucas and Vee are lounging on leatherette sofas in the bar of the Hotel Rus.

'So how's Rachel?' asks Vee. She stubs out a cigarette and pushes her fingers through her hair. 'Did she finish the survey already?'

Lucas lifts his glass of beer, checks it in the dull, flat light from the chandelier above their heads, and takes a sip.

'The survey's done, though it took quite a while. Don't worry – I fed her some numbers. Kiev is a hardship posting, no question. Your diplomat buddies will get their allowance.'

Vee sighs. 'Did you hear the Finns are opening an embassy in the building next to mine? Sorin told me, though I don't know why he bothers. Maybe he wants me to get him into some parties.'

'Hmm.' Lucas hopes Sorin hasn't told Vee about his film industry feature, where progress is frustratingly slow. He imagines Sorin accompanying Vee to a party, brushing the small of her back with his bureaucrat's palm and staring at her cleavage. Lucas can see the serpentine curve of her right breast as she leans back against the sofa and yawns without covering her mouth. What would she do if he made a pass? He's been playing this game more often lately, eyes fixed elsewhere so as not to betray the inevitable direction of his thoughts: how it would go, how it would feel. Not that anything would happen; if visions appear uninvited in his head, then he is hardly to blame. Besides, Vee would be scathing.

Or maybe she wouldn't.

'How about a proper drink?' he asks. 'Vodka?'

'Kicking back, are we?' Vee smiles, raises an eyebrow. 'Then you should call Rachel, get her to join us. She must be going crazy in that flat.' She leans forward, her blouse falling open a little. 'How does she do it? I mean, with Ivan, and *you*, for chrissakes . . .'

Lucas looks over his shoulder, searching for a waiter, but the bar is deserted except for a man who is just leaving via the revolving door of the lobby. He steps into the darkness. It's no one Lucas knows. 'Yeah, well, it's been hard for her. Not just Kiev, but being a mother. Her focus has shifted. She worries about stuff. She's promised me she'll see that new embassy doctor.'

'Philip Alleyn?' Vee pushes her hair back from her face. 'Seems like a thorough kind of guy.'

'Right.' Lucas frowns at her choice of words. 'Anyway, it's funny – all of a sudden she's friends with the *dezhornaya* – the one who's been complaining about Ivan's nappies. She comes up most days to see Ivan, and they watch TV together. Rachel says it's good for Ivan to be around someone else, though I have to say I'm surprised. She makes it pretty clear that she hates the crap out of me – the *dezhornaya*, I mean. What is it Teddy calls her? The Baba Yaga—'

'Hey!' says Vee, sitting up. 'That reminds me.' She slips her hand into the shoulder bag on the seat beside her and pulls out a red-bordered copy of *Time*.

Lucas glances across, sees the full-page image of a pavement stall. It is a familiar Kiev scene, though only the vendor's hands are showing: an old person's hands, fingers bound in dirty strips of fabric, held out as if in supplication. Most of the frame is taken up with the meagre vegetables on a sheet of damp newspaper: a couple of wrinkled carrots, a cabbage or two and, in sharp focus in the foreground, a single banana, dotted with flakes of fresh snow. The text beneath reads 'Ukraine – crisis or stasis?'

'Nice,' he remarks, to hide the dismay that rushes up each time he sees a story about Ukraine that someone else has written.

'The pic's one of Teddy's,' says Vera, smiling, pinning him with her gaze. 'Clever boy. He's made the front cover.'

Rachel is sitting on a hard chair in the new doctor's office at the British Embassy on Desyatynna Street. Ivan wriggles in her lap and she reaches nervously for his hands. She hasn't seen a doctor for over four months.

'So, baby first, then you,' says Dr Alleyn – Philip, as he has asked her to call him, though she would prefer him to maintain his professional distance. He looks like a doctor, she thinks, with his wiry grey beard, dark, bright eyes and a tweedy tie that swings forward as he manoeuvres round his over-sized Soviet-era desk and lifts Ivan out of her arms. When he speaks his vowels curl at the edges, the hint of a past life in Australia, perhaps.

'Let's get him undressed. Seven months, hey? He's a good weight! Had all his jabs, I take it, eating well . . .'

'Shall I do that?' asks Rachel, rising to her feet as the

doctor lies Ivan down on the narrow consulting bed and starts to unzip his snow suit.

'No need. Means I can check his joints and his reflexes . . . You sit down, have a rest.'

Rachel does as she is told.

The consulting room is taller than it is wide. There is a long, wooden-framed window behind the desk and freshly-hung net curtains, still with their horizontal creases, open slightly. Beyond Rachel can see a small courtyard and the trunk of a plane tree, its bark patchy as if it has a skin disease: impetigo or psoriasis or another of those words that used to fascinate her as a child. There's an austere quality to the room – the thin February light, the pale blue walls, the high ceiling with its airy cornicing – that lightens the weight on her shoulders, opens up her lungs. She takes a deep breath, then exhales slowly.

'Nasty rash,' says Dr Alleyn, as he opens Ivan's nappy. 'I'll give you something for that. But the best treatment is plenty of fresh air. Put him on a mat on the floor and let him go commando.'

'Okay,' says Rachel. Here is the doctor, she thinks. He is telling her how to look after her baby. This is what she has been missing. This is what she needs.

'He's sitting well. Pulling himself up to stand, yet? Wouldn't be surprised if he's a late walker. He's got long legs. Higher centre of gravity. Super chap!'

Rachel smiles, nods. She remembers the way the security guard had squinted at Ivan's passport photo when they arrived. The photo had been taken when Ivan was six weeks old. The photographer had lain him down on a white sheet on the counter in the shop near Clapham Junction, then stood on a step ladder above him. When the flash went off Ivan's arms and legs had shot out in surprise. The result was an image of a moon face – white, hairless, eyes half-closed and that wide, searching mouth. He looks quite different now, she thinks, as the doctor hands her son back to her, nappy re-taped, vest flapping about his long, strong thighs. Ivan swings his torso forward, fists open, reaching to grab something from the desk. She glances down to see what has caught his attention and notices a copy of *Time* with a picture of a snow-flecked banana on the front cover.

'Look, Ivan!' she says, as a memory flickers. 'Banana.'

'Likes them, does he?' asks Doctor Alleyn, washing his hands at a sink behind a curtain. 'You've done well to keep breastfeeding. Those journalists are a tough crowd – not like us coddled Foreign Office types! But you – well, not many western wives and mums out here, I should think. Everything else all right?' He turns off the tap and pulls a paper towel out of a dispenser, before returning to his chair behind the desk and writing something on a pad of paper. A silence settles around the room. Rachel realises she is expected to answer.

'I'm fine.' She chews her lip. 'My back aches a bit. We don't have a washing machine, so I do the laundry in the bath . . .'

Doctor Alleyn looks up at her.

'Quite.' He frowns a little; just enough to suggest sympathy, should she need it. 'Are you sleeping?'

'Well, yes, mainly. The dogs wake me sometimes. And I still get up twice a night to feed Ivan . . .'

'Try letting him cry. Tough love, and all that. It's not easy, but it works. Are you eating properly?'

She thinks of the soft folds of flesh across her abdomen that won't shift, despite all the walking and lifting and bending. 'Yes. Too much, probably.'

'I shouldn't think so.' He notes something down, then regards her with a calm, practised gaze. 'Do you ever feel weepy? I mean, cry for no particular reason?'

A pause.

'No.'

'Are you more irritable these days? Do you feel any more angry or more lethargic than before you had your baby?'

'I don't think . . . No,' says Rachel, carefully, as she realises, too late, where these questions are heading.

'Don't mind me asking. I'm sure you are on top of things. Anyone who brings a child to Kiev must be pretty resilient . . .'

Rachel, however, is struggling to concentrate. The room's height, its airy spaces are pulling her away from her chair, her heavy stomach, the baby on her lap. If she stands now, he'll fall to the floor and the magazine he is grasping will fall too. *I know this picture,* says the voice in her head. *I've seen those bandaged hands, I was there, this is Teddy's photograph taken outside the monastery and Ivan and I are just out of shot, beyond the red border . . .*

'I have to ask . . .' The doctor is still speaking. 'It's all part of the service – no stone left unturned. Have you ever had thoughts of harming yourself or your baby, Rachel? Even for a moment?'

Rachel looks up and sees that one of Dr Alleyn's eyes is not quite level with the other, as if an invisible finger is tugging at the side of his face. She resists the urge to laugh, though she must bite the inside of her cheeks if she is to remain composed. A lie isn't always a lie. Sometimes you simply nudge the camera sideways.

'Everything's fine,' she says, pushing Ivan's legs into his snowsuit. 'I'm just tired. Thank you so much for seeing me. You've been very reassuring.'

She stands quickly, holding Ivan against her hip. Doctor Alleyn stands too.

'Take my card,' he says. 'For emergencies. I have to tell you I won't be in Kiev for most of the summer, though I can recommend a good private clinic . . .' He hesitates, but Rachel is in control of herself now and her grasp, when he holds out his hand, is swift and firm, as if to say *you do not know me, I am not what you think and now I am going to step back outside the frame.*

Outside on Desyatynna Street Rachel breathes in the freezing air. Ivan is still grasping the copy of *Time*, the top corner damp and ragged where he has mouthed it. She takes it from him and taps on the window of the security guard's concrete booth.

'For Doctor Alleyn,' she says, pushing it under the glass.

The guard looks at her strangely.

'Your baby is bleeding,' he says, touching his own lips.

Rachel checks her son. There's no blood, just flecks of red magazine paper round his mouth.

She wipes them away with the back of her glove.

CHAPTER 13

LUCAS ONCE TOLD Rachel that he loved her for her secrets. They were lolling beneath a tree on a prickly stretch of New Forest heath, gazing at the clouds piling up like over-yeasted dough and eating cherries from a bag. He said that Rachel had hidden depths and he wanted to be the one to plumb them.

Rachel had laughed. 'My head is empty,' she said. 'I'm just an airhead. Any thoughts pass straight through me, and out the other side.' But even as the words slipped from her lips, both knew this was a lie.

❦

One afternoon, just after lunch, the telephone rings in the apartment. Rachel, folding washing in the bedroom, thinks it must be Lucas. It isn't Lucas. It is Zoya, her voice flat and tinny on the poor local line.

'A driver wishes to deliver six boxes of nappies. I told him we cannot take them at the office.'

Rachel's grip tightens on the receiver. She closes her eyes and breathes deeply. Suzie has done what she asked.

'I *said*,' repeats Zoya, 'a driver wishes . . .'

'Sorry,' says Rachel, collecting herself. 'Sorry. Are they Pampers? Is Lucas there?'

'Yes, and no,' says Zoya. 'Lucas has an appointment

at the Ministry of Finance. This is why I am calling you.'

'Right.' Rachel is already imagining the nappies with their neat folds and self-sealing fastenings, their soft elastication and velvety, leak-proof coating. She wants to touch them. Count them. 'Can you ask the driver to send them up to Staronavodnitksa Street? And pay him, please – use Lucas's emergency dollars. I'll pay it back.'

'I have told the driver to return tomorrow. He has no paperwork. No invoice.'

'Zoya!' Rachel tries not to shout. 'I need them now! Tonight!'

'Then I tell him to come back. Lucas can drive them up later.'

Rachel is still absorbing the fact that the nappies have arrived at all. Lucas doesn't know about the order. He'll hate the fact that she's buying them from Rob, but she won't let him refuse to take them as he refused the washing machine.

'Zoya, listen. Lucas is trying to save money, but I need those nappies and I ordered them without telling him. Please can you drive them here for me? I –' she hesitates – 'I can give you ten dollars if that helps.'

Zoya doesn't reply and the phone goes dead. Rachel assumes she has gravely offended her and weeps at her own stupidity, until forty minutes later the doorbell rings and she spies Zoya standing on the landing with several cardboard boxes balanced on top of the washing machine.

'I have done this for Ivan,' says Zoya, when Rachel opens the door, still blowing her nose. 'Clearly, if you don't receive Pampers, you will become insane.' The two women stare at each other, Zoya frowning as she always does, her plucked eyebrows a line of rebuke, a line that will not stand a challenge, yet perhaps can bear a truce.

'Thank you,' says Rachel.

⁂

At four o'clock Lucas returns home with a slab of pork wrapped in newspaper. He seems buoyant in the way he used to be, before he and Rachel came to Kiev.

'I'm going to the Dovzhenko studios tonight,' he says, jiggling Ivan's bouncy chair. 'They're doing some voice edits for A Golden Promise.'

'For what?' Rachel looks up from the button she is sewing on to an old denim shirt.

'A Golden Promise. That's the title of the film. The one I'm writing about. Keep up, Rach!' He grins, too fired up to care that his wife doesn't remember. 'It's the perfect time to get some background sound for my feature, and Sorin says the director has guaranteed an interview. He's been hard to pin down, so I'm not going to miss him. I'm sick to death of churning out bulletins from Parliament, when all London thinks it needs is the nuclear story.'

Sorin, remembers Rachel. This is the man who took Jurassic Park.

'Will he – Sorin – be there?' she asks.

'Probably. I bet he'd love to hook up with an actress or two. Hey, why don't you come with me?'

Rachel considers the possibility that she might recover her book. 'What about Ivan? We can't take him to a sound recording.'

'Why not?' Lucas opens the fridge door and pushes the

meat inside. 'It's a huge place. You can wander round with him while I get what I need. I've got the car tonight. Zoya says she'll meet us there.' He sucks his lips into a pretend pout and puts on a fake Russian drawl. 'You, baby, should be star of blockbuster film – screen goddess and wife of Hetman!'

Rachel has just secreted sixty-four perfectly pure Pampers nappies in the drawer under the bed and hidden the other four boxes under a blanket on top of the wardrobe. Their value is incalculable to her; they help keep the danger at bay. If she could only get her book back – if she could complete the ritual – then all might be well.

She looks at her husband. Go with him, she tells herself. Don't overthink it. In fact, don't think anything at all.

⚜

Lucas is driving with the interior light on. He is holding a street map above the steering wheel and peering at the blank-faced buildings that flicker past them like a spool of Kodak Super 8 as the twilight deepens and the bare trees crowd in.

Rachel, sitting in the back of the Zhiguli with Ivan on her knee, is struggling to read her husband's script in the gloom.

'What does freedom mean to Kievans doing a little late shopping down on the city's main street, Khreschatyk?

[clip: demonstrators chanting]

Some say they write poetry, while others join the singing in Independence Square. A few daub nation-alist slogans, while many simply apply for a passport,

140

rent out their flat or cross themselves as they pass their local church.

[clip: get some nationalist music here – folk singers outside St Sophia's?]

But if you are a true Cossack you revive a legend. Everyone here knows the story of Hetman Polubotok, who in 1723 deposited 200,000 gold coins in the vaults of the Bank of England and bequeathed them to an independent Ukraine. Back in 1990, the poet Volodymyr Tsybulko did the maths. He declared that the interest amounts to sixteen trillion pounds sterling. According to his calculations, every man, woman and child from Donetsk to Lviv is owed precisely thirty-eight kilograms of the Hetman's treasure. Director Viktor Lukyanenko has been quick to seize on the story for one of the first post-independence films to be produced at the Dovzhenko studios here on Peremogy Prospekt. Mr Lukyanenko, I'm told you are describing the film as a romantic epic . . .

[clip: interview with Viktor Lukyanenko] . . .'

'So, what do you think?' he asks.
Rachel is trying to catch hold of her husband's breezy tone.
'Great,' she says, nodding. 'Great!'
'It's just the intro,' says Lucas. 'A bit of scene-setting. I need to interest different audiences, not just the World Service lot.' He yanks on the wheel so that the car turns sharply left. 'Peremogy Prospekt. Over there.'

Rachel drops the script and grasps sleeping Ivan more tightly. The Zhiguli bumps over the fissures in the concrete and comes to a halt outside some sort of warehouse. She peers out of the window. The building might be a sports hall or a House of Culture or a hospital or a market: they all look the same from the outside with their closed-up, peeling frontages and their lack of lights and signs. She thinks of the old amusement halls on the seafront at Southsea and mouths the Cyrillic letters that hang lopsidedly above some padlocked doors until she makes the right sounds.

'Dov – Dovzhenko *keeno*studio . . .'

The passenger door is wrenched open.

'Why have *you* come?' asks Zoya, frowning with no trace of their earlier complicity.

'She's an extra!' declares Lucas.

Rachel climbs out with Ivan in her arms and follows Lucas and Zoya across the icy crust of the car park towards a steel door. The metal is dented as if someone has given it a kicking. Zoya stops to stamp the snow off her boots.

'Ready for your debut?' Lucas asks.

Rachel hears Zoya grunt, but as they step inside and walk down a narrow corridor past a wall light that softly fizzes, she sees that Zoya is wearing eyeshadow. Green eyeshadow. She hasn't changed her clothes; she's still in her padded coat and her heavy, lumpen boots. Yet the eyeshadow changes her. It makes her look younger. Or older. It makes her look *something*.

The corridor is long and smells of molten wire. Ivan is wriggling inside his snow suit. Rachel pulls off his balaclava as they turn a corner, and soon they are passing open doors and stepping round old women sitting on stools. The women have spongy, swollen knees and wear slippers on their feet.

A man in brown overalls squeezes past. He is carrying an old-fashioned suitcase.

'In here,' says Zoya, nodding towards a side room with shiny green walls and a single lightbulb dangling from a flex. There's a curtained recess at the far end, and people are pushing in and out, creating a bottleneck. She hands Lucas his audio recorder along with a neat coil of cable. 'Don't lose this – you have no spare.' Then off she goes, swallowed up by the huddle. Lucas hooks the recorder strap over his shoulder and pushes the cable into his pocket. He takes Ivan from Rachel and holds him up above his head as they push their way through.

'This is the sound stage,' whispers Lucas, as they emerge into a cavern-like room the size of a school gymnasium. Its high roof is crisscrossed with pipes and drooping wires. In the centre is a big tent made from swathes of grey felted fabric suspended from the ceiling. People mill everywhere, some in small groups, others forming a long line that snakes around the walls. A few men are playing cards at a table by the light of a fringed lamp that seems better suited to an old-fash-ioned cloakroom or a seedy sort of club. At another table, two women count out bundles of small paper notes into piles. The line of people shuffles forward.

'Are they filming this?' Rachel asks.

'I shouldn't think so,' says Lucas. 'It's pay day! Those people must be crew, or extras.' He hands Ivan back to Rachel and points at a man wearing headphones. The man is stand-ing half way up a ladder, near the tent. 'There's the director, Viktor Lukyanenko. He's the one I'm here to interview.'

As Lucas finishes speaking, the man with the headphones raises his arms and sweeps them twice through the air.

Immediately the hum of conversation pulses more intensely. Then he presses one hand down and Rachel realises that he is orchestrating the sound, directing small clumps of queuers whose voices rise and fall in response to the signals he gives them. They are being recorded even while they line up to collect their wages.

Lucas raises his eyebrows and turns to talk to someone – a woman with short, silver hair wearing owlish glasses and a crumpled cotton jacket. He gestures towards the tent and starts fiddling with the dials on his recorder. Rachel steps out of his way. It doesn't seem like the right time to ask him whether he has spotted Sorin.

A young man with thinning blond hair pulls gently on Ivan's foot.

'*Malchik?*' he asks, smiling.

Rachel knows this word. Boy. She nods. The young man puts his head on one side.

'Ameree-can?'

'Oh no,' whispers Rachel. 'English.'

'Engleesh,' repeats the young man, grinning. His forehead is inflamed with acne, its surface like the woodchip that lines her mother's front room. 'London. Film London.'

She nods again, but now the director on the step ladder is speaking, his voice ringing over the crowd's swelling chorus. It is only when the chatter reverts to its usual formlessness that she realises the segment has ended. Lucas has disappeared, so Rachel watches while two women clear a space in front of the tent, shooing people away and frowning. Inching sideways, she sees that an old-fashioned microphone is suspended from wires just inside the tent. She stands on tip-toe as a shortish man steps forward and positions himself beneath it. The director signals to the crowd to stop talking. At this point, however, few people are watching, so he claps, twice, his palms cracking like a starting pistol. Instantly, everyone falls quiet.

It is the silence that upsets Ivan, not the clapping. He is seven months old, already settling into the life-long yearning for pattern, the fear of the broken rhythm. Silence jolts him into self-awareness. He makes a fretful droning sound. Rachel, alerted, pushes her finger into his mouth, but he doesn't want a pacifier. He wants milk. She looks around, eyes searching for an exit. Not now, she thinks. Then, *of course now*. Anxiety prickles along her arm and provokes her son still further. The more she bounces him on her hip, the more his limbs resist. Ivan leans back, arching away and then, before she can raise her hand to stop him, he smashes his forehead into her cheek-bone. The blow is so sharp that Rachel actually stumbles sideways. She utters a short cry, then clamps her mouth shut and tries to move back so she can steady herself against the wall. She knows what is coming. Ivan's eyes are wide with shock. His throat is opening.

He screams.

'So,' says the man from the white goods shop as he leads Rachel down the passageway. 'I will take you to a quiet place. Here it is, to your left.'

'Mykola,' she mouths, her skull still pounding. She is unsure whether she is speaking out loud but relieved she has remembered his name. At least Ivan's cries have slowed; he hiccups and starts to suck his fingers, calmed by the dim lights and his mother's steady pace. The man opens a door.

Beyond it she sees a small store room with shelves and a mop and bucket in one corner. Two middle-aged women with dyed hair sit on stacking chairs with a picnic laid out on their laps.

'*Eezvenitye*,' says Mykola, motioning to the women to continue with their meal. He turns to Rachel. 'Your baby is hungry.' He gestures to a third chair. 'Sit.'

Rachel stares at this man with the rounded shoulders and dark, soft eyes. She cannot fathom why he is here, but the stillness envelops her and the warmth from a small electric heater makes her sigh and sit down.

'You will not be disturbed,' he says, placing his hand on the door handle. 'I will wait outside.'

Rachel looks at the two women. They are laying out strips of pickle. 'Thank you. I'll be fine.'

'You are safe here.'

'Yes . . .'

He nods, then closes the door with the gentlest of clicks. She doesn't hear a key turning, but neither does she hear his footsteps retreating. Even Ivan has fallen silent. A strange kind of peace settles across her shoulders, like feathers, soft and weightless. As the two women politely incline their heads, then dip their black bread in a little pot of salt, chew their sausage and wipe their fingers on yellow cotton napkins, she opens her jacket and feeds her son.

Some time later, when Ivan is asleep and Rachel's head is nodding with tiredness, Lucas opens the door.

'Hey! Are you okay?'

Rachel looks up. The two women have gone. There is no

trace of their picnic, no heater, no yellow napkins. They must have slipped out while she was dozing.

'Yes, yes, I'm fine.' She tries to remember who else entered the room. 'Did you see anyone come in – or go out?'

'No. I've been tied up with Lukyanenko for the past hour. Got a great interview, though we all heard Ivan bellowing. *Kashmar!* as the babushkas say. Mind you, I'll probably keep him in my piece. These sound accidents often create a more authentic audio experience.' Lucas walks over and lifts Ivan out of Rachel's arms, settling him into his shoulder. 'Your first brush with fame, son of mine! Just as well you managed to tuck yourselves away in here. Hey, what happened to your cheek?'

Rachel touches her face, wincing where her skin feels tender, then stands up and checks Ivan's forehead. His skin is white, unmarked.

'Ivan head-butted me.'

'Ouch – that's quite a bruise,' says Lucas. 'This'll make you feel better. Sorin brought it.' He fishes something out of his pocket with his spare hand. It is a paperback book with a silhouette of a T-rex on a yellow disc on the cover, scored by a familiar white crease. Her copy of *Jurassic Park*.

Rachel stares, caught in a moment's disbelief. She takes the book in both hands and grips it, testing its density, its solidity beneath her thumbs. Her arms tremble. She will not let it go again. Quickly she pushes it into the inside pocket of her coat.

'Thank you.'

'Thank Zoya,' says Lucas, hoisting Ivan a little higher. 'She remembered to ask for it. She told Sorin you needed to know who gets eaten at the end.'

Back at home in the flat on the thirteenth floor, Rachel settles Ivan into his cot and runs a bath while Lucas steps out for a smoke. Lying in the tepid water with the door locked, the back of her neck against the unforgiving rim, she takes up her book and turns the pages, her lips mouthing the numbers as she counts the words, the now-familiar see-saw of anxiety and release pulsing across her synapses.

After forty minutes, when the letters start jumping and the terror of dropping Ivan over the balcony is temporarily in retreat, she is almost too cold to stand up and rub herself dry. She shivers on the edge of the toilet seat with a towel wrapped around her and closes her eyes.

Things happen for a reason, she reminds herself. You see a man. You find your book. Mykola is a real person, though sometimes she imagines him. Perhaps she ought to watch for him again.

CHAPTER 14

THE COLD SNAP breaks at the end of February. Grey clouds barge across the sky, northwards now, and the mounds of shovelled snow soften like ancient boulders worn smooth by the passing of millennia.

Lucas is relieved that Rachel seems more settled. Every Sunday, news permitting, he takes his wife and son on an outing. Family time, he calls it, and laughs at how they have arrived at something so suburban. Sometimes they take a trip in the car to the Architectural Park where they stroll around the little wooden huts and the drinks kiosks and show Ivan the life-size blue whale made of concrete. At Respublikansky Stadion they wander past the displays of cheaply made t-shirts and sweatshirts boldly proclaiming 'Hugo Boss' or 'Gucci' beneath drooping plastic awnings, or they hop on the 62 bus that runs along the river, then take the stately funicular past the Barbie sign and up the hill to St Andrew's or St Sophia's. When Lucas catches Rachel staring into crowds or turning her head towards strangers, he assumes she is merely curious. The two of them talk about Ivan, or about Lucas's work, but they don't discuss the future or their shared past. Those places are fraught with danger. Sex is a rare midnight fumbling; Rachel goes to bed before Lucas gets home and she's up with Ivan at six. Anyway, Lucas needs his sleep. The agencies want news of disarmament treaties and the Black Sea Fleet, but instead there's just rumour, stalling and a nudge off a

149

sub-editor's schedule. Each short bulletin takes its toll. He tells Zoya he'll hold back his feature about Lukyanenko's film until *A Golden Promise* is released. Then he can tell the whole story, rounded off with reaction from the premiere.

Rachel, meanwhile, sticks to her routine. After breakfast she soaks the washing in a bucket with water boiled on the stove. Next she takes Ivan out to the *universam* or rides the trolleybus down to the shops along Khreschatyk, trawling the Bessarabsky market or the empty booths of the central department store within its grand carapace on the corner of Bohdana Khmel'nyts'koho Street. She marks her path across the city by tearing off the little handwritten slips from notices pasted to lampposts and walls. She doesn't know what they say: they could be adverts for language lessons or prostitutes or pleas for lost children. Soon her pockets are full of telephone numbers.

After lunch, Ivan naps while she keeps him safe by counting her words from *Jurassic Park* at the table in the kitchen until Elena knocks on the door for their daily dose of *Simplemente Maria*. Sometimes Elena brings a gift for Ivan – a musty-smelling balloon, a teething ring made from hard, unyielding plastic or, once, a pair of red nylon socks with a border of little yellow hens. Rachel wishes she could speak Russian or Ukrainian. She's learned a long list of nouns, but conversation is much harder. There are things she wants to ask the caretaker.

One afternoon in early March Lucas comes home for dinner with twelve dark red roses in a crackly cellophane bouquet.

'Happy International Women's Day!' he says, kissing Rachel on the mouth with the tang of his last cigarette still strong on his breath. The roses aren't fully opened, yet already their heads droop on flaccid stems, petals browning at the edges. 'I couldn't move on the trolleybus – wilting flowers everywhere. The woman who sold me these swore they'd been flown in from Tbilisi this morning! I bought chocolates for Zoya. She'd have sulked for a month if I hadn't arrived at the office with a box of cherry liqueurs the size of a small table, and you can bet the *dezhornaya* was watching to make sure I'd remembered flowers for you. I suppose I should have bought some for her.'

Rachel unwraps the roses and trims the ends from the stems before placing them in a tall jug of water. 'They might revive,' she says, as several petals fall to the floor. She is surprised to find she cares about a custom in which scowling, sheepish men do their once-yearly duty by their mothers and wives and female employees.

Lucas tickles Ivan in his bouncy chair and peers into the fridge.

'We should go out really, but I'm working again tonight. There's interest in my *Golden Promise* feature from Radio Four. I've been speaking to a couple of programme editors. They all say I should go on a camera course. Start filming my own stuff. Become an all-rounder.' He pokes at a tray of eggs. 'Have we got enough eggs for an omelette? Good to see the washing machine has finally been taken away—'

Rachel turns, sharply. 'What?'

'The washing machine. It's gone.' Lucas straightens up, a carton of UHT milk in his hand. 'Didn't you notice? Your dodgy salesman must have had second thoughts – or found a buyer.'

Sure enough, when Rachel hurries along the hallway and pulls open the front door, there's nothing next to the doormat except a square of unwashed lino. Has Mykola been here to remove his troublesome gift? The space left behind leaves her strangely hollow inside so she stands there for a minute or two in her stockinged feet and wonders what would happen if she stuffed her husband's grimy shirts and her own rancid nursing bras into the rubbish chute and sent them tumbling down to Elena.

Nothing escapes the caretaker. She will know who took the washing machine away.

Then something else occurs to Rachel. Maybe it hasn't moved as far as Lucas thinks.

After breakfast the next morning Rachel scoops up Ivan and takes him downstairs in the lift. The day outside is dull and misty. She can't see the river from the windows in the foyer and even the Motherland monument is shrouded from view. The snow on the ground is pocked and grey, and the hunched women on their stick legs at the tram stop make the street look like a Lowry painting. The Siberian freeze may be receding, but winter has not yet left for good.

Elena is not in her cubicle. Her chair is pulled out and the dregs of her morning coffee sit darkly in the bottom of her usual cup. A newspaper lies flat on the desktop with lists of Cyrillic letters like shorthand jotted in the margins, and a neat row of plastic yoghurt pots from Denmark or Sweden, each filled with soil, sit on the shelf beneath the window. One or two seedlings are just starting to poke through, their pale backs still bent, still bearing the burden of the seed case from which they have just emerged.

'Elena?' Rachel says, not loudly, for the empty foyer is full of echoes. Ivan starts kicking her thigh. '*Da*,' he says, '*da-da*' like a good little Ukrainian boy. She kisses his head and wishes she had brought him down in the baby carrier. Instead she wraps her thick cardigan around her son's shoulders and ventures outside.

Rachel has never been down to the basement. The door is round the side of the apartment block, at the bottom of an external service stairway. It has a broken metal rail and there are lumps of congealed salt on the concrete. She taps on the metal door which drifts open at her touch.

'Elena? It's Rachel . . .'

Her voice is drowned by a sudden acceleration of sound, a deep, juddering roar. Ivan's back stiffens and his fists grasp her shirt, pinching her skin. Elena and another figure are standing beneath a strip light with their backs to the door. Lines of nylon rope strung from the ceiling pipes droop with strange, disembodied articles – dresses, trousers, pairs of sagging pants. In front of a stainless steel sink plumbed against what must be the bottom of the lift shaft she recognises the familiar bulk of the washing machine, shimmying sideways across the floor as its spin cycle peaks.

The figure next to Elena turns, and Rachel sees that it is Zoya, her arms full of soiled sheets.

⁂

We are all compromised by the washing machine, thinks Rachel, as she extracts another load of clean vests and pillow cases from the drum. She and Zoya have both lied to Lucas, who believes she still soaks the washing in the bath and takes it down to the basement merely to dry it. Elena appears to have banished her disgust for the machine – or with the man who sent it – and twists the dial to set the cycle as if she has been doing this for years. Ivan, meanwhile, watches the spinning washing from his bouncy chair with mute fascination until the rhythmic churning and plashing send him off to sleep. Rachel's back no longer aches at night and her clothes smell fresh – fresher than before, at any rate, now that she's discovered a Norwegian brand of washing powder at the black market kiosks near the football stadium. The box with its picture of a fjord on the front is emptying at an alarming rate. Zoya seems burdened by endless dirty sheets. Rachel wonders if she's taking in her neighbours' washing on the side.

'Do you have children, Zoya?' asks Rachel one day, a couple of weeks after the washing machine is moved. Rachel is less wary of Zoya since she recovered her copy of *Jurassic Park* and kept the secret about the nappies.

Zoya shakes out a pair of nearly dry jeans. The fabric cracks like a whip.

'No.'

'Any family at home?'

'One relative, yes.'

'Your mother? Father?'

'No.'

Rachel gives up and squats down to hand Ivan a bread ring. Her son is sitting on his blanket on the floor, his chubby knees splayed out like a little Buddha's, surrounded by the clothes pegs that the women have placed there for his amusement. He is safe like that she thinks – close to the ground. His trunk is sturdy and already he is trying to pull himself up if a chair is placed next to him. Soon he will be crawling.

'What about Elena, I wonder?' asks Rachel, peering into the gloom. Elena stands at her workbench beside the fuse boxes coiling torn strips of newspaper into cones for her spring seedlings. 'Elena!' she calls softly, adding the Russian word for children as a question. '*Dyeti?*'

Zoya stops sorting clothes and looks up, folding her arms beneath her breasts.

Elena carries on coiling. '*Nyet,*' she says.

Rachel frowns, frustrated by her inability to communicate. 'What's the word for niece, or nephew?' she asks, turning to Zoya, but Zoya isn't in the mood for conversation.

'There are plenty of underpaid teachers in this city,' she says. 'You should take some lessons.'

CHAPTER 15

VEE THROWS A party on the evening of Lucas's twenty-eighth birthday. Vee's own birthday falls two days later, so she calls it a joint celebration and invites all her friends. Teddy and his boyfriend will be there, and the usual crowd – journalists, plus a scattering of the diplomats and European Bank types that Vee always seems to attract.

Rachel lays out her dangly earrings and washes her hair in the sink. She is worried about taking Ivan to the party. There will be smoking and noise and he'll have to stay up long past his bedtime.

'The smokers will stay in the kitchen,' says Lucas as he takes two bottles of cheap Russian fizz out of the fridge and sticks half a litre of vodka in his coat pocket. 'Vee has promised. And Ivan can sleep in her bed when he gets tired.'

'You know that won't work,' chides Rachel.

'But it's my birthday,' says Lucas, only half-joking. 'And that means everyone does what I say.'

Vee's apartment is at the top of the stairwell in a brown building near the Dnipro Hotel. The invitation says eight o'clock, but Rachel and Lucas are late because Rachel wanted to bathe Ivan first and get him into his pyjamas. She is already peeling him out of his snowsuit as Lucas presses the bell. The landing smells of garlic and dill, and there's a handwritten sign stuck above the spyhole in Vee's shiny steel door.

'*Sshh! Baby sleeping!*' it reads, in thick, cartoonish letters.

'So thoughtful!' says Lucas, tapping it when Vee opens the door. Vee puts her fingers to her lips and pulls a Betty Boop face, then laughs. She is wearing a clinging top over jeans and stylish high-heeled boots. The hallway behind her is jammed with guests; the clamour of voices rises over a pounding europop beat.

'Happy birthday!' she shouts, waving them inside. Lucas shrugs off his coat, then, while Rachel removes hers, he lifts Ivan up on one shoulder and ploughs into the crowd.

'Don't let him get over-excited,' murmurs Rachel. It is too late. Ivan's eyes are wide and bright, his legs kick enthusiastically and his fists reach out towards every passing thing. The apartment is warm with bodies and breath, there's a string of gold tinsel dangling from the ceiling light and Vee is passing round plates of blinis garnished with baby gherkins, sour cream and a dollop of red caviar. She holds them high over everyone's heads.

'Hello!' says a man with a beard as Rachel inches past a wardrobe in the cramped hall. It is Dr Alleyn from the embassy. Rachel, startled, slips into the dim cave of the living room that doubles as Vee's bedroom. Lucas passes her a tumbler of sweet *champanskoye* and points past a couple trying to dance in a tiny space in front of Vee's dressing table. He is motioning towards the bed where Teddy and his boyfriend Karl are sitting with their backs against the wall, clutching their knees. They are talking to an older, balding man in a white shirt who looks as if he has only recently removed his tie.

'What's Sorin doing here?' Lucas mutters, before turning to greet an acquaintance from Interfax. Someone has given Ivan a plastic spoon. More guests squeeze in through the doorway – pale faces – no one Rachel recognises. The near-darkness in the living room, the crush of bodies and the noise create a cocoon of anonymity. She tips back her glass and drinks.

৵৺

An hour or so later, Rachel is clutching a bottle of beer and squatting on the floor next to Teddy.

'Where have you been?' she asks, her eyes re-focusing on Ivan, who has fallen asleep in the crook of Karl's arm. He looks so perfect, she thinks, so trusting and fragile.

'Oh you know,' says Teddy, rubbing his hand down his shin. 'In the café, mostly.'

The café. Rachel remembers the photographs of figures standing still in the street, carefully positioned like statues or chess pieces, each staring at something outside the frame.

'I want to ask you,' says Rachel. 'I mean,' her head is a little fuzzy, 'about that picture you took at the monastery, the one on the cover of *Time* . . .'

'It was shit,' says Teddy, pulling a face.

'No it wasn't . . .' soothes Karl. His finger traces the edge of Teddy's ear.

'It was shit,' insists Teddy. 'A cheap shot. Old woman, snow, banana. State of the nation. God – I hate it all – hate the way we *tell* a story, as if it is just waiting for us to come along and scoop it up. Because story is king, right? Let's all worship the story king.'

'I hated it too,' says Rachel.

'Exactly,' says Teddy. Then, after a moment, 'What did you hate?'

Rachel takes a sip of beer and wipes her hand across her mouth.

'That picture! I don't know – it was wrong. Maybe because Ivan and I weren't in it. We were there. We were part of that scene as much as the old woman.'

Teddy looks taken aback. 'You *wanted* to be in it?'

'No,' says Rachel. 'I don't know, maybe. You made it look like she was begging, but I bought that banana and took it home and Ivan ate it. You didn't show that. It sounds stupid, now . . .' She peeks again at her sleeping son. 'I like your gallery pictures better.'

'Not stupid,' murmurs Karl, stroking Ivan's soft cheek. 'You two should be on all the front covers.'

                                   ✵

A few minutes after midnight Teddy climbs on a chair in the hallway to get everyone's attention and Karl hands him a tray bearing a large pink iced cake.

'Vee made me hide it in the bathtub,' he says, laughing. 'Happy Birthday, Lucas!'

'You're too late!' shouts a voice from the kitchen. 'It's already tomorrow!'

Then someone starts singing 'Happy Birthday' in a comically deep tone and someone else turns the music down, while a handful of others join in. Soon they are calling 'toast!' and looking round for Lucas, because no one has seen him for a while, but then Rachel hears the front door open and sees her husband walk in from the outside hallway. Behind him steps Vee.

'We were *smoking*!' she cries. 'Not having sex in the lift like

159

you two, you squalid pair!' She throws her pack of Marlboros at Teddy and Karl, and everyone laughs. Rachel laughs, too, and kisses her sleepy son because she is at a party with lots of different people and her fear is waiting quietly on the landing behind the door. By the time she has knocked back another shot of vodka the music has been turned up once again.

Later, as the night slowly unravels, as Teddy and Karl are curled around each other like two brown mice and Sorin is drinking Johnnie Walker with Lucas in the kitchen, Rachel opens her blouse and gives Ivan a discreet feed. A young stringer from *The Telegraph* sits next to her, his hand resting in a bag of pretzels; he has round, wire-framed glasses and an earnest expression and he doesn't know where to look, so he shuts his eyes and reels off the latest IMF statistics.

'Fifty per cent by the end of the month,' he intones with a slow shake of his head. 'You can't shift from a command economy overnight,' and Rachel nods, while her gaze wanders to the doorway. Vee is standing there, her lips still matt and red; she is listening to a woman whose bleached hair, backlit by a wall light, has become a frizzy halo. Rachel shuts her eyes for a moment to make sure she isn't imagining things, but it's Zoya, all right, dragging on her cigarette and blowing smoke past Vee's ear as she talks in English before switching to rapid Ukrainian.

Ivan pinches Rachel's breast; he hasn't finished his feed and she is already adjusting her blouse. Something has happened – a murder or a strike or another presidential stand-off. The party is over. The journalists are reaching for their coats.

∂℘

It is almost two a.m. when Zoya, on Lucas's instructions, drops Rachel and Ivan back at the apartment block. Once her passengers are safely indoors Zoya sits motionless in the driver's seat for a minute. As a few drops of sleety rain splatter across the windscreen, she reaches beneath the glove compartment for her wipers and climbs out of the Zhiguli to attach them. A stray dog – brindled and leggy – sidles across the car park. Zoya bends down to give him a stroke. His coat is rough and one of his eyes is infected, but his ears are silky smooth. Out in the darkness another dog barks. She looks up. It sounds as if the animal is high above her head, maybe on one of the apartment balconies. Her grandfather used to keep an Alsatian on the balcony. When Zoya was fourteen the dog ate rat poison, but he didn't die. In the end, a brain tumour killed him.

The trolleybuses have stopped running when she turns the key in the ignition and pulls out on to Staronavodnitska Street. On impulse she turns left and drives up towards Lesi Ukrainky rather than right towards the river. She stops at a red light, the engine ticking over as she waits, though there are no other cars at the junction. When the light changes to green she turns right, puts the gear stick into neutral, switches off the engine and coasts down the hill. If anyone were to ask she might say it was to save petrol, but the truth is that at this hour she would rather listen to the wind. There is no one here to make crude gestures because she is a woman driving a car, no one to shout insults or say she cannot do this thing or that thing. She is alone on the six-lane boulevard, carried by the silence of the buildings and the trees.

Back on Khreschatyk, the prostitutes in their shiny leggings lean against the wall that leads down to the metro. A black Mercedes winks as it jumps the lights. The Zhiguli coughs after free-wheeling, though soon it is passing the new Seagrams store with its marble pillars, its Canadian maple panelling and blue satin presentation boxes of cognac costing two hundred dollars apiece. The stores patronised by the new elite take their place between the book shops and the bread shops and the shops selling machine-embroidered tablecloths and hand-daubed plates. Bribes flow like vodka. The suits and the watches may be flaunted more openly, but their new visibility makes it easier to steer Lucas round the pot holes of corruption, keeping him safe. Rachel is a different matter. She is secretive, like most mothers, though her cow eyes and her way of watching the world without looking straight on unsettle Zoya. Rachel counts buildings. She asks questions without purpose. Sometimes, she walks as if she is afraid of the floor.

The river is black as Zoya crosses over. In summer, the old communists and the young and the foolish who have stopped caring about radioactive contamination picnic and bathe on its islands. Now, though, the lights on the bridge are too dim to illuminate the water. On she drives, past the cement works and the tower blocks, past the schools and the Houses of Culture and the stretches of waste ground with their rusting see-saws and dented slides, until finally she reaches her own neighbourhood.

Upstairs in the little flat her neighbour Tanya is asleep on her sofa.

'Wake up,' says Zoya, giving her a shake.

'He's crapped himself,' mutters Tanya, reaching for her coat. 'You need to get some diapers.'

Zoya, cleaning her grandfather, holds her breath against

the stench and grips his leg just a little too hard. Sometimes the need to squeeze and crush overwhelms her. The old man groans and she releases her grip and wipes her hand, relieved that she can still let go.

'Forgive me, Grandpa,' she whispers, as she dabs at his thighs with a towel. 'Forgive me.'

CHAPTER 16

L UCAS, WHO HAS stayed out all night, phones the next
morning to say there's an Interior Ministry briefing. He
asks whether Zoya mentioned anything as she hasn't turned
up for work and he's pretty furious actually as he hasn't seen
her since she drove Rachel home from the party.

'No,' says Rachel. 'What happened?'

'A leak at Chernobyl.'

Fallout, thinks Rachel. Seepage. Half-lives. She takes a
quick breath. 'Is it dangerous? What should I do?'

'What? Oh no. It's contained. A mammoth fuck-up, all
the same. Not what Kravchuk needs while he dithers over
nuclear warheads.'

Rachel is silent. She has lots of things she wants to say to
her husband: things like 'come home' and 'don't come home',
but sometimes it is as if there is a fine mesh in front of her
mouth, catching her words. She tries to single out one question, push it through.

'Will Vee be there? At the briefing?'

'I should think so, if her hangover can stand it. Why?'

'Pass on my thanks for the party.'

'Right. I'll see you later. It's going to be busy.'

❦

When Rachel goes down to the basement mid-morning with

Ivan on her hip and her laundry bag in the baby carrier, she expects to find Zoya and Elena. She is greeted by darkness, but it doesn't matter. The basement calms her. It feels safe to retreat to below ground level, surrounded by concrete and earth. No vertiginous balconies. No radioactive cloud. No journalists with their high heels and complicated laughs.

She flicks the light switch, but the fluorescent tube spits and dies so she fumbles her way over to the desk lamp Elena keeps on the workbench and turns that on instead.

The bare bulb's glow illuminates Elena's sheets of old newspaper and neat coils of twine. It reaches into the shadows, exaggerating concrete uprights and draped washing and the warm, humming bulk of the boilers. Almost immediately Rachel knows she and Ivan are not alone.

'Allo . . .' she says cautiously, as something swings backwards and forwards near the base of the far wall, half-obscured by a pillar. Then she hears the sound of tearing paper. Elena must be here somewhere. 'Elena?'

'Good morning,' replies a strange voice – a boy's voice. It lingers over the first syllable of 'morning' as if savouring its unfamiliarity. 'Ciao baby!'

Rachel blinks for a moment, gripping Ivan so that he wriggles and complains. She knows this voice: it belongs to Stepan, the boy from upstairs, the boy who stares at her in a way that seems too old for his years. He's been sitting in the darkness.

'I'm sorry . . .' She takes a step backwards. 'I didn't know anyone else was down here.'

Stepan doesn't speak for a moment. Instead Rachel hears a rustling sound, and then the sudden *sheesh* of a sneeze. Now she can see him; he is sitting on a tall metal stool, swinging his legs and fiddling with a paper packet in his hands. As she watches he lifts the packet up to his mouth and shakes it to dislodge its contents. She can smell something, too – a sickly strawberry smell, a synthetic tang that takes her back to the formica kitchen table of her childhood.

'Baby, want some?' he asks, offering the packet.

'No thank you. I'm – I have to go.'

'Why go, Mum?' The boy swings himself off the stool and strolls towards her. He passes three of Ivan's vests dangling from a line and she wants to leave, she wants to tell him not to call her 'Mum', but she also wants to take the clean laundry with her. 'You bring clothes here I think,' he continues. 'This is your – ah, *steeralnaya mashina*.' He nods at the washing machine, its tubes attached to the taps of the sink like a cow in a milking parlour. 'I know that shop. Okay for shop, but no for Elena Vasilyevna. She like machine, she don't like shop. She don't like man in shop.'

Mykola, thinks Rachel, remembering how Elena had spat at the delivery man.

'You seem to know Elena Vasilyevna quite well . . .' She dips quickly under the line and bobs up next to the vests.

'Quite *well*.' Again, the boy lingers over the second word, as if he is tasting it in his mouth. Rachel, uncomfortable, changes the subject.

'And you aren't rollerblading today?'

'No. It is difficult. Before I train in Soviet system, compete with many countries. Learn English! Now, no money. No papers. No compete.'

Rachel is still holding Ivan. She tugs a vest from the line with her free hand.

'What about school?'

'No school. I leave school.'

166

'But your uncle?'

'He not my uncle. He, ah – coach.'

Stepan continues to stare, though his cheeks slacken for a moment. Lucas is right, thinks Rachel. The old man is his keeper, or worse. She tries to imagine how difficult Stepan's life must be and how abandoned he must feel. She'd like to reach out to him, to show him she cares as she truly *wants* to care, even while he is reverting to his habitual brazen smirk.

'What will you do?' she asks, but Stepan is stretching out his arm, offering Ivan the packet he's been holding. Before she can stop him, Ivan grabs it and brings it towards his mouth. It is only as she pushes it away that she recognises English words, the branding of Bird's Angel Delight, the same pudding her mother used to make every Saturday, whipping the pink powder with milk until the lumps disappeared and the mixture thickened. There were other flavours – chocolate and butterscotch – though her mother only ever bought the strawberry.

'From UK,' he says, ducking beneath the last row of pegged washing. 'Nice gift.'

'Stepan!' she calls sharply but the boy is through the door and gone.

Rachel wants to believe that Angel Delight is another of those out-of-date consumables that wash up, by some circuitous route, in the kiosks by the war memorial. She has never seen it for sale though, and she has scoured the city for western goods. No. Already she understands, she *knows* that this boy is stealing packages sent from England by her mother.

🙠

The line crackles and pops. Rachel pushes the receiver closer to her ear.

'Mum?'

'Who's that?' The voice, so familiar, makes Rachel's breath catch in her throat.

'It's me, Rachel.'

'Rachel? What a terrible line. I'm watching the one o'clock news.'

'Mum . . . Thank you for sending me things. I'm sorry I haven't called. I didn't know.'

A pause.

'Someone else was opening them. They didn't reach me.'

'I see. I thought you must have given me the wrong address.'

'No, they arrived, but – I had no idea you were sending packages.'

'Well I thought perhaps Customs were stopping them. You can't tell.'

'I'm sorry Mum. How are you?'

'I'm very well. How is my grandson?'

'Fine! He's got long legs, and a gorgeous smile, and he's sitting! He sits in front of the washing machine, and if I leave the hall cupboard open he pulls all the shoes out.'

'He ought to be crawling.'

'He is, sort of –'

'You'd better bring him home soon. I don't know what you do out there. I never see your husband on the news.'

'He's not that kind of journalist, Mum. He's radio. Not TV.'

'Well you know what I think; you should never have gone.'

Now it is Rachel who says nothing. Instead she makes

pictures in her mind's eye, the old habit from childhood, in case her mother can still invade her head. The fifteen hundred miles between them really isn't so far. *Here I am going to lots of parties. See? I have friends here. I am living a grown-up life.*

'Is this call expensive?' asks her mother. 'It must be expensive.'

Rachel clears her throat. 'Thank you for the Angel Delight . . .'

'I shan't send any more. Not if someone else is opening it. Is that the baby I can hear? He sounds fretful. You'd better see to him.'

'What? Okay – well, bye-bye Mum . . .'

'Bye-bye.'

There is silence, then a click as her mother replaces her receiver. Rachel can almost hear her sighing as she reaches for her cup of tea and settles back to watch her programmes. She stares at her three reflections in the mirror above the telephone, at her sagging corduroy skirt with its creases across her hips. Ivan is sitting at her feet, reaching for the edge of the low table. His fingers grip the veneer as he tries to pull himself up, a bubble of saliva shining on his lip.

'That was your grandma,' she says, scooping him up before he knocks his chin. There is something about his wide eyes, open, trusting, that reminds her of the hand-written notices on the lampposts on the road up to the monastery: all those flaps of paper, waiting to be torn off, waiting for someone to call the number on the slip, waiting for a connection. 'She used to be a mind reader,' she whispers, into his soft ear. 'But not any more.'

A couple of days after Vee's party, Rachel wakes up to a ringing sound.

'Do you hear it?' she asks Lucas, as he sits on the side of the bed to pull on his socks.

'That's tinnitus,' he says. 'I used to get it on night shifts when I was subbing. Like a worm in your ear. Bloody annoying.'

Rachel shakes her head. It is as if someone is standing by her shoulder, running a wet finger around the rim of a crystal glass. She thinks of Stepan, for some reason, though this is no squeak from a pair of rollerblades. The sound is most insistent when she reads *Jurassic Park*, counting the words and memorising entire pages. When she descends in the lift the ringing fades, and when she walks outside into the dense grey fog that has rolled up from the river it stops altogether. The sound isn't unpleasant, but it does confuse her. 'What?' she asks Lucas, as he says goodbye.

When Elena arrives to watch TV Rachel turns up the volume, which in turn wakes Ivan from his nap. Elena draws a circle with her finger next to her temple in a gesture straight out of *Simplemente Maria*. 'Vesna,' she mutters as Rachel pads off to the bedroom. 'Loco'. And perhaps Elena is right, perhaps Rachel has inhaled a little spring madness, because later that afternoon, before she can think twice, she is digging out the credit card that Lucas has asked her not to use and taking a trolleybus down to Khreschatyk to buy a pair of imported jeans from the place under the stone archway Suzie calls the 'hookers' boutique'. She can't try them on because she has Ivan in the baby carrier, so instead she shakes them out, holding them against her legs and inspecting the seams, frowning and tutting like the women she has watched buying clothing in the musty corridors of the central department store. However, these jeans are not made of the cheap, bleached denim that everyone wears; they are cut from a dark indigo, good quality fabric, with tiny metal studs in the shape of a curvy 'S' on each back pocket.

'One hundred twenty dollars,' says a bored-looking young saleswoman with pushed-up breasts and piled-up hair.

Rachel's hand shakes a little when she hands over her card; she must wait as the woman picks up the phone and reels off the long number, rolling her eyes at the incompetence of the operator down the line or maybe Rachel herself, who ought to know better than to waste her husband's dollars on a tired, sagging backside.

Back at the apartment the jeans button digs in to the soft flesh of Rachel's stomach and the fabric strains tight across her thighs. Nevertheless, when she squints she looks taller. When she closes her eyes she hears the high, ringing note, and imagines she is a Mexican polo player's mistress, or a kohl-eyed violinist or a journalist throwing a party and smoking out in the hallway with someone else's husband.

CHAPTER 17

T HE FOG LINGERS across Kiev for five whole days.
Like a cocoon, thinks Rachel, opaque and animal. The
landscape is already morphing into spring by the time the sunlight glimmers through. A slick of green spreads between the
apartment blocks. The lilacs that grow through the chain link
fence by the military academy are in bud, and the air smells
of wet earth and oily potholes and a more ancient smell – last
winter's thawing detritus, or maybe gas from the tunnels that
once burrowed beneath the streets. The ground is sloughing
off winter.

Lucas groans about the mud by the dump bins but otherwise pays little attention. His story about *The Golden Promise*
is snagging – the general release has been pushed back to July
and Lukyanenko won't let him sit in on the editing. Lucas
has asked Teddy to take pictures for an *Observer* feature
he's hoping to bag, but Teddy has problems of his own.
Karl's café has been vandalised; disgusting graffiti have been
daubed on its walls. They are thinking of shipping out to the
Balkans, or so he tells Lucas one evening at the apartment on
Staronavodnitska Street. Events in Bosnia aren't fixed yet,
he says. He wants to document a more fluid, less predictable
story.

'The story's not fixed here, either, unless we make it so!'
says Lucas.

'Everyone makes it so,' argues Teddy, with uncharacteristic

sourness. 'Politicians, editors, readers. Journalists are the worst. I want something else.'

Rachel, meanwhile, is preoccupied with Ivan. When she takes him outside he throws off his mittens and his hat, again and again, chuckling like a maniac, playing the game that always gets her into trouble with the old folk on the trolleybus. He is starting to look more Ukrainian with his cowlick of blond hair, the vests with strange fastenings and some woolly leggings made in Korea. He is crawling now, too – a sort of lop-sided scoot. One moment he is under her feet in the kitchen and the next he has vanished along the hallway. If she doesn't intercept him he will pull out the drawer from under the bed and fling nappies across the parquet with frowning concentration. She keeps the living room door shut, of course, and when Lucas is out she always wedges a chair under the handle.

Nevertheless, there are some difficulties that Rachel cannot keep at bay with her rituals and her barriers and her pages. When Ivan sits on the bedroom floor and his eyes spill swollen tears, she thinks he's starting to peer into the future. When she opens the cupboard door and slips behind it to stow his vests, perhaps he thinks she will disappear like Lucy Pevensie, away to Narnia, and never return. She tries playing peekaboo with the door, but Ivan won't be tricked. Sometimes he howls for hours. The only remedy is to take him out in the baby carrier or the pushchair, down across the waste ground, over to Podil by way of the river or up through Tsarskoye Selo to the monastery, with its winding cobbled paths.

༺ঌ

'Do you know of any parks?' Rachel asks Zoya, next time she meets her in the basement.

'Parks?' Zoya snorts. 'Are you not looking? There are parks everywhere in Kiev.'

'I know,' says Rachel. 'But I want a quieter space, away from all the kiosks and monuments.'

Zoya turns and mutters to Elena, who is emptying used teabags onto newspaper at her workbench. Elena no longer seems to sit in her cubicle upstairs, but spends most of her working day foraging in the dump bins for eggshells and banana skins. Not that she ever had much to do other than twitch her curtain and bang on the glass whenever someone forgot to wipe their feet. Elena and Zoya are becoming friends, it seems; Rachel often finds them talking together – not chatting, exactly, but murmuring and nodding with their arms folded across their chests. Now when the old woman hobbles forward her fingers are caked in dirt and the deep pockets of her overalls are actually full of the stuff she's dug up from somewhere. Rachel has noticed that her cubicle is full of seedlings sprouting in cones of newspaper or in yoghurt pots ranged on the windowsill and the shelf above the desk. Her own private greenhouse.

'You could try the Botanical Gardens,' says Zoya. 'Though you'll have to pay. They charge tourists.'

Elena, however, is interrupting her, her eyes bright in the lamplight. '*Botanicheskiy sad?*' She grips Rachel's arm. '*Bas – pesyat shest. Pesyat. Shest.*'

Rachel nods, this time understanding.

Take the number fifty-six.

As the creaking trolleybus approaches the stop on Kutuzova Street, Rachel, waiting on the pavement, lifts Ivan out of the pushchair, folds it down and picks it up with her spare hand. Ivan is becoming too heavy for her to manage for more than short periods in the baby carrier. She hopes the Botanical Gardens live up to Elena's enthusiasm. She hopes she will be able to find them.

The bus is crowded, as the buses always are. She climbs on board and stands near the front, wedging the concertina'd pushchair between her hip and the edge of a seat. The man sitting there balances a pale green porcelain toilet bowl on his lap. His arms are folded across the rim; its weight must surely press into his thighs, yet the man's eyes are closed and his head lolls. He doesn't notice when Ivan tugs off his knitted hat and drops it past his ear into the bowl. Rachel will have to fish it out, but the woman behind her makes a sucking noise with her teeth as if to say this bare-headed foreign *malchik* will now catch pneumonia or scarlet fever or whooping cough and it will be its mother's fault, for no baby should be out without its head covered and at least one sour-faced granny in attendance. Rachel blows a soft raspberry on Ivan's forehead. She has read her pages. She has checked the piles of nappies. *We are off on an outing*, she thinks, *and no one can stop us*.

Outside, the watery sunlight glances off the car wind-screens as the bus sighs and heaves its way into the flow of traffic. Rachel tips forward, then shifts her weight so as not to fall. People begin to shuffle and mutter as someone stands up and starts moving along the aisle, but she takes no notice and looks out of the window, ticking off the traffic lights, counting the plane trees that line the boulevard. At the tenth tree she hears a low voice behind her.

'Pazhalsta.'

Rachel looks over her shoulder. She recognises the speaker

straight away, but it takes her a moment to realise that his thick black moustache, his dark eyes are real and not a silent conjuring from her dreams. This time he is wearing his Astrakhan hat. A camel-coloured coat, probably cashmere, swings from his shoulders.

'Oh!' she exclaims. 'Mr . . .'

'Mykola,' he reminds her, flicking his hand to rouse the man with the toilet bowl and let him know he should vacate his seat. The man says nothing, but after the briefest hesitation he locks his hands together around the toilet bowl and stands so that Rachel can slip into his place.

'No!' she protests, though it is pointless. Mykola is leaning in and his hand is on the pushchair. The man with the toilet bowl shows no expression. He shifts his feet further apart, his arms grip his burden and she wishes he would rest it on the floor.

'Good afternoon,' murmurs Mykola, smiling down at Rachel when she has settled in the seat.

'Why are you here?' she asks, then quickly looks down; the question seems a little too direct.

Mykola, however, has no problem avoiding an answer.

'It is a beautiful day,' he says. 'Your little boy – he is well? You are well?'

'Yes, thank you,' she replies, as Ivan wriggles on her lap. She lifts him up so that he can stand on her knees.

'I am glad to hear this. Spring has come. So much better for mothers and their children. But you, you are not afraid of the cold!'

Rachel doesn't know what to make of his small talk. People are staring, and Mykola and the man with the toilet bowl are blocking the aisle. She doesn't know if she'll recognise the stop at the Botanical Gardens. She is hoping to see something that looks like a park, but her view is obscured by the woman sitting next to her.

'Tell me,' says Mykola. 'The washing machine I sent to you. Is there a problem? You have not yet installed it in your flat?'

'Oh, no.' She bites her lip, wondering how he knows this. 'Not in the flat. My husband – he wasn't sure . . .'

Mykola puts up a hand as if to say she doesn't need to explain.

'These things can be difficult.' He smiles at Ivan yet doesn't try to touch him. 'Now, I think you must be going to the Botanical Gardens. We will arrive there in one minute, God willing, but it is better if you stay seated until the bus has stopped. Don't worry about this,' he adds, as the bus makes a sudden lurch and Rachel reaches out for the pushchair. 'I am getting off myself. I will look after it.'

And when the bus wheezes to a halt and the doors jerk open, that is exactly what happens. Mykola even retrieves Ivan's hat from the toilet bowl and nods politely to its owner before following Rachel down the steps. He stands a little apart on the pavement while she settles Ivan with a bread ring and clips him into his safety belt.

'Well, thank you again,' she says, straightening up and looking round at the road lined with horse chestnuts, their sticky buds swollen and ready to burst. The tower blocks have given way to older buildings with tall, thin windows. A wall made of concrete panels snakes into the distance. Rachel wonders what business Mykola has in this part of town and if he, too, was already going to the Botanical Gardens, or whether this has only now become his aim. Her sense of freedom is fast evaporating.

'This way,' he says, indicating that she should walk in the direction of the disappearing trolleybus. 'It really isn't far.'

A dozen or so yards along the road, before Rachel has worked out how to part company politely, they arrive at the entrance to the gardens. Several other people walk through a gate in the wall, and then it is their turn. They pass in front of a small kiosk and straight away a woman behind the little glass window flicks it up and demands 200 *kouponi*. Rachel worries that Mykola will offer to pay, but he stands back and admires some bird wheeling high above their heads while she fumbles for her purse and hands over the money. A hand-written ticket is passed back to her, and they walk on. Mykola, Rachel notices, doesn't buy a ticket. Indeed, no one else passing into the gardens is stopped at the kiosk. She is the tourist. Tourists pay.

Because Mykola is walking beside her, his strides measured, the sound of his leather soles discreet yet persistent, Rachel doesn't at first take in the view that opens out ahead. She sees the long brown flower beds, some tulip leaves starting to push their way out, the fissured tarmac paths, the ever-present horse chestnuts and some spindly, still bare birches. She sees a dirty yet ornate greenhouse to her left and a fountain with no water to her right and it is only slowly, after five minutes or so, that she notices the way the gardens stretch downwards across the hillside, paths winding and criss-crossing through clumps of newly flowering cherry and magnolia. Some contain little detours, steps that lead to benches with views across the bright grey-blueness of the Dnieper. Gold onion domes rise above the railings – there's a church below them somewhere.

'It's beautiful,' she says, stopping for a moment. The sun feels warm across her shoulders so she shrugs off her coat and slings it over the handles of the pushchair. It occurs to her that this is the first time she hasn't worn a coat outside since she arrived six months earlier. She breathes a long sigh of relief as Mykola strolls on. This is fine, she thinks. This is where he leaves her and she can discover this place on her own.

Except Mykola isn't leaving her. He pauses in front of a budding lilac bush and breaks off a bough that is almost in bloom, its cone of purple buds quivering as he snaps it clear.

'For you,' he says, walking back towards her. 'In Kiev, spring means two things. The horse chestnut – our beautiful *kashtan* – and the lilac.'

The buds and the heart-shaped leaves tremble on their stems.

'We probably shouldn't pick things here,' Rachel says nervously.

Mykola laughs and shakes the flowers for Ivan's amusement. 'Why do you think all these people come?' He gestures towards a woman with a headscarf tied at the back of her head. She is crouched low in the middle of a flower bed. Rachel shades her eyes with her hand and sees that the woman is in fact digging with a spoon around the base of a scrappy-looking corm that has only recently emerged from the snow. Where are the gardeners? Where are the babushkas shouting *nyet*? The woman discards the spoon and starts to dig with her fingers, feeling around the corm's roots and then prising it out with a grunt. She wraps it in a sheet of newspaper, before pushing herself slowly back up to her feet.

'There's plenty to go round,' says Mykola. 'Maybe in a year, two years, the flowers will be gone but in *Ukraina* we grow things and their descendants will live on – though perhaps not here.'

Rachel thinks of Elena, with her seeds and her pockets of compost and the earth beneath her fingernails.

'Did you follow me here?' she asks suddenly, surprising herself.

Mykola stops smiling.

'I saw you get on the bus,' he says. 'I come here often. Sometimes, things happen that way.'

Ivan whimpers. She looks down, sees that he is fidgety and starts to push him again, slowly, with Mykola walking beside her. He is still holding the spray of lilac that she won't accept and she knows she has upset this man with whom she has spoken only once before. Or twice, if she counts what she still thinks was a dream of him at the film studio. She isn't afraid, though – not yet. There are plenty of people around, strollers, lovers, young men lounging on benches, legs splayed, and old women wielding pruning knives in the bushes.

'Elena,' she says, 'our *dezhornaya* – she spat at the man who delivered the washing machine. Do you know her?'

Mykola doesn't answer straight away.

'Elena Vasilyevna.' When he does speak, he says her name as if it is something he hasn't spoken for a long time. 'You must not approach her. You must not let her touch your child.'

'Oh, but she is much kinder than she seems!' exclaims Rachel. 'At first I thought she was a dreadful old witch – she was so cross and unfriendly and the spitting is disgusting – but really she's just lonely, and she's helped me with the flat, and—'

'You invite her into your apartment.' Mykola interrupts her sharply. He is not asking a question. He stops walking, so that she must stop too. 'You must not let her in. You are a beautiful mother, remember? Your child is your gift to the world. I have allowed much, too much and this I cannot overlook. Promise me – do not let her in.'

Now Rachel is afraid. Mykola doesn't touch her; he is standing a clear two yards away from her, but she sees the anger in his eyes, feels it in the distance he maintains so carefully between them. She hasn't told him about the basement, she remembers. Yet he knows that they haven't installed the washing machine in the apartment. In which case, he must know it has been moved downstairs.

'I will be honest with you,' he says. 'I noticed you some months ago in the restaurant where you ate with your husband and your friends. You were nursing your baby. You wore a *platok* – a veil.'

He sweeps his hands across his shoulders, and Rachel realises he is talking about the shawl she wears when breastfeeding in public. *You were in the corner, by the bathroom*, she thinks. *You heard me crying.* She glances sideways and takes in the wide path to her right that leads back towards the entrance. There are people about, though they might not help her. Her heart is racing. Her legs feel heavy, as if a low swell of water is pressing against her calves.

'The veil protects, you see. Our Most Holy Lady holds out her veil and shelters her people beneath.' Mykola holds out his arms. 'But who protects her? Who protects our Blessed Mother?'

'Please leave me alone,' Rachel murmurs, gripping the pushchair's handles. 'I don't know what you want. I am not a blessed mother. Just leave me alone.'

Mykola remains still for a few seconds. Then he nods once and walks away, down the hill towards the gold domes of the church. When Rachel tugs the pushchair round to move in the opposite direction, she sees he has laid the lilac branch carefully across Ivan's lap.

CHAPTER 18

'Zoya,' says Rachel, the next morning, when she has checked to make sure they are alone in the basement. 'What do you know about the man who gave me the washing machine?'

Zoya is folding sheets but she's in a hurry, swinging her arms out and back in and flapping the green polycotton into submission.

'Gangster,' she says, without missing a beat. 'Bad money. Black market. Corruption. Extortion. Sometimes violence.'

The words snap like flicked tea towels. They are frightening words, but also distant, make-believe. They don't explain why a virtual stranger in a cashmere coat is following Rachel.

'He came to the Botanical Gardens,' she persists. 'He might have been at the film studios. He said strange things about me being a mother.'

Zoya shakes her head.

'Probably you are imagining it. You are -' she concentrates, searching for the right expression, 'tightly strung.'

'No,' says Rachel, firmly. 'He sent me the washing machine, remember? And yesterday he actually followed me to the Botanical Gardens. I think he's spying on me. He warned me to stay away from Elena.'

'Elena Vasilyevna?'

'Yes, Elena,' repeats Rachel. 'Why would he do that? How does he know her?'

Zoya drops the folded sheet into the laundry basket on the floor, but her face is a mask in the dim light and for a few moments the only sounds are the sighs and the soft clunks from the pipes that lead to and from the boilers.

'I will try to find out something. Do not tell Lucas. He would not handle it well.'

'I know,' says Rachel. 'He would be a nightmare.'

⁂

'Opposites attract!' laughed Lucas's mother when Lucas and Rachel announced their engagement. And it was true, in a way, for both were curious about the other. Sometimes, though, in the first weeks of their marriage, Rachel felt herself peering into the cracks between them, fearing what she could not see.

Once they had a fight about a lottery. They had gone to Spain for their honeymoon. Not the package version, but somewhere Lucas called 'undiscovered Spain', the north-west corner, because Rachel had expressed a wish to visit the end of the world and he had a yen to indulge her. The fog hadn't lifted since their arrival. They had stopped for breakfast in a café on the outskirts of Vigo, where the streets stank of cooking oil and diesel.

'Christ,' said Lucas, folding the copy of *El País* he was attempting to read and stabbing at an article with his finger. 'People here go crazy for the lottery. "El Gordo", they call it. The Fat One!' He leaned back and stretched his legs out under the table, which wobbled and made Rachel's pen jump across the postcard she was writing.

She looked up. 'Pardon?'

'The lottery. It's plastered all over the place – posters on the windows, ads on beermats. A throwback to Franco, maybe. It gives people a little hope, stops them thinking about the big stuff.'

Rachel nodded. Nodding was becoming a habit.

'There's an old boy here who won a million pesetas,' continued Lucas. 'He died of a heart attack the next day. Poor bastard! Never even got the chance to buy a decent bottle of Cava.'

'Oh, that's awful!' murmured Rachel, staring out past the peeling posters on the window to the ghostly cranes of a storage depot and longing for a sun-drenched beach. 'I'd never buy a lottery ticket.'

Lucas put his arms behind his head.

'Wouldn't you? Why not?'

'Well, I'd never be able to decide what to do with the money if I won.'

'Yes, you would. A big house, straight off.'

Rachel frowned. 'I suppose . . .'

'I know what I'd do,' said Lucas, glancing over his shoulder for the bill as he slipped his cigarettes back into his shirt pocket. 'I'd invest in a couple of properties, give some to both our families and put some in trust for our kids.'

'Well, where would you draw the line?' asked Rachel. 'I mean, how much would you give your family? And where does 'family' end? You've got all those second cousins!' She tried smiling but Lucas was busy rummaging for coins.

'There'd have to be a cut-off, obviously. You'd have to be professional about it – get proper advice. A pot for personal use, a pot for family, a pot for other stuff.' Now Lucas looked at her, ready to deliver his *coup de grâce*. 'Because wouldn't it be great to make a difference, you know? Give to worthwhile causes; give to charity?'

The woman behind the bar wasn't bringing the bill. This time Lucas waved, making a little signing gesture with his hand, though Rachel wasn't finished: all sorts of thoughts were tumbling around her head. Couples were destroyed by this kind of thing – you read about it all the time. Wills causing disputes; disagreements between siblings or parent and child – why didn't you give *me* a bigger share? Why aren't *my* needs as important as theirs? It was human nature, to want more, to have more. Money is power, and power corrupts, as her O-level history teacher had never tired of repeating while he scratched his litanies across the blackboard.

'I wouldn't claim it,' she said, turning towards the window again. A young man in a leather jacket glistening with damp sauntered past, his hand quickly checking his flies. 'Or I'd give it all away. I'd have to do it quickly.'

'Thanks!' Lucas rolled his eyes. 'Never mind your wretched husband, pissing peanuts all day long to keep you in overpriced coffees!' He stood up, scraping back his chair so that an old man at a seat in the corner looked across, then looked away. 'We're going to have to abscond to get some attention . . .'

He walked over to the bar, where the woman was re-filling a tray with some greasy-looking pastries in between flipping eggs on the griddle behind her. Rachel, meanwhile, looked around for a loo, not knowing how long it'd be before they found another.

The cubicle was tucked away behind a drinks cooler. When she emerged Lucas was impatient to leave. As he held open the door he pushed something into her hand.

'Here,' he said. 'I got you one. If you win, I want half!'

Rachel looked down in dismay at a slip of paper with a drawing of a church in coloured ink and the number 700321 above the words 'Loteria Nacionale'.

'I don't want it,' she said, but he wouldn't take it back.

'If you win and don't claim, it would be an abdication of responsibility.' He was teasing still – laughing and needling. 'Think of all the anti-malarials it could purchase. Think of all the sex workers you could save or the slum children you could educate! Or maybe you'd rather do nothing? Now that would be something to feel guilty about.'

Rachel scrunched the ticket in the palm of her hand and thrust it into her shoulder bag. Lucas was right and he knew it and was already forgetting, moving on to the next thing, striding across the road, peering through the fog to the hire car. She, on the other hand, was culpable now, whichever way she looked at it.

The ticket stayed in her bag until the weekend. She checked the numbers at a roadside kiosk in La Coruña without telling Lucas and when she discovered she hadn't won anything, she almost cried with relief.

⁂

Rachel is watching *Simplemente Maria* one afternoon when the phone rings in the hall. Elena has not joined her today – she has missed a few episodes lately, but Rachel tunes in, regardless. She doesn't care about the storyline – Maria's eyes fill with tears, Maria wears a jacket with big shoulder pads, Maria's old love comes calling with flowers. The routine helps her breathe inside the flat. It helps calm the high-pitched sound in her head.

'Hello, Rachel!' says a soft voice. It is Suzie. The two have seen each other once or twice for coffee since Suzie sent the nappies, always at Suzie's flat – never on the thirteenth floor. The nappies aren't a secret, exactly, but Rachel tells herself that because they aren't paying for them, Lucas doesn't need to know.

Today, Suzie has some news.

'We're moving!' she says, brightly. 'Not far – to a little old house in the Tsar's Village! It's rotten and full of mice and God only knows what skeletons, but we're going to do it up – the full *remont*! The rent is a ludicrous amount – I could see the dollar signs popping in the owner's eyes. Rob will beat her down. You must come and see it. I need to know what you think!'

A house, thinks Rachel. Not a flat up in the sky, but a house on the ground.

'All right,' she says. 'I'd love to.'

'Next week,' says Suzie. 'When Rob says it's ours.'

෯

Rachel meets Suzie in the car park and they stroll across the tramlines together, Ivan in the pushchair, no need for his snowsuit today. Suzie is wearing grey wool trousers that show off her slender legs and a cream ski jacket with a neatly cinched waist. Rachel is wearing her new jeans, even though she told herself she'd save them for parties. The sun is shining. A few petals of pink apple blossom float above the dump bins. It's a beautiful April day.

'He's growing so fast!' observes Suzie, as Rachel stops to pick up the hat Ivan has tossed down to the tarmac. 'Soon he'll be walking, won't he?'

188

Rachel remembers what Dr Alleyn told her. 'He's tall,' she says. 'So he has a higher centre of gravity. Maybe not yet.'

She and Suzie pick their way past the burnt-out Lada on the corner and on up the lane through Tsarskoye Selo. Rachel has walked here countless times, up and down from the monastery and the kiosks by the war memorial at the top of the hill. She has counted the wooden gates hinged with twists of wire and the battened and boarded cottages, each with a single upstairs window like a blank eye peering out from under the steeply angled eaves. Some are more dilapidated than others, with a scrawny cat lying on the steps or torn netting hanging from untended trees. There may be people inside, though Rachel never sees anyone – just a lick of paint on the fretwork above the doorways, a bright piece of sanitary ware sitting under a tree or a freshly concreted path, shovelled hastily, its edges already crumbling. Others appear uninhabited, their shutters tightly closed, though their gardens suggest otherwise: neat rectangles of tilled earth beside the steps; green shoots just emerging; fruit trees showing signs of recent pruning, their bare stumps painted an alarming dark red.

'Can you imagine?' says Suzie. 'Me, in one of these? Rob says it'll take three months to make it habitable. Then I can decorate it how I like, but you know me, it'll be white, white, white!'

'Fairytale houses,' says Rachel, thinking of trails of breadcrumbs. 'You'll be like Hansel and Gretel.'

Suzie laughs her smoky, throaty laugh. 'Oh, I was thinking more Sleeping Beauty! Ivan's my prince. Look, this is us!' She pulls Rachel down a stony track and they pass between two cottages towards a more isolated house beyond. It has a mansarded roof, a long, thin orchard displaying the first dabs of blossom, and a peeling waist-height picket fence painted the usual faded blue. There's a figure bending over by the steps, but Rachel knows it isn't Rob because Suzie has promised her that he is out of town. Besides, the figure is too short. It looks more like an old woman wearing baggy trousers. Her hair is tucked beneath a sort of knitted beret; thin scraps of it are escaping.

When Suzie and Rachel approach, the old woman straightens up slowly, as if it pains her.

'That's the woman we're renting from, some old communist,' whispers Suzie. 'I didn't know she'd be here.'

Rachel, however, needs no introduction. 'It's our *dezhornaya!*' she says, taken aback, for she realises she has never asked where the caretaker actually lives, assuming it to be a one-room flat somewhere past the monastery, or even a dark corner in the basement of her own block of flats. 'Elena, *privyet!*'

For a moment Elena seems bewildered. Then her eyes narrow and she nods to them both.

'*Dobrey ootra,*' she says - good morning - a rebuke to Rachel's over-familiarity. Ivan bounces with excitement, stretching out his arms. The old woman leans forward but checks herself and pulls back, rubbing at the dirt on her hands. She and Suzie converse awkwardly in Russian while Rachel unclips Ivan from his pushchair and settles him on her hip. It's obvious Elena is unhappy to meet them here and this makes Rachel feel uncomfortable. She wonders if renting out the property is distasteful to the old woman, or whether it is the intrusion she objects to. Then she remembers what Lucas said about the houses being built for Party officials. Perhaps Elena had been a spy, as Rachel had first suspected, though she struggles to believe this now that she knows her a little. Elena's face and body language give too much away.

Elena is waving her hand towards the front door.

'She doesn't want us here,' whispers Rachel, as she and Suzie climb the steps.

'Too bad!' laughs Suzie. 'It's ours! Rob got his lawyer to draw up a contract and we've paid for the first year in cash! She asked for used dollars, which wound him up no end.'

Despite her misgivings Rachel finds she is curious about the house. There isn't much to see: a living room with an old table pushed against the wall and a couple of beaten-up chairs; a lean-to kitchen with an old-fashioned stove and a sink; and a downstairs bathroom, its tiles cracked and its floor covered by a piece of curling lino. The bedroom upstairs is spacious enough but instead of a bed a single mattress rests on the floor. Rachel cannot imagine how the old woman manages to heave herself up from it each morning, or how she escaped being frozen to death in the winter. There are few personal touches and no photographs. Elena's cubicle at the apartment block seems more homely. Suzie, meanwhile, chats about her plans for the *remont*: she will arrange to import a ready-made kitchen; she will introduce a utility room; there will be re-cessed lighting, roman blinds, a shower room off the bedroom and a fully glazed veranda on two sides of the house.

'Rob wants a sauna in the garden,' she says. 'That's why we're moving. The house itself will still be smaller than the flat.'

Rachel feels as if she is trespassing.

'It's a lot of work,' she says, 'for a place you're just renting.'

'Yes, but Rob says that Ukraine's property laws aren't fit for purpose. He'd rather buy, always. We should be in by August, if the workmen pull their fingers out. Rob's got them on a penalty for late completion.' Suzie smiles, her eyes bright, full of trust that all will be well, that white goods and white walls will prevail. 'Then you can bring Ivan to toddle around the garden.'

'Where will Elena go?' asks Rachel. 'Do you think she's lived here for long?'

'No idea. Now she can afford somewhere nice, though,' says Suzie, her brow creasing in a brief flash of anxiety. 'We're hardly throwing her out on the street.'

No, thinks Rachel, but she'll stop working at the apartment block. No more *Simplemente Maria*. No more tea in the kitchen, keeping Ivan safe.

As they leave the house Rachel looks over her shoulder towards Elena, who is now working at the far end of the orchard. The old woman bends down over the ground, digging up the deep-rooted dandelions, her legs planted firmly apart, her back rounded like a seedling as it emerges, inexorable, from the earth.

CHAPTER 19

EVERYTHING CHANGES WHEN the warmer weather comes. As the sticky buds of the horse chestnuts burst into leaf and their creamy candles reach up to the light, as the breeze wafts the scent of lilac along the boulevards and the dandelions flower for a day, people pour on to the streets. Secrets are hard to keep without winter coats and fur hats. Arguments leave the stale one-room apartments and step out on to balconies. Lovers roam the sidewalks and drunks lie spread-eagled on the benches. Even the man playing tennis with his son at the edge of the car park thrashes him openly with his racquet when he fails to demonstrate his commitment to the game. By the first week in May, when the schoolchildren on the trolleybuses are sneezing from the drifting pollen, all things are laid out, laid bare, made open and exposed. This is how it is in Kiev's summer months. This is how it is for Lucas and for Vee.

'So,' Vee says one night, as she and Lucas sit on stools at the bar of a shiny new place in a back street behind the Foreign Ministry. 'Have you booked a room?'

'What?' asks Lucas, looking stricken.

'Sure you have,' says Vee. 'But there's something I must tell you first. I've been sleeping with Sorin, and he has told me everything about your secret story, and you know what? It's a good one! Don't look so surprised.'

Lucas doesn't know what to think, so Vee helps him.

'We could have sex,' she says, pushing the slice of lemon in her vodka tonic under the surface with her finger. 'And it would go badly because you would feel guilty and I would despise you for that. We might meet again, but I would sleep with other lovers and you would be angry and hurt and then Rachel would find out and she'd go crazy and try to jump off the balcony or leave you or something much worse and then you'd be in pieces and follow her back to England and your career would be finished.'

'That's funny,' says Lucas, his heart pumping so loudly he fears she might hear it. 'You're funny.'

'I know,' says Vee. 'I'm pretty hard to take.'

Lucas is silent for a while. His drink is too warm; the bar needs a new refrigerator before the weather gets hot, and he wants to scream at someone – the sullen waitress who poured it, or the bandit on the door or maybe just that weird guy in the corner with the moustache and the doleful eyes like a po-faced Omar Sharif. Instead he stays silent, knowing he must ask a question, hating how it is going to make him sound.

'Don't use my story,' he says, trying not to beg.

Vee licks the finger she used to stir her drink, then reaches up to trace the line of his eyebrow.

'Stop frowning,' she says, solemnly. 'I wouldn't dream of it. I'm not a total bitch.'

❦

The ninth of May is Victory Day. Zoya buys her grandfather three red gladioli and places them in a vase by his bed. She pins his Order of the Patriotic War, second class, to his pyjama jacket, even though tourists can buy them for a dollar apiece outside the metro at Arsenalnaya. She pours two glasses of vodka, raises one toast to the heroic survivors, another to the glorious fallen, and drinks them both before checking her watch. She's due to meet Lucas at the Tomb of the Unknown Soldier in an hour. He is hopeful the communists will make a showing, waving their pension books and their framed pictures of Stalin, though this isn't Moscow, as she never tires of pointing out. There's no front page story being orchestrated in the hills above the Dnieper. In Lviv the holiday has been cancelled altogether.

Tanya arrives a quarter of an hour late. Zoya, irritated, picks up her bag and yanks the door shut behind her without saying goodbye. Two minutes later Tanya is opening the window and shouting down to her in the street.

Her grandfather isn't breathing.

Zoya drops her bag and runs back up the stairs.

Elena Vasilyevna stays away from the commemorations, though the long finger of the war memorial is only a short walk from her cottage, across the summit of the hill. Today she has her possessions to pack up and a new flat to occupy. The flat she is moving to is on the second floor of the apartment block on Staronavodnitska Street. It's been empty for a while. The locksmith who helped her gain entry didn't ask questions. She has always been the caretaker, ever since the block first opened two decades before. That stinking gangster Mykola can threaten her – he can send his thugs to torture dogs as much as he pleases and replace her with someone whose husband or son owes money and who thus has no ears, no eyes – but Elena isn't going anywhere.

Elena has enlisted some help with the removals. The boy Stepan will arrive soon with the handcart that she keeps in the basement at the apartment block. Her belongings are few even by Ukrainian standards: a mattress, bedding, two chairs, a chest of drawers and a couple of lamps. There are pots and pans, some crockery and a plastic laundry bag full of clothes. She rolls her old fur coat with care – the coat she hasn't worn for four decades. It was given to her by the same man who drew up papers in her name for this house, with its strip of earth for growing vegetables and for planting fruit trees. She has already wrapped her gardening tools in neat parcels of newspaper after oiling them the night before.

Then, as she folds a blanket, another memory rolls up from her gut like the dark waves of the Dnieper. This memory belongs to a time before the war, when she was still a child. It washes over her, blocks out the present moment and takes her breath away, so that she must sit down on the stairs.

The blanket in her mind is knitted from rough yarn. It is grey and moth-eaten. Even now she can feel the looped wool between her fingers and sniff again the smell of sickness and mould. At dusk she takes it down to the river with her sister. The two girls wade out through the shallows until the current pushes up against their hips. They stretch the blanket between them, gripping its corners, and they stand there for hours, thin bodies numb with the cold, even though it is summer, arms aching, burning, then dropping with hunger and exhaustion as they wait for a fish.

There are no fish. As the sun rises they stumble out of the river and lie in the mud. When their mother comes to find them she falls down and weeps, and they gnaw at the blanket, gagging and sucking because the great famine is upon them and their stomachs contain nothing but leaves.

Memories are burdens. Elena, old now, sits on the stairs for some time, the blanket clutched in her fingers. She has never wept for her mother and her sister. When they died, they were saved.

⁂

At last Stepan arrives with the handcart and helps Elena to her feet.

'Come on,' he says in Ukrainian, impatient to load up the mattress and the chairs.

As they trundle down Panfilovtsev Street, the faint strains of piped military music start up on the hill behind them. The tramlines at the bend on Staronavodnitska Street prove tricky; they almost lose a soup bowl, but they finally reach the apartment block and Stepan carries her possessions up the steps, then stacks them in the foyer by the lift.

When Elena gives him a fifty dollar note he sniffs it before stepping back outside and inspecting it in the sunlight.

'*Eta vsyo*,' she says, more to herself than to Stepan. *That's it.*

⁂

Across the tramlines and up the hill, in the lee of the Motherland monument, Rachel and Ivan are out with the crowds. There's a fresh breeze and it's chilly in the shade, yet the sun itself is hot. Faces grow pink, while the ice cream sellers and the *kvas* trucks are making a killing. Ivan is having the time of his life, shrieking at the bouquets of tulips and gladioli, the dandelion seeds that waft across the concrete, the uniforms with their burnished buttons, the sense of occasion. Rachel buys him a pretzl to suck on, even though it is stale and full of salt. She walks slowly, one hand on the pushchair, watching the old men leaning on a grandchild or a great grandchild – the boys in v-necked jumpers lugging their replica assault rifles, the girls' hair tied back with patriotic blue and yellow pompoms. Really though, she is looking out for Mykola. She's been seeing him everywhere since her trip to the Botanical Gardens. Zoya hasn't told her anything, and now it is as if his face carries something archetypal, something she seems to recognise in the expression of every man she passes: a glance, the twist of a mouth, the shadow of a moustache. She wanders for ages, yet he doesn't materialise and this both relieves and dismays her. He is watching, she decides, but he is concealed.

Instead she glimpses Lucas in the distance, striding about, bending down to speak with someone, trying to balance his notebook on his knee. He starts to shake his biro up and down and she almost goes to him, almost reaches into her bag for a spare, but then a family strolls across her sightline and he is gone. Anyway, she won't interrupt him while he is working. She certainly doesn't want to talk to him.

Up ahead she spots a bench in the shade, one half unoccupied. She sits down next to a middle-aged couple and fumbles in Ivan's nappy bag for his lidded beaker. The beaker is an innovation. She bought it at the House of Children in Lipki and Ivan hated it at first. He threw it to the floor and splashed the water Rachel had carefully filtered and boiled and cooled all over the kitchen. Now the warmer weather has arrived he is thirstier and glugs at it noisily, gripping its two handles with his moist pink fingers, his eyes rolling slightly. The sight of him sucking triggers the let-down reflex in Rachel's breasts and she pulls her thin cardigan across her chest.

The couple next to her are talking in low voices. The man, who is wearing brown polyester trousers and a carefully pressed short-sleeved shirt, holds the woman's hand and the woman presses her knee against his leg. To Rachel they seem sweet – demure, unshowy in their solicitude. They smile at her child and make encouraging noises, and the man reaches forward and gently pats Ivan's head.

Then the woman leans round her companion and speaks directly to Rachel in a quick burst of Ukrainian.

'Nye panimayu,' says Rachel, shaking her head apologetically. 'I don't understand.'

Her response seems to agitate the woman, who says something to the man. They both point at Ivan, who has kicked off his knitted slipper. He beams at the pantomime these strangers are performing for his amusement.

'Fut!' says the woman, then again, more sharply, 'Fut!'

'Oh,' says Rachel, smiling politely, though with no intention of covering up his toes. Her new strategy for batting off the imperatives from every woman over forty is to gabble at them in a language they can't decipher. 'It's a lovely day,' she says. 'Bare feet won't kill him. In England, unlike in your country, we know about germs and vitamin D. We know how to bring up our babies quite safely in the fresh air, with no hat on, with no boots on and, sometimes, would you believe it, with no clothes at all!'

This time something is wrong. The man looks angry. He stands, and so does the woman.

'Then consider yourself fortunate,' he says, in precise English. 'My wife wished only to help you. We did not expect an insult in return.' And with that the couple move away.

Rachel gets up, too, a low mood upon her, exposed and ashamed by her outburst. She wants to be at home now, she wants to read her pages and she wants to hang her washing out in the basement in straight lines, tightly pegged, as tight as she can possibly stretch the towels and the vests and the sheets. She picks up the dropped slipper and rushes away from the park, out through the gates, across Lavrska Street and down the lane towards the tower blocks on Staronavodnitska. Building Number Four still broods there like a standing stone. She looks up, as she always does when she passes into its shadow. As she raises her head someone throws something from one of the balconies. Whatever has been thrown falls clumsily, straight at first, then wheeling and unfolding as it approaches the ground. Rachel sees it is a piece of cardboard or packaging of some kind. She swallows down the bile that has risen in her throat and hurries inside, wishing that Elena was here to shout and summon the lift in order to bang on the door of the offending apartment.

When Rachel walks across the foyer there's a different old woman sitting in her cubicle.

'*Gdye Elena Vasilyevna?*' she asks. Where is she?

The woman shrugs and scowls at the pushchair's dirty wheels.

❧

Lucas marches along Khreschatyk, too much energy in his legs. There's a pink flush below his cheekbones and he wants all the strollers around him to get out of his way. This city is too much, sometimes – the queues at the kiosks, the endless holidays, the wide blank faces. Take Zoya, who didn't show up at the War Memorial today. He wants to find her, to tell her straight that he is going to hire someone else, that he'll be paying someone else to do the job instead of her. She thinks she's so good he won't fire her, and that's his problem, as usual, because he does need her. Back at the office he took a call from Sorin. There's an obstruction with some of the permissions he needs for his film feature. Lucas could go ahead anyway, but he doesn't want to upset the director at this point in production – he needs to be invited to the premiere, now scheduled for July.

He passes a woman pulling along a grizzling child and thinks of Rachel, which doesn't help. Her silences, her de-liberateness, her superstitions depress him. When she was pregnant, he loved her softness, her needs. Now, everything is weighted and weighed – a touch, a caress – nothing is gifted to him, nothing is free. He needs to act. He needs to take control of their lives and the emptiness he feels where there used to be attention and ardour. All the same, he wishes Rachel would decide to go back to England without his urging. Nothing permanent – not yet. He'd miss Ivan, but a break would allow them both to breathe. There's the cost of the flight, though if she stayed with her mother it needn't be too expensive.

He'll try to steer her round over dinner.

⁂

In Rachel's dream she neither flies nor falls. Instead she sits on a chair in the middle of the living room, looking out beyond the balcony to the white gauze of the sky. In her dream everything is still. She sits still; her bones inside her skin rest lightly, her feet skim the surface of the parquet.

When she wakes she is disoriented. The furniture spins around her with a speed she cannot match. She sits up and *Jurassic Park* slides off the bed to the floor. She must have fallen asleep while counting so she'll have to start again later. Ivan isn't in his cot and now she hears noises – the opening of a cupboard, the judder of a tap. Lucas is home. She looks at her watch. Seven-thirty.

Her husband is standing at the kitchen counter with his back to her when she reaches the doorway. He is hacking at a pimply-skinned chicken.

'Coq au vin,' he says, with a wave of his knife. 'I wanted to do chicken Kiev, but I couldn't find a recipe.' On the table sits a bottle of plastic-topped wine and some vegetables – carrots, onions – along with a sizeable heap of peelings. Ivan is sitting on the floor underneath waving a thin coil of potato skin. Rachel scoops him up, presses her lips against his hair and stares at the mess, still dazed from her nap. Back in London Lucas sometimes made dishes like lasagne or shepherd's pie. He always wanted her to guess the secret ingredient he'd added – fennel, or coriander or something just as unfamiliar.

'How did things go at the War Memorial?' she asks. 'Did you get what you needed?'

Lucas grunts dismissively. 'There was no story. Just the usual reminiscences, rose-tinted recollections of comrades. Even the protests were half-hearted. People don't want to re-member the truth. There's no mileage for me in that kind of self-delusion.'

Rachel thinks of the set faces on the trolleybus, the sagging shoulders and shuffling in the queues and feels a ripple of affinity with the city's pensioners.

'Elena has moved,' she says. 'The caretaker – she's rented out her house to Suzie and Rob. She's not working here anymore.'

'So I heard. Funny to think of her as the landlady for those two. You did pretty well to get on the right side of her. She always looked like she wanted to murder me.' He turns around. 'Dinner will be a good hour or so. If you stick Ivan in the bath I'll bring you a beer. I won't do any more work tonight. We should talk.' He pulls a long face for his son, then smiles, and Rachel sees that this costs him, which makes her both sorry and wary.

'Okay,' she says. Then, when she's sitting on the loo seat with her feet on the edge of the bath and Ivan is kicking his legs in the yellowish water and shrieking with delight at the sound of his own echo bouncing off the tiles, she chews her lip and wonders what Lucas has planned.

Sure enough, when Ivan is asleep and the chicken has been eaten, Lucas asks her to come out onto the balcony while he has a smoke.

'It's a beautiful evening,' he says. 'Come and talk to me. Look at the stars.'

'You know I don't like the balcony,' replies Rachel, trying to keep her voice even. But Lucas, who has already deviated from the script he has rehearsed, can't leave it there.

'I'm not asking you to take Ivan outside. Just us two. For five minutes.'

Rachel doesn't move, doesn't uncross her legs. This is what happens when you fall asleep, she thinks. There are consequences when you don't read your pages.

Lucas scrapes back his chair, gets up, paces down the hall to the living room, then returns to the kitchen. 'Look,' he says, his voice tight. 'I get the fact that the height gives you vertigo. Never mind that the balcony is perfect for some fresh air and sunshine and that maybe it would be nice to sit on a couple of chairs and drink a beer and not have to leave you to go out by myself for a smoke – I get that you don't want to.'

Rachel stands up now. She has to do something, so she puts the kettle on the stove, tilting her head as she tries to settle the ringing sound behind her left ear.

Lucas ploughs on. 'But what I don't want is for Ivan to grow up with your – issues.' He sucks in some air, as if drawing on a cigarette before blowing out the next words in a rush. 'I don't want him to be afraid of heights. I don't want him counting shops or lampposts under his breath and I don't want him getting a headache if something isn't in a neat pile. I want him to be normal and healthy and happy. Why don't you just do it? Why don't you make yourself stand on the balcony? Fetch Ivan, do what any new-agey counsellor would tell you and take him out there, for all our sakes, Rach! I mean, what exactly do you think is going to happen if you do?'

Rachel's fingers grip the kettle handle. Ivan, she tells herself, is safe in his cot in the bedroom; she remembers closing the door. A vision of her mother's hardboiled egg slicer rises unbidden in her mind. You place the naked, glistening egg in the little hollow and push down the handle and the row of fine wires presses into the whiteness and all the way through. What you hope for is a perfect cross-section – no grey rings – just white and sunny yellow, still slightly warm, the fanned segments cradled by a leaf or two of lettuce, a dab of salad cream.

'Things are fucked up,' says Lucas, quieter than before. 'I'm sorry – I know it sounds harsh, but maybe you should go back to England for a while.' He clears his throat as if a cough might, even yet, make everything clear and right. In the old days Rachel would be crying by now. Then he could go to her – he'd know what to do, knowing she wanted it too. Now, though, he keeps pushing on, saying they both need a break and maybe she should patch things up with her mother. 'You could think this whole thing through,' he continues. 'Ivan ought to play with other children. You could stop nursing him, get your hair done, see some friends. Then, when you're ready, we could work out what comes next.'

'What about you?' asks Rachel when he stops talking and her hand is steady, and she can set the kettle safely on the hob and turn round to face him.

'Me?' He adjusts his expression as he retreats to safer territory. 'I'll work, like I always do. I'll get my feature out, report twenty-four-seven, start making some decent money so that you – we – have some options.'

'What if I don't want to go?'

Lucas stares at his wife, uncomprehending.

'I'm not going to force you!'

'Then I'll stay here.'

Lucas doesn't say anything for a while. He opens the kitchen window and leans out as the sound of the first cannon booms from the war memorial and the fireworks around the Motherland statue wheeze and blossom and pop.

'Why put ourselves through this?' he mutters, as the night air trembles.

Why indeed? Rachel's closest acquaintances are Suzie and Zoya and Elena. There's Teddy and Karl, of course, and she might even count Mykola, as he knows so much about her. These people aren't her friends, though sometimes they seem more real than her own husband.

But they are not why she cannot retreat from her struggle with the balcony. They are not why she needs to stay.

CHAPTER 20

ELENA SHOWS UP a week after Victory Day. She knocks on the door of Rachel and Lucas's apartment one lunch-time as if nothing has changed – as if she isn't now a landlady with Suzie and Rob's hard currency to spend. When Rachel, surprised, lets her in the old woman squeezes Ivan's chubby calves, fishes her slippers out of her string bag, accepts a cup of tea and sits down in the kitchen to watch the latest episode of *Simplemente Maria*.

Later, while Rachel feeds Ivan and Elena rinses the cups in the sink, the two of them manage through the usual mix of mimed verbs and stabbing nouns to establish that Elena is not living across town, but has in fact moved into a flat downstairs.

'*Kharasho!*' says Rachel, nodding vigorously to express the rush of relief she feels. Elena, who quickly tires of Rachel's attempts at conversation, shuffles into the bedroom and strips Ivan's dirty cot sheet before moving to the living room and folding the crumpled bedding she peels off the sofa. Rachel peeks in from the hallway, dismayed that Elena should find evidence for the disharmony between herself and Lucas, but Elena doesn't seem to notice. She stuffs the laundry into a basket and puts her shoes back on, before indicating that Rachel must take it downstairs to the washing machine.

When Rachel is alone with Ivan once again she wedges a chair against the living room door, tidies the bedroom and retrieves *Jurassic Park* from under the bed. It seems that everyone is busy in their separate spheres. Zoya doesn't bring her sheets to the basement any more – perhaps she is working elsewhere, as Lucas has so often suspected. Suzie, meanwhile, is preoccupied with the renovations of Elena's old house. Lucas is out most of the time, chasing interviews or drinking or confessing his sins to Vee or maybe just walking the streets. His absence allows him and Rachel to put further confrontation on hold. Instead they move around each other with a determined solicitousness, meeting only in the hallway or at the threshold of the bathroom or in the wedge of electric light in front of the refrigerator.

CHAPTER 21

ACROSS THE RIVER in Darnytsia, Zoya, standing in the kitchen of her flat, sets the telephone's receiver back in its cradle and sits down at the table.

She can guess the identity of her caller. The man had told her in his low, soft voice that he knew a great deal about her. He knew, for example, that her flat was still registered in her grandfather's name, that she'd had three abortions in the mid-1980s and that she had been questioned about the provenance of her car at a road block the previous winter. 'So what?' Zoya had said, ready to cut him off. Then the man said he had copies of her grandfather's medical records, that he knew about the morphine levels in his blood and his urine and that such things could be misconstrued if she was not more careful and continued to sniff like a bitch around the private affairs of legitimate businessmen. He also warned her not to discuss this conversation with the likes of that dried up whore Elena Vasilyevna.

Zoya lights a cigarette and blows smoke towards the open window. She doesn't fear for herself, but Elena is another matter. She is going to have to be careful.

CHAPTER 22

JUNE ARRIVES LIKE a pulsing heart, pink and glistening. There are swift thunderstorms and sudden showers, after which the city's shining streets expand beneath the trees to accommodate the makeshift stalls with their blushing radishes and tender carrots, strawberries, *smetana* and clear linden honey. Meanwhile the hot water is turned off for a fortnight's maintenance in the apartment block on Staronavodnitska Street. As the pipes bleed they make sad sounds, like whale song. Lucas starts shaving at the office, while Rachel boils pans on the stove and holds Ivan as he splashes in the sink. Sometimes she takes him to Suzie's flat, whenever Suzie wants Rachel to examine her swatches of fabric samples or discuss the merits of pelmets or moan about the fact that the old woman who leased them the house still appears every evening to water the vegetable patch. Most of the time, however, Rachel walks, and as she walks she stares at the passers-by who seem, every day, more strange and more familiar.

One afternoon, as Rachel is watching a man buy raspberries from a fruit stall on Khreschatyk, Teddy spies her from across the street. He runs over to her, dodging a truck with flapping tarpaulin sides. It beeps its horn and makes Ivan shriek.

'Hey,' he says, planting a kiss on her temple. 'Raspberries! The first of the season. I want some.'

'Do you think they're safe to eat?' asks Rachel, who knows

that if she asks the stallholder he will swear they've been grown in the Caucasus.

Teddy smiles. 'I hope so. I've given up worrying.' He glances at Ivan. 'Seriously, it's too early in the season for them to have come from the exclusion zone. Don't they smell fabulous?'

They both pause for a moment, waiting as the man at the front of the queue refuses the little newspaper cones offered by the stallholder and instead opens up his peeling vinyl briefcase so that she can heap the soft fruit inside.

'I should have brought a bag,' says Teddy. 'Those cones are going to leak.'

Rachel pulls a pastel blue nappy sack out of her handbag. 'Would you like one of these? They're quite hygienic. I use them all the time.'

'Rachel,' exclaims Teddy, 'you are beautiful *and* resourceful! We must have raspberries with ice cream. And meringue – Karl loves a Pavlova. I'm going to tell Vee that's what I want at my leaving dinner. Not cherry dumplings. Dumplings are for winter.'

Rachel feels a little unsteady on her feet. She grips the handles of the pushchair.

'Are you leaving?'

Teddy looks down at her, surprised. 'Didn't Lucas tell you? That boy is something else! Well, I'm off to Bosnia with Karl. New adventures! Hey, don't look so sad! We're having a last supper at Vee's. Next Saturday. You better come – I refuse to sit next to anyone else!'

'Dinner is difficult . . .' murmurs Rachel. 'With Ivan – now he's older it's harder to take him out at night.'

'So let's find you a babysitter,' says Teddy. 'How about that caretaker – the one who's retired with a suitcase of cash. She's fond of Ivan, right?' He smiles, rueful, sympathetic. 'Lucas needs to show you off.'

'Lucas wants me to go back to London.' The words rush out of Rachel before she can stop them; for a moment she doesn't recognise the woman discussing her husband with a man she barely knows. But this is Teddy, she reminds herself. Not Mykola.

Teddy rubs his chin.

'Then please come for my sake, and yours.'

Rachel thinks about Teddy's suggestion as the trolleybus rattles up the broad boulevard of Lesi Ukrainky. She doesn't want to leave Ivan with someone else, but neither does she want Lucas to visit Vee's flat without her. Teddy knows something; he's just too loyal to pass it on.

As she pushes Ivan across the waste ground she spies Stepan. He is lounging in the grass; she can just see his shorn head and shoulders through the tangle of stems and weeds. He is with that horrible man, his minder. That they are outside is not, Rachel reminds herself, so unusual. These days she often encounters bodies sprawled in the sunshine. Sometimes she passes lovers grappling silently, like molluscs, or she steers the pushchair round a pair of mottled legs sticking out across the path. Old men slump on the benches and chat softly or stare down at their hands. Young girls with their skinny arms and bright hair accessories sit cross-legged and play clapping games or chalk neat rows of sums on the concrete, and several times she has seen the same middle-aged couple enjoying a picnic of gherkins and sausage laid out on a blue handbag amongst the dandelions.

She could skirt around Stepan. She could remain out of sight, but she has things she wants to ask him and it is better to do it here, out in the open, than down in the basement or in the shadows on the stairs.

As she approaches, she wonders what the pair are looking at, for Stepan's shorn scalp and the older man's bulging neck both bend towards the ground. She is almost upon them when she sees the chick. It is golden brown and fluffy and it makes little cheeping sounds as it shuttles between them in the space they have flattened out in the grass. Yet what strikes her most is not the chick itself, but the way the two of them use their bodies to fence in the tiny bird. Stepan makes a wall with his legs, while the older man is squatting like a broody, dishevelled hen.

'*Ciao!*' says Stepan, raising his head. '*Cik cik!*'

'Hello,' says Rachel. She is facing the sun and puts her hand up to protect her eyes.

'You want to look?' he asks. 'Show your baby?'

Rachel glances down at Ivan, who is nodding off in the shade of the pushchair's canopy. 'He's sleeping . . .'

The older man doesn't acknowledge her. He is wearing a grey vest and a pair of shiny tracksuit bottoms. The flesh below his jaw sags and glistens. He mutters a few words, then puts his hand to the ground, palm up. The chick obligingly steps on to it.

Rachel grips the pushchair handles. She hasn't spoken to Stepan for weeks – not since she found him in the basement eating the Angel Delight her mother had sent. She wants to make sure he hasn't stolen anything else, but her courage is quickly fading.

'Have you seen Elena today?' she asks.

Stepan shrugs.

'Well, if you do see her, will you please tell her I need to talk to her?' Rachel hopes the boy thinks she is going to tell Elena about the intercepted parcels. Stepan breaks off a stalk of grass and sticks it in his mouth; he looks like a drawing she once saw of Huckleberry Finn.

'Okay Mum. You want baby-sit?'

Rachel frowns. He must have spoken to Teddy. She hates the way he knows what she wants. Before she can contradict him, however, the older man lifts his hand off the ground and curls his fingers around the chick.

'Don't!' says Rachel, stepping forward, imagining the crushing of its tiny breast and bones.

Stepan's companion takes no notice. Carefully, gently, he places the chick behind him in the long grass and lets it topple off his hand.

'*Cik cik!*' repeats Stepan as the chick shakes itself off and scoots out of sight.

Now Rachel wants Stepan to go after the chick and rescue it, because she knows it won't survive alone in the killing fields of the waste ground with its starving strays and sharp-beaked crows. But Stepan doesn't move.

'I've been meaning to ask you,' she says, trying to sound self-assured. 'Why did you open that parcel addressed to me – with the packets of pudding mix? Have you opened other parcels, too? I don't understand why you would do that.'

Stepan sticks his tongue between his bottom lip and his teeth.

'Someone tell me to,' he says.

This is not what Rachel is expecting.

'Who? Who told you?'

'I don't say,' says Stepan. 'Not someone. I make it up, like story.'

Don't lie, thinks Rachel. She is still distracted by the lost chick, still looking for movement in the weeds behind him. 'Was it someone called Mykola?'

Stepan shrugs. 'No one!'

'Him?' she presses, nodding at the older man. 'Did he make you? What else have you stolen?'

For the first time Stepan looks surprised.

'Not stolen, Mum. I looking.'

Rachel feels the heat spreading across her neck. 'Don't call me "Mum".'

'Okay,' says Stepan. 'Queen Mum. Mrs Mum. Not you. You not Mum. I tell Elena Vasilyevna you want baby-sit.'

Sensing she is being dismissed, Rachel stares, exasperated, as Stepan lies back in the long grass and drapes his arm across his face. The older man grunts and rolls on to his side.

It isn't until she regains the path that she sees a small thing skitter through the grass towards the dump bins and hears its plaintive cheep.

Elena is walking up the hill to the *universam* when she notices the car slowing to a crawl beside her. She doesn't turn to look; rather, she does her utmost to ignore it. It is a foreign car – silver, with a long sloping bonnet and windows you can't see through. A gangster car.

Elena isn't feeling so well today. Her hips ache and now her stomach is upset. She doesn't want to be out for too long in case her bowels loosen. It's the new flat, she tells herself, with its strange echoes and hard floors. She keeps the windows open despite the flies, because she knows how the vents work in these apartment blocks and she doesn't want to breathe in air that has incubated its germs in the lungs of a stranger.

The lights are green at the busy intersection, but the silver car doesn't accelerate. Instead it continues to creep forward beside Elena, keeping pace with her slow shuffle, holding up the traffic behind so that other drivers lean on their horns. When the lights turn red it doesn't brake, staying abreast of the pedestrians as they flow across the street.

Elena keeps walking. She needs oil and scouring powder, and may perhaps buy a bag of bread rings for the little boy, but the afternoon is warm and her feet feel swollen and heavy. She turns right down a side street and the car glides right too, hugging the curb, nosing level with her legs.

Now she is beginning to feel breathless. The city is full of fumes and each day the walk to the *universam* gets a little harder. She stops for a moment and steadies herself beneath a plane tree. The car stops moving, too. The passenger window slides down with a soft electric hum, though because of the shadow cast by the tree she cannot see who sits inside. It doesn't matter. She never sees, never looks. She bends down as if she is about to pluck a weed out of the soil, but instead she scoops up something in her hand and quickly, awkwardly, throws it into the car: a dog turd, not as fresh as she would like, yet still stinking.

On Saturday night, when Elena taps at the door of the flat on the thirteenth floor, Rachel is having second thoughts about going to Vee's without Ivan. She arranged the time with Elena the day before, holding up seven fingers and repeating 'syem!' but now she has more or less decided to send her away. However, as she opens the door Elena thrusts a small carton of peach juice at her and slips quickly inside, divesting herself of her thick cardigan and shoes. The old woman smiles and shuffles down the hallway as if she is the housekeeper or Ivan's elderly godmother.

'Ivan is sleeping,' whispers Rachel, cutting Elena off at the kitchen, miming and pointing to the closed bedroom door. Lucas is in the bathroom so she switches on the television, keeping the volume low. Elena nods and sits down at the table while Rachel, unsure what to do next, sets the kettle on the hob and puts biscuits on a plate. Ivan won't wake, she reminds herself. He's become a deep sleeper like his father.

When Lucas appears she asks him to explain that they will be back at ten-thirty and if anything is wrong she must call Vee's number, which is written down on a sheet of paper next to the telephone.

'Ten thirty?' mutters Lucas. 'This is Teddy's leaving dinner! Well, I suppose Zoya can bring you back earlier.'

Rachel doesn't risk a last peek at her son. She closes the front door softly behind her.

'Hurry up,' says Lucas, stabbing at the button of the lift. 'I don't want to be late.'

※

Rachel stands in the hallway of Vee's flat and stares at the homemade bunting that hangs along the wall. Each triangle is cut from a photograph of Teddy or Karl, or both. In all the pictures they are laughing, sometimes with Vee, sometimes posing with other people, sometimes caught unawares. These are snapshots of lives that are busy and sociable; lives that mean something.

'Look, here's a picture with you in it,' says Vee, pointing at a dark image. It is a little out of focus and shows Rachel with her eyes half shut sitting next to Karl and Teddy on the bed at Lucas's birthday party.

'It's a nice idea,' murmurs Rachel, as she glances along the row and sees a picture of Lucas, smiling through a cloud of cigarette smoke, one arm around Teddy, the other round Vee. What was it Lucas told her they used to call themselves? The *Troika*.

Rachel, having assumed the dress code for the night would be 'expensively understated', is wearing the jeans she bought with her credit card and a pale blue shirt she has carefully ironed. Tonight, however, Vee is wearing a low-cut dress made from some silky, stretchy material that clings to her hips and shows off the creamy lustre of her breasts. Lucas keeps glancing towards her as he chats to Karl beneath a triangle of Vee and Teddy pouting at the camera.

Vee has dragged her kitchen table through to the bed-sitting room. Rachel looks in and sees candles and linen napkins and counts places laid for eight. The doorbell rings. Vee's other guests have arrived, and Rachel is surprised to find she recognises all three of them: Sorin, Dr Alleyn from the embassy, and Viktor Lukyanenko, the young film director, who pulls Vee close and kisses her on the mouth.

Vee serves black caviar with the bottle of proper champagne that Sorin has presented to her. Rachel, squeezed between Teddy and Dr Alleyn, isn't feeling very hungry. She needn't have come, she thinks. Vee has moved on to someone else. Her husband, sitting opposite her between Karl and Lukyanenko, looks wary in the glow of the candlelight. For a moment she pities him.

'Our hostess is spoiling us!' stage-whispers Teddy, as he scoops up a spoonful of the sticky beluga eggs and smears them across a freshly-made buckwheat blini.

'Ah, but I have a friendly supplier who gives me a discount,' laughs Vee.

Dr Alleyn raises an eyebrow. 'Of course you do,' he says, to no one in particular.

'Well, I should like to raise a toast to these intrepid adventurers – Teddy and Karl!' says Sorin from the end of the table, waving his glass.

'To Teddy and Karl!' repeat the others. '*Nazdarovye!*'

The main course is a platter of fresh perch along with baby potatoes and herb butter. Wine and vodka appear, and before long the table has divided into separate conversations all happening at once. Dr Alleyn talks to Sorin about isotopes and river contamination. Teddy tells Rachel about Bosnia, and how he and Karl hope to get into Sarajevo, despite the fact that it is under continual bombardment.

'There's a tunnel,' Teddy says. 'From UN-controlled territory right into the city. Paid for with cigarettes, I heard.'

'But it's too dangerous, surely?' asks Rachel, as she picks through the fish on her plate. She thinks of the mortar bombs and the weeping women and skeletal men she has seen on the news.

'Maybe,' says Teddy, serious for a moment. 'But I'd rather take my chances there than get my head smashed in by some queer-basher down by the Dnieper.'

Rachel is shocked. 'Has something happened?' she asks.

'No,' says Teddy, though his glance over to Karl makes her wonder. Karl is quiet tonight, which isn't unusual, but now she sees how one side of his face is slightly yellow. He seems to be holding himself in, his left arm crossed over his chest. She draws a deep breath, ready to probe further.

'Shh,' whispers Teddy, watching her carefully, holding a finger to his lips. 'Out of the frame, remember?'

Lucas seems to be getting into a discussion with Vee and Lukyanenko about the film industry and the progress of his feature. Lukyanenko is talking about financing, his face serious, his tone sombre, yet he is holding Vee's hand and they are pushing against each other's thumbs, each bending the other's back with real force. Suddenly Lukyanenko's thumb gives way and he laughs.

'What's funny?' asks Lucas, clearly unsettled.

Lukyanenko sits back; he is now caressing Vee's fingers. He isn't the kind of man Rachel expects Vee to choose as a partner. His face is too pointed, his head too small; but his expression is intense, and Rachel finds herself staring.

'Everything is funny,' he says, looking round the table. 'I am here, eating dinner, sitting next to my – ah, that phrase – "whip-ass" girlfriend. Yet my movie is very far from secure. Everything is paid for – wages, post-production, PR -' he nods at Sorin – 'yet I depend on the . . . *protection* of my backers to ensure the film is released and is shown in our cinemas. Now I have a problem. Someone is making threats.'

'Who?' asks Lucas quickly.

Vee leans back and studies Lucas from behind Lukyanenko's head. 'See there's the real story, Lucas. Haven't I always said so? It's not the production you should be interested in, but the money flow, the gate-keepers . . . I know a guy with a white goods store. Nothing too fancy – take a look at his sort if you want to dig deep. He's connected, all the way. Not even Sorin here can touch him!'

Sorin is grinning, uncomfortable, but Lucas looks horrified. 'The film *will* be distributed, won't it? On general release? The premiere—'

Lukyanenko turns to him and now there is no trace of irony. 'I want you to have your story,' he says. 'Good for you, good for my movie, good for our industry. You will come to the premiere, I think, and I hope you bring your wife, though maybe not your little boy, whose performance I remember at the sound stage!'

'Oh God!' Vee laughs, offering cigarettes around the table. 'The kid's adorable, but what a responsibility! Rachel has managed amazingly with him here.' Her eyes fix on Rachel in the candlelight. 'Gotta love him, but it's great you found a babysitter. It must be quite a deal, leaving him for the first time.' She raises her glass, still holding Rachel's stare. 'Now it's my turn to make a toast. To all moms. To Rachel!'

'To Rachel!' echoes Teddy, then Karl and Sorin.

Rachel, however, isn't feeling well. A painful pressure has been building at the back of her eyes since Vee mentioned the owner of the white goods store. The ringing sound in her ears has returned. This is the first time she has experienced it away from the apartment block. She shouldn't be here, she thinks. Mykola warned her not to leave her child alone with Elena. She drops her fork on the floor.

'Hey,' says Teddy, instantly attentive. 'What's wrong? Do you need some air?' He looks over to Dr Alleyn. 'She's kind of pale – do you want to lie down?'

'I need to go home . . .' she mumbles.

With some reluctance, Dr Alleyn pushes back his chair.

'It is a little warm in here.' He reaches out for her wrist, tries to feel her pulse. Rachel tugs her hand away.

'I need to go home. Lucas, I have to go now.' She stands, leaning against the table so that glasses wobble. Lucas stands too. 'Please. I'll wave down a car . . .'

'Don't be stupid,' says Lucas, aware of everyone watching. 'I'm sorry. We'd better go. I'll come back later if I can.' His dismay increases as murmurs of 'no, stay with Rachel' pass around the table. Teddy and Vee see them to the door.

'Call us!' they urge, as Lucas follows Rachel down the stairs. But Rachel has already forgotten the party.

Her baby. She needs to save him. She needs to reach page twenty-seven before it is too late.

❧

The tropical rain fell in great drenching sheets. All the way back to Staronavodnitska Street, Rachel mutters under her breath, sentence after sentence, line after line: see the words, count the words, miss nothing. She pays no attention to the driver who is staring in his mirror or her husband, who keeps asking her what's wrong. When they arrive at the car park she scrambles out before the car has stopped moving and Lucas is still fumbling for the fare. Inside the building the light shows the lift is stuck on the sixteenth floor, but Rachel is already running up the stairs, gasping for breath, lungs breaking, counting and counting, don't miss, don't repeat, page twenty-five, three hundred and twenty, page twenty-six, two hundred and ninety-two. Her legs are stronger than she knows, yet weaker than she needs; they crumble on the last flight so that she half crawls, half drags herself to the landing on the thirteenth floor.

The key is in her pocket. She fumbles and almost drops it. Finish page twenty-seven. Finish it. *Elena opened the door . . . the lizards crouched like gargoyles . . . the child must be dead . . .*

As she enters the apartment Rachel bites her tongue until her mouth tastes of blood. She must be quiet now, so quiet, for the living room door is gaping wide and all the lights are on. The breeze is cool on her face and she knows the balcony door is open on the other side of the net curtain. A figure is out there, diffuse, indistinct against the darkness of the night. Rachel must slow her own heart and the high-pitched ringing in her ear and not raise the alarm. Like a ghost she moves across the floor of the living room. She hears the old woman murmuring to herself, sees her stoop down. A squeaking noise, something scraping on the lino – *what is she doing . . .*

On the threshold of the balcony, poking through the net curtain, a face appears – a plastic, gurning face from a TV cartoon, rolling on wheels. Rachel stares, first in horror, then bewilderment as an old, arthritic hand pulls the curtain aside. Ivan, her baby, is standing in the doorway, gripping the handle of the Donald Duck baby walker Rachel bought at the *universam* all those months before. Elena is bending over him, ready to catch him should he fall.

'*Privyet!*' says the old woman, looking up, and then her face falls and her hands shield the child's mouth and eyes, because Rachel is leaning over, retching and retching, all the sickness pouring out onto the living room floor, spattering across the shiny parquet along with little spots of caviar, pale fizz and some half-digested perch.

CHAPTER 23

THINGS HAPPEN, DREAMS Rachel. You say, it was like this, and so it becomes that way. You think something, and then it gets stuck if you don't blink it away. But the stories you tell yourself, they are not fixed, they can be unmade. Anything might happen, or not, or maybe. Not knowing is something you fall into and falling makes you weightless. It doesn't hurt – not much. Sometimes when you fall the wind lifts you up like a puff of white dandelion seed and then you are clean again, and new.

The ringing has stopped. There is silence, then there is noise, but nothing is constant. Squeaking from the ceiling, a baby crying, a balcony door opening – these things start, they stop and they start again. Elena is there, bringing peppermint tea. Ivan, her child – she can hear he is near.

Rachel tries to sit up. There is someone she must speak to. The man with the black hat made from unborn baby lambs – where is he?

༺✦༻

Rachel is sick for three days. Her fever is high, her body is wrung out, yet still she leans over the side of the bed and retches into a bowl.

'Food poisoning,' says Dr Alleyn, who pops over to the flat on the second day. 'Not the worst, but bad enough. Call this number if she's not better by Wednesday.' He tells Lucas his wife needs a holiday back home and a visit to her GP when she is up on her feet. He leaves his card, together with some sachets of Dioralyte.

'Must have been some ropey perch,' murmurs Lucas, from somewhere near the window.

Rachel is too weak to tell him it wasn't the fish.

༺

'Hey,' says Lucas. He lowers himself onto the edge of the bed near Rachel's feet. 'You're looking better.'

Rachel nods, carefully. It has just taken all her strength to shuffle to the bathroom and back again. 'I feel empty,' she says, and it's true, she *is* empty – her milk is all gone. She hasn't nursed Ivan for three days, and now there's nothing left. Lucas shows her the powdered formula he bought from the pharmacy in Lipki – some American brand she's never heard of, but the date on the base of the tin is still good and Lucas says he read the instructions, boiled the water for ages, and even found the sterilising tablets Rachel kept beneath the sink.

'He didn't like it at first,' Lucas tells her. 'But he hasn't been sick and now he slurps it up from his beaker like a pro.'

Rachel rests her head back against the pillow. Ivan is sitting on the floor by Lucas's feet, brandishing a rope of cotton reels that Elena has made for him. Her hand reaches through the space until she touches the top of his head. This isn't how she wanted to wean her son. In truth she hadn't known how she would do it and the loss leaves a physical ache, as if a piece of

226

string is knotted beneath her sternum and someone is tugging, but it keeps catching between her ribs. Ivan is separate from her now; yet, unexpectedly, the ache of separation is tempered by relief. He survived out on the balcony even though she wasn't there. If she died now he would live.

'Where is Elena?' she asks.

'Elena? No idea. She was here earlier, though. I know you weren't sure about leaving her with Ivan, but she's been a godsend while you've been ill. She's taken the washing away, taken him for walks. Don't worry – I've told her not to take him out on the balcony.'

'It's okay,' says Rachel. 'I don't mind.'

Lucas is taken aback. 'Really? I thought it would upset you!' He doesn't know about Mykola's warning, or the gravity-invoking weight of her own fear and none of this matters to Rachel any more, because Elena has taken her baby out to the edge and proved them all wrong.

'Look,' continues Lucas. 'I've been thinking. I said some stupid stuff before you got ill, and I'm sorry. I really am. But you do need to go back to England for a couple of weeks – nothing more, I swear – just a bit of time for a rest and some food that won't poison you.' He takes her hand. She doesn't pull away. 'Zoya's been useless – I think a relative died and I've got behind with work. Not your fault, obviously. So I've booked you a ticket. For next week.'

Rachel blinks quickly, her old habit, the one she has always used to push away difficult thoughts.

'Anyway,' continues Lucas, 'when you come back my story will be finished and we can take a holiday together, maybe down to Crimea like I promised at Christmas. I could get a feature out of it – make it pay for itself.'

'I suppose.' So many other things are stretching, twisting, re-forming into a way of thinking that is as yet unclear. For the first time in months Rachel peers out at a pressing, insistent future. England, and the fact of its continuing existence, is beginning to reassemble itself.

CHAPTER 24

O N   T H E   M O R N I N G of Rachel's departure she wakes early and stands in the kitchen in her bare feet. The sun is already high above the river. She can feel its warmth on her face as she sips her tea. Her suitcases are packed. Ivan's changing bag is ready. The cupboard is full of dried pasta and tinned tomatoes so that Lucas won't starve. Soon she will wake Ivan, give him his morning milk and dress him for the journey, but she won't move until she hears Lucas pull the light switch in the bathroom. Her own stillness calms her. In a few hours she will be in England, knocking on her mother's door. She hasn't told her mother she is coming. Neither has she mentioned this fact to Lucas. Baby steps, she thinks. First one foot, then the other.

Lucas, however, doesn't go into the bathroom. Instead he steps in behind her and stands just an inch or two away. She can feel his bed heat between them. She can smell his morning breath. He can't take her to the airport, he tells her. Lukyanenko has called a breakfast press conference. Lucas wasn't given any warning; he has to go. He is sorry, but this is big. Soon he is dressed and gone, leaving only an awkward kiss next to her ear and a plea that she will call the office number from Heathrow when she lands.

Rachel watches from the window as he strides across the car park. Soon he is a tiny figure like the other tiny figures moving across the road, milling at the tram stop, combining and separating, impelled by some law of mutual proximity. She stows her copy of *Jurassic Park* in the bottom of Ivan's changing bag and waits for Zoya.

When Zoya arrives, Rachel tells her how sorry she is to hear about her bereavement.

Zoya is wearing a green shirt today, tucked into the high waist of her jeans. She looks different – the outfit is more casual than her usual skirt and boots as if she was dressed for a stroll in the park.

'My grandfather was old,' she says, with a quick shake of her head. 'Dying was all he had left.' She spots Rachel's suitcase. 'Let's go. You have your passport, your ticket, money?'

'Yes, thank you.' Rachel clips Ivan into his pushchair and loops the changing bag over the handles. When she closes the front door behind them and rattles it to make sure it is locked a shiver passes through her, a sense of severance, as if the time she has spent here is shaking itself out. She will be back in two weeks, she tells herself. Nothing will have changed.

Downstairs in the foyer Elena is waiting to say goodbye. She bends forward to give Ivan a kiss and a squeeze. When she straightens up she is smiling, but her eyes are watery with tears. Zoya speaks to her quickly in Ukrainian and Elena bows her head.

'What did you say to her?' asks Rachel, as they exit through the door.

'I told her to stay out of your flat.'

'What?' Rachel looks back at Elena, who is already retreating up the stairs.

Zoya sighs. 'Your flat. She has a key. Lucas gave her one while you were ill.'

Rachel thinks about this for a moment. 'I don't mind if she lets herself in for a bit,' she says. 'Lucas wouldn't like it, but he gave her the key. Imagine – he comes home, and Elena is sitting on the sofa watching *Simplemente Maria!*' She starts laughing, surprising herself, while Zoya rolls her eyes to hide her smile.

＊

Rachel's mood changes as they drive out of the city. She sits on the back seat of the car with Ivan on her knee and winds down the window. Zoya glances in her mirror and tuts, but Rachel takes no notice. The day is calm and warm, with a high blue sky. The smells of scythed grass and tar compete with the exhaust fumes as they drive along the boulevards. The trees are in full leaf now and the sun is glancing off the empty windows of the shops announcing *Khleb* or *Kneegi* or *Myaso*, so that people walking past in the shade look blurry, like the figures in Victorian photographs who moved while the plate was exposed. Everything in Kiev is alien to Rachel – the cars, the people, the noises, the language, the smells – yet it feels more real to her than anywhere else.

'I don't want to go back to England,' she says softly, to the back of Zoya's head.

Zoya studies her in the rear view mirror.

'Then don't go.'

The wind is blowing Rachel's hair across her face. She pushes it away. 'What are you doing today? I mean, after you've dropped me at the airport. Are you going to the office?'

'No.'

Rachel is used to Zoya's curtness. She adjusts her son's legs – he is falling asleep and she tries to make him comfortable. However, just as she resigns herself to silence, Zoya takes one hand off the wheel and winds down her own window a little way.

'As a matter of fact,' she says, 'I am going to my grandfather's place in the country.'

'Oh.' Rachel tries to imagine Zoya in the woods; she struggles to picture her anywhere but the city. 'Do you grow things there? Can I come with you?'

Zoya snorts. 'I have things I must do. You have a plane to catch.'

'Well, *you* said, "Then don't go," and I don't want to.' Rachel leans forward, gripped by the possibility that she might be allowed to change her mind. 'We could go back and fetch Elena. She'd love a day in the country – she must be missing her little house in Tsarskoye Selo!'

Zoya says nothing for a while. She drives around a pot hole, then pulls over beneath a hoarding and eases up the handbrake.

'You don't belong here,' she murmurs, not unkindly.

'You may be right,' says Rachel, as a flush burns across her cheeks. 'But you aren't the one who decides.'

꧁꧂

The little Zhiguli sways and bumps along the track around the edge of an untended field and on into the straggle of birch wood, where the light flickers through the leaves and the air smells of moss and something vaguely medicinal. Elena sits beside Zoya in the front, while Rachel remains in the back with Ivan dozing in her lap and Stepan beside her. No one says very much. Perhaps, thinks Rachel, they are as surprised as she to find themselves here together on a jaunt to the country. Once again, Elena almost cried when they drove back to fetch her, and Stepan – well, he was loitering by her door and Elena said he must come too, despite Rachel's head-shaking and his insistence on going back upstairs to fetch his anorak. Zoya stopped at a roadside kiosk a few miles out of Kiev to buy a picnic of *kvas*, rye bread and sausage, but otherwise they've come as they are. Elena is wearing a heavy cardigan around her shoulders, Stepan a blue tee shirt and his skimpy footballer shorts. He has bunched up his anorak to make a pillow. His narrow thighs jut outwards so that Rachel must point her knees towards the door. He has grown in the past few months; his shoulders seem more angular. There is new hair on his lip.

'Are we nearly there?' Rachel asks, breaking the silence. Her words echo memories of childhood trips to the seaside, never knowing whether the blue-grey plate of the English Channel lay just beyond the next hill or whether, in fact, she would never arrive, lost in the chasm between home and away. It mattered to her, as a child. It still does.

Zoya doesn't answer – no surprise there. As Rachel looks about her, the track widens and the spindly trees thin out. A wooden dacha comes into view. It has pretty carved shutters, but they don't stop beside it; neither do they stop at the others that follow, all in varying states of upkeep, all with panelled fences and low, drooping roofs. The place seems deserted, despite a couple of rusting Tavrias parked up along the road-side and the crowing of a cockerel in someone's backyard.

Just as the little settlement begins to peter out, Zoya slows to a halt and turns off the engine. She says something to Elena, then opens the door and steps on to the verge.

'There are ticks,' she says, eyeing Rachel through the open window. 'It is good you are wearing trousers. Push the legs inside your socks.'

'What about Ivan?' asks Rachel. 'And Stepan? They've both got bare legs!'

Zoya is tying a scarf around her head. It makes her look like a woman in a Soviet propaganda poster – a factory worker or a peasant. 'You will see if something crawls on to your son,' she says.

'I burn them so they *pik, pik!*' adds Stepan, flicking his fingers.

'I will take tweezers and pull them out,' warns Zoya.

Rachel tries to open her door without waking Ivan. 'Where is the house? Is it far?'

Zoya sighs. 'If you get out of the car, I will show you.'

❧

Rachel sits Ivan on her hip and picks her way along an overgrown footpath. Stepan follows behind with the bottles of cloudy *kvas* while Zoya walks ahead with Elena, who treads carefully, shuffling along in her outdoor shoes and nursing the newspaper-wrapped sausage. After a few minutes they leave the line of trees behind and descend into a valley. A tin roof protrudes beyond some reeds, and now Rachel can see that the house is not a house at all. There are no shutters, there is no veranda, no mansarded roof, no quaint fretwork. To Rachel it is a shed: a single room dwelling raised on concrete blocks. Its windows are made from thick plastic sheets and the metal door has clearly been salvaged from somewhere, cut and welded to fit. There is no sign of a toilet, no plumbing, not even a pump.

Zoya makes the rules clear straight away.

'If you need to answer a call of nature, climb back up the hill and go in the woods. Bury, please.' She yanks out a small spade from the space beneath the steps.

'What do you do out here?' asks Rachel, as Stepan pulls his trainers off and hops across the stones and rough grass towards a shallow stream.

'Do?' Zoya looks amused. 'We sit. We drink and eat.' She turns to watch Elena, who is hobbling around the side of the building to inspect some remnants of soft fruit bushes and an ancient plum tree with thick branches that twist outwards like flailing arms. 'My grandfather used to grow things here. Many things – fruit, vegetables – sometimes even flowers when I was a child. Elena won't like the way everything is now wild, but I could not manage it when Dedushka was sick.' She pauses, her twitching smile gone, her face empty.

'I'm sorry . . .' says Rachel, wishing she had better words to offer. She is an interloper, standing uselessly in the fresh-ly-trampled grass with Ivan wriggling in her arms. She shifts him up her hip and looks around. 'What can I do? Can I help with anything?'

Zoya is fiddling with the padlock on the door. 'You can help me find the vodka.'

⚜

The five accidental *dachniki* eat lunch on Ivan's nap blanket, spread out in the long grass. The sausage is full of chewy lumps of gristle, though Rachel finds she is hungry and the salty fat isn't so bad. Ivan eats the two pots of yoghurt she was saving for the plane, and for dessert she raids her son's changing bag for biscuits and some sliced pear and apple. Elena sniffs the fruit and won't touch it, but she takes several biscuits and slices the sausage with a small paring knife Zoya hands to her, managing surprisingly well with her broken teeth and a jaw that folds in on itself as she masticates each mouthful. Zoya then insists they all drink the vodka she has brought out from its hiding place in the hut. They have no glasses, but by now Stepan and Elena seem convinced that Ivan's changing bag is a cornucopia of abundance and usefulness, so once again Rachel burrows amongst the nappies and fishes out Ivan's spare beaker. She takes off the lid and pours a finger's depth for Elena and herself, while Zoya swigs straight from the bottle. The vodka is unfiltered and slightly gritty; it burns Rachel's throat and oesophagus as it slides its way down. Elena takes a sip, then passes the cup to Stepan.

'I am baby!' jokes Stepan, picking up the lid and pushing it back on to the cup.

'No!' pleads Rachel, helplessly. To her mind there is something repulsive about watching this boy suck vodka from the spout, though Zoya is smiling at her squeamishness and Elena is laughing so much that tears squeeze out of her eyes.

And so the day gently unwinds. Rachel lies back in the grass and closes her eyes while Ivan pulls up handfuls of weeds in his chubby fists or tries to catch the flies gathering on the greasy crumbs, and Elena naps, snoring, then gets up and shuffles off towards the rear of the hut to rummage amongst the bolting vegetables and broken canes. Perhaps she is searching for something to prune back or harvest. Time slows, memories fade, the sun inches across a soft blue sky. Rachel feels her son scrambling over her hips. She puts her hand out, touches his dense, warm skin. This is real, she thinks, this bond of blood and survival. Today they are all saved and she could lie here forever with Ivan's head on her stomach, pinning her down, his legs twitching gently against her own, even the weight of his wet nappy a reassurance that now, right now, she has everything she needs.

She wakes with a jolt when Ivan bashes something hard against her collar bone. Her head is spinning a little, from the sunlight or the blood-rush or possibly the vodka, but as her eyes readjust she sees that he is clutching the pot of Sudafed she always keeps in her handbag. Other items lay strewn across the blanket: keys, a couple of tampons, a pen with the ink starting to seep into the fabric. And her well-thumbed copy of *Jurassic Park*.

Zoya is lighting a cigarette on the steps behind her.

'I remember that book,' she says, blowing smoke towards the stream. 'You were reading it when you first arrived. Then Lucas gave it to Sorin, and you wanted it back.'

'Yes,' says Rachel, frowning.

Zoya stretches out a leg and pushes the book with her foot. 'Dinosaurs. The dangers of men playing god with science. You read it a lot, but what does it say? I think it is rubbish.'

Rachel wishes the book had stayed at the bottom of the changing bag. She picks it up and flicks the pages slowly, as if the book is unfamiliar, until she finds one with the corner folded over. The fold is on page twenty-seven, marking the part where Elena the midwife leaves the window open at the clinic and the baby raptors climb inside and eat the newborn's face. She must have counted the words of that section a hundred times at least.

'I thought I needed this book,' she murmurs.

'And you have changed your mind?' Zoya's tone is neutral, but her questions, Rachel knows, are always loaded.

'Elena helped me,' she says. 'I don't need it anymore.'

'Then get rid of it.'

Rachel thinks for a moment. Ivan is safe. Now when she looks at the cover it seems ridiculous.

'All right,' she says. 'I'm going for a walk in the woods. You can come if you like, though I warn you, I'm taking the spade.'

Zoya offers a hand and pulls Rachel to her feet.

Up beneath the trees, the air is still and cool. They have left the wasps behind them and the ground is springy, made soft by decades of leaf fall. Light pools haphazardly between the birch trunks that stand white and straight like postulants stopped in prayer. Rachel feels as if she has stepped into a church.

Ivan, whom she has once again carried on her hip, is trying to get down, so she sits him on the weedless grass and looks around her.

'Anywhere will do,' she says, taking the spade from Zoya. She thrusts it into the earth near a small anthill. 'Here.'

When a small hole is dug and the ants are scattering amongst the pale tree roots, Rachel tips her book inside, quickly, as if now she cannot wait to be rid of it, as if burying it is part of the ritual she never wanted, never craved. As an afterthought, she bends down and removes Ivan's sodden nappy and drops it on top of the book.

'There,' she says, aware that Zoya is watching her.

'You are killing two birds with one stone,' remarks Zoya dryly.

'Multi-tasking,' says Rachel, as she kicks the soil back into the hole with her foot. 'When I was little, we used to say, "good riddance to bad rubbish".' She pauses. A memory comes back to her, the love notes to the boy she'd left behind, hidden within those dark waxy sleeves. When her mother discovered one and confronted her with it, Rachel had collected up all the others and pushed them down amongst the chicken bones and broken eggshells at the bottom of the dustbin. 'I hope it rots quickly.'

Rachel scoops up Ivan and the two women turn and walk back to the edge of the trees, where the sun is strong and bright, the air full of heat. They raise their hands to their eyes and squint down the slope towards the little hut and the stream. The place appears deserted, but then a small movement to the left catches Rachel's attention and she sees Stepan peeing, directing the arc of his urine at a flat stone near the edge of the reeds.

Zoya sees him, too.

'He likes to win, that one,' she says. 'If there's no one to play against, he competes with himself.'

'He seems very attached to Elena,' says Rachel.

Zoya snorts. 'She gives him money.'

'Oh.' Rachel remembers how the boy looks at her sometimes. She wants to feel sorry for him; she knows that back in London he'd be in and out of children's homes or on the streets. He is alone, and lonely teenagers must, of necessity, probe the limits of their power. 'He steals parcels from my mum. He eats the stuff she sends me. Why did you let him come with us today?'

'Why not? You came.' A pause. 'I thought I would be here alone. Then you wanted to see and I thought, okay, but not just you. You are too much for one person by yourself.'

Rachel is never sure if Zoya means to offend her. 'Well you know how to wind Lucas up,' she says. 'And I have to listen to him afterwards. So perhaps that makes us even.'

'Ah, Lucas!' Zoya lifts the spade and lets it rest across one shoulder. 'He runs around Kiev, looking for his stories, listening in the wrong places . . .' she stops, eyeing Rachel as if to gauge whether or not she has said too much.

Rachel is nodding her head, slowly. 'That's exactly what Vee says . . .' Her voice tails off. She hasn't thought of Vee or her husband all afternoon. Lucas's longing for something better is a dead weight, dragging him under. She should have found a way to call him. She should have left him a note. Her flight would have arrived at Heathrow by now.

Somewhere through the trees, perhaps nearer the village, a bird screeches a warning.

'Vee is a magpie,' says Zoya.

'Magpies steal.'

'And this is what frightens you?'

Rachel blows a little soil out of Ivan's hair. Without his nappy his bottom is small and bony. He feels light, almost weightless, like a bird.

'I'm not frightened of Vee,' she says. 'But I should probably go back to Kiev.'

'Now?'

'Soon. After I've dipped Ivan's feet in the stream. His first paddle.'

'*Tak*,' murmurs Zoya, as Rachel sets off down the hill. 'At first I did not like you. Now I do.'

CHAPTER 25

ZOYA HAS BEEN driving for half an hour. Elena, sitting in the front with a bunch of cornflowers across her knees, snores gently, her chin bobbing against her chest. Stepan is sleeping, too, his head lolling against the dusty window as he sprawls on the back seat next to Rachel. His anorak lies discarded by his feet.

Rachel's arms ache from holding Ivan. Her left elbow is wedged between the seat and the door and the basket on her right is digging into her thigh. Elena actually managed to unearth some self-seeded carrots, thin and misshapen with feathery tops. Their smell is strong and earthy and Rachel's stomach rumbles. Boiled and mashed for Ivan or chopped into a soup – she could live on soup quite happily if she had to – a few onions, a little garlic, some potatoes, a pan on the stove, tipping scraps in, a pinch of pepper or some of Elena's homegrown herbs . . .

Ivan stirs and kicks his legs out. His thigh, Rachel notices, is marked with pinpricks of bright pink. Not ticks, though – ant bites. She licks a finger and dabs the raised skin as she remembers her mother once doing.

'Oy!' mutters Zoya, pressing on the brake in her careful, measured way, though they haven't yet reached the city.

Rachel peers around Zoya's headrest. There's a vehicle about fifty metres in front of them and it isn't moving; instead it straddles the single-lane road. It is a silver car, sleek and foreign. It looks out of place in the birch woods.

'Is it an accident?' she asks, squinting as the late afternoon sunlight glances off the bonnet.

'Maybe the engine has overheated,' says Zoya, slowing the car to a stop while they are still some metres away. 'Or they have no fuel.' She eases the handbrake upwards, but she doesn't turn off the ignition.

Rachel shunts Ivan up against her left shoulder, wincing at the stabbing pins and needles in her hand. Cars don't run out of fuel at right angles to the road, she thinks. There are no other vehicles in sight. This block to their progress is deliberate, and it is probably the police because Lucas is always complaining about the cursory checks they make, the bribes they require. But the man stepping out of the trees doesn't look like a policeman. His hair is dark; he has sloping shoulders, a measured gait. She recognises him straight away.

'Mykola!'

'Mykola?' repeats Zoya, turning her head a little, as if she might have misheard. Stepan opens an eye, yawns and pushes his knees into the seat in front so that they leave dents in the vinyl. Elena stirs also, muttering something as she wakes. She covers her eyes with one hand and gathers the cornflower stems with the other. The skin on her knuckles is stretched thin like tracing paper as she clutches the stalks. Rachel remembers how she spat at the man who'd delivered Mykola's washing machine. She remembers Mykola's warnings. There is unfinished business between these two. Now he will see that she and Ivan are with Elena, out here in the woods, when he told her to stay away. Rachel's chest tightens. He has been waiting for them here.

Mykola skirts round the Zhiguli's bonnet.

'Lock the door,' instructs Zoya. 'I will deal with this.' But Rachel is too slow; Ivan is fully awake now, stamping his feet on her thighs. The door is already being opened.

'Hello Mykola,' she says, keeping her voice bright. 'Has your car broken down?' Zoya glares at her in the rear-view mirror.

Mykola peers in. He is wearing a white shirt, no jacket. His head is bare. 'Good afternoon, Rachel,' he says. He looks at Ivan before staring briefly at the other occupants. 'You have had a pleasant afternoon, I think. Please get out of the car.'

Rachel shifts Ivan onto her lap. 'Is there a problem?'

'Yes,' says Mykola.

'No,' says Zoya, with a warning pump on the accelerator. 'Stay where you are.'

Now there are two people telling Rachel what to do. Zoya sounds strained, furious. Mykola, on the other hand, remains impassive, his dark eyes upon her.

'These are bad people,' he says. 'The boy, I know him. I have no problem with him, if he keeps his mouth shut. But your driver, and *her* –' he pauses, raising his chin towards Elena, though his gaze doesn't shift. 'You must come back to Kiev with me.'

Insects buzz around the car outside, but inside there is silence. Stepan is examining a scab on his elbow while Elena just stares down at her lap, her grey hair sticking out and her shoulders hunched forward. She is still gripping the cornflowers, though their baby-blue heads are beginning to wilt.

'Zoya and Elena are my friends,' says Rachel, carefully. 'I'm not going anywhere with you. I don't need your

243

protection.' She wants to shut the door, but Mykola is in the way. He is patting the car roof with his right hand: one, two, three.

'All right,' he says. 'If you will not come with me, then I shall tell you about her because she is a mother, like you, and also nothing like you.'

This man is talking about mothers again, yet Elena and Zoya don't have children. Zoya won't catch Rachel's eye, so she glances across to Stepan and although he has turned away, staring out through the glass towards the woods, it is as if he holds her gaze in his reflection. His pale eyes are unreadable, unreachable.

'You think that Kiev is a hard place,' continues Mykola. 'You pity us for what you imagine we have endured. The women, you believe they have seen too much and that is why they shout and scold when you appear with your fine healthy baby. Yet *she* is not part of this story of yours. *She* is outside all of that and I can see that you won't ask why because you are afraid. Well, a mother should never be afraid. You will hear what I have to say. You will hear what she has done.'

Mykola has lowered his voice. It is as if he is telling them a story. Rachel wants to stop him, yet her own dread prevents her.

'Once, there was a woman who had a baby. She was unmarried, but that is how it goes sometimes. When the war came, she took up with a partisan who promised what he could not deliver. Then the fascists arrived. They pulled her lover out of the cellar where he hid and they marched him to a place outside the city to be shot. Well, the woman did not want to lose what she desired. So she pleaded with the soldiers to take her baby, to swap her baby for her lover. The guards laughed at her at first. Then they tossed her baby to her lover and while he held the infant they murdered him and he was the first to fall into the pit. The child was buried alive.'

When Mykola stops speaking Elena is still staring into her lap. Her lips are pushed forward and Rachel almost cries out as she sees what the old woman is really gripping amongst the flowers. A knife – the small paring knife from the hut – sharp enough for slicing through thick, fatty sausage. Zoya sees it too and reaches across, covering it with her own hand. An old woman holds a knife while a man tells a story no one asked to hear. Such things don't belong in Zoya's car and Rachel blinks too late to bury them, already grieving for what has been lost: the warmth by the stream, the picnic, the stroll up to the trees. What remains is impossible, unfathomable.

'This woman is a murderer,' says Mykola. 'I tell you this, Rachel, to keep your son safe.'

Safe.

The word is a lie, one that breaks Mykola's spell. With a sudden grunt, Zoya rams the gear stick into first. When she releases the handbrake, the car lurches forward so violently that Elena drops the knife and Ivan's head is thrown backwards. The door is hanging open and it clips Mykola's hand as Rachel leans out to yank it shut. She holds Ivan tight as the car skids across the potholes, spitting up stones from its wheels. The silver saloon is blocking their path but Zoya doesn't slow down and instead pulls the steering wheel to the left so that they swing cartoonishly across the verge, into the narrow gap between the car and the trees, crushing a small sapling as it catches on the bumper. When they finally regain the rutted concrete, Zoya is shouting and even Stepan is leaning forward, yelling 'Top Gun! Top Gun!'

Rachel, twisting her head, glimpses Mykola's white shirt and dark hair on the far side of his car.

'He's not following us,' she says.

Zoya leans over the steering wheel, her head almost touching the windscreen.

'Why would he? He knows where we live.'

The little Zhiguli shakes and rattles as it moves onto the dual carriageway. Zoya re-sets her mirror and wipes the perspiration from her neck, but she doesn't slow down until they reach the outer suburbs. The car makes a thudding sound on its right side, towards the rear. Zoya mutters under her breath, then brakes to a stop by the tramlines and leans over the back seat to open Stepan's door.

'*Ubiraysya otsuda!*' She spits out the words like a curse.

'*Nyet!*' cries Elena – the first word she has uttered since she climbed into the car. The two women start to gabble in Ukrainian. Zoya shakes off the old woman's hand.

'Stop arguing,' pleads Rachel. 'I don't understand! Tell me what's going on!'

'I am not moving until that boy gets out!' says Zoya. 'He is spying on us! Who do you think told that man where to find us, eh? He didn't need to go upstairs to fetch his coat!' She slumps down in her seat, the anger suddenly gone out of her. 'Elena still protects him. She says if I abandon Stepan, I abandon her, too . . .' Her hands fumble with her cigarettes. She lights one and sucks hard, her eyes flicking to Rachel via the driver's mirror as if she can't make up her mind what to say next. Sweat glistens in the creases above her nose and when she speaks again her

246

voice is low, hoarse. 'You know what I discovered when I tried to find out about that gangster? He looks at my hospital files, at my grandfather's files. He pays the doctors, he pays the typists, the officials, the boys like Stepan, then he calls me at my home and says I must be punished.'

'Why? What for?' Rachel looks at Stepan who is scratching his ribs, a smile twitching at the corner of his mouth. Stop it, she thinks, but he doesn't.

'Abortions!' says Zoya. 'Two – three – why not more? It is not a crime, the state allows, and why would I want a child to be born who was made in our poisonous air? But my grandfather – well, I tell you, that Mykola of yours is a liar, a disease. He says I am the one who killed him – my own grandfather! With black market morphine. He thinks he is a god – the one who decides, the one who passes sentence, but is he the one nursing his grandfather? Does he have to listen as an old man shrieks with pain in the night and shits himself in the only bed while his neighbours' children grow sick with cancer of the thyroid or cancer of the blood? Why does he think he must protect you? *You* – as if you are so innocent . . .' Zoya takes a deep breath, flicks ash out of the window. 'Do not believe him, Rachel. He wants to control you.'

Rachel cradles Ivan close to her chest. He is starting to cry, upset by the distraught voices, the car that isn't moving. She wants to get him home, to feed him and bathe him and rock him to sleep and then count her pages, except that she has buried her book amongst the tree roots in the woods.

'He is not *my* Mykola,' she murmurs. 'He can't control me. Please, let's go.'

Stepan shifts in his seat, his bare legs making a sticking sound against the plastic. 'You cannot go,' he says, to Rachel.

'There is broken tyre.' He shrugs. 'Maybe Zoya want to wait for Mykola to fix it?'

His provocation galvanises Zoya, who jumps out of the car, reaches in to the back seat and hauls the boy out on to the sticky tarmac by his t-shirt. He sits where she dumps him, pulling faces and complaining as she inspects the rear tyre then thumps her fist on the roof.

'Out! Out!' she shouts, waving her arm at Elena and Rachel. '*Bystra!* I cannot change the wheel while you sit there.'

Rachel struggles out of the car and rests Ivan on her hip. He is grizzling, leaning his head backwards so that she almost loses her balance. She can feel the heat from the road on her legs as she reaches into her bag for her son's hat. The tram stop is no more than a sign – there is no shelter, no tree, just a long, etiolated shadow cast by the concrete post. Zoya is muttering, rummaging in the boot for the jack and the wrench and the spare wheel as lorries behind her thunder past, creating blasts of dry wind. Elena, however, isn't moving. The flowers and the knife lie in a heap on the floor of the car, but she is staring straight ahead through the dusty windscreen, as if she is in shock.

'Elena,' murmurs Rachel, opening her door for her. She touches the old woman's arm and is taken aback by the feel of bone beneath the skin. No muscle, no fat. Mykola said she'd had a lover and a baby – that she'd watched them both die, or worse. He'd been speaking in English, so Elena can't have understood him, yet he has reached in and eviscerated her somehow, trailing her insides across the concrete – intimate, vulnerable, stinking. Rachel doesn't know whether to believe him, and because of this she feels ashamed.

Zoya stops what she is doing and leans in through the

driver's door to murmur something to Elena. 'Come here,' she says to Rachel, as Elena slowly swings out one leg and holds on to the door frame, refusing Rachel's hand. 'Elena must hold the baby. You and Stepan must help me take off the wheel.'

Certainly, fixing it will require them all to work together. Rachel hesitates for a moment before handing Ivan to Elena. Elena moves back from the verge, holding the child stiffly, not looking at him. It is as if she doesn't know him or is afraid to rest her eyes on him. Instead she peers off to the left in the direction from which they have come, while Zoya jacks up the car and puts the wrench in position. Stepan steps onto its jutting arm, gripping Rachel's shoulder for support, jigging up and down, his bare toes poking out of his plastic gym flip flops until the nuts loosen and Zoya can prise off the wheel and bolt on the spare.

By the time the damaged wheel has been stowed in the boot, all four of them are done in.

Zoya takes them back to Staronavodnitska Street. She drives carefully, silently, continually checking her rear-view mirror without moving her head. The sun has dipped behind the apartment block and in the shade the car park is gloomy. Stepan slips out before Zoya has turned off the engine and disappears behind the dump bins in the direction of the waste ground. Elena moves more slowly, pulling her cardigan around her before hobbling towards the steps.

Rachel hauls her suitcase out of the boot, too tired to do anything except drop it onto the tarmac. Nevertheless, she is reluctant to leave Zoya without some sort of reckoning.

'I am sorry . . .' She stops, seeing Zoya's scowl.

'*Sorry*? For what? This isn't your business. I have already told you so.' Zoya hooks out the pushchair and shuts the rear passenger door. 'You are a good mother, Rachel. Believe this, look after your little boy, but stay away from Elena, yes? Or Mykola will hurt her.'

Rachel sucks in a breath, remembering the knife and the way Elena gripped it. 'Why? Why would he do that?'

'Because he wants to control everything! What she did in the past, we don't know. You understand that, don't you? She cares for Ivan and she cares for Stepan, too, though I cannot think why when that little shit betrays her. I will stay with her tonight. You must go upstairs. Find Lucas.'

When Zoya dismisses her in this way she makes everything sound so simple. Mykola's words can't be unsaid, but he is too young; he couldn't have been present at the events he described. None of them can guess what torments Elena suffered. The war was a different time. A terrifying time. None of them has any right to judge.

Nevertheless, as Rachel lugs her case and Ivan's pushchair up the steps, as she waits for the lift, as she puts her key in the door of their apartment, she counts the floors, counts the walls, and though she has buried her book, she comforts herself with the fact that its pages are filed like an insurance policy in her head.

⁂

Lucas doesn't yell, or make a fuss, or even get up when Rachel parks their sleeping son's pushchair in the hallway. She finds him sprawled on the floor in the bedroom, curtains pulled against the early evening sun. He is lying on his side, blowing smoke rings under the bed, with the half-empty bottle of Vee's Christmas Stolichnaya near his ear.

'You didn't go then,' he says, tipping his head back to see her. 'I called your mum. She said you hadn't told her you were coming, so I phoned the airline and they said they couldn't tell me whether you had checked in.'

'I went to the country with Zoya.' Rachel looks at her husband, at his half-closed eyes and supine limbs stretched out on the parquet at her feet. He is blocking her path to the wardrobe. She wants to tell him to move, to stop smoking; she wants to feel his anger towards her for not catching her flight, yet his torpor makes her hesitate. Something has happened. She retreats to the kitchen to prepare Ivan's milk.

As the pipe coughs and the water spurts from the tap into the kettle she hears Lucas kick the wardrobe door.

'Rach,' he calls, his voice thin and hoarse. '*Rach!*'

'I'm here,' she says, turning off the tap.

'The film has been cancelled. Lukyanenko announced it this morning on the steps of the House of Artists. Then he set fire to the master reel. There won't be a premiere, or any distribution. Nothing at all.'

Rachel leaves the kettle in the sink. She wasn't expecting this. She steps back to the bedroom and stands in the doorway.

'Why?'

'Some politician said it was incendiary, an incitement, so no licences would be issued. Then the backers started pulling out. Vee knew it was going down the pan but she fucking lied to me. She's just published a piece in *The Washington Post*. She must have been working on it for a week or two at least. Maybe longer. Maybe from the start.' Lucas's voice rises like a child's. 'She's gone for the corruption angle. She even mentions me: "A naive English freelancer" like she's writing my epitaph . . .'

'Lucas . . .'

'She played me,' he says, groaning and rolling on to his back. 'Lukyanenko must have known. I can't stay here now. I can't work here. I need to get out. This place has been a disaster. I've not made any money, I've got no credentials, I'm sleeping on the sofa . . .' He twists his head to look up at her, but he is facing the wrong way and Rachel realises it must seem as if she is towering over him.

'Shh,' she says, stooping to pick up the vodka bottle. Lucas flails and grasps her wrist. His eyes struggle to focus, he stinks of cigarettes and alcohol and she recoils a little, yet he doesn't let go. Hold on then, she wills him. Hold on. He is hiding nothing from her, though the day has been full of betrayal: Vee, but also Stepan, and Mykola with his terrible words about Elena. Zoya has always insisted that Rachel and Lucas don't belong in this city, with these people. Lucas, on the other hand, knew Rachel before she became a mother. He had loved her when she was still a girl.

'Shhh,' she whispers, softer now. There is a kind of release in solace, in the comfort of the familiar, even if that comfort is more like the caress of a mother to her child. Lucas is willing, and soon he is eager. She is cautious at first, but then she unzips his trousers and holds him in her hand and she knows she could do anything at this moment – anything – and he would acquiesce. When she moves down to brush her lips against his skin, faces appear: Mykola in his white shirt, staring through the rear window; Zoya at the edge of the birch trees, watching her when she doesn't think Rachel can see her; Elena; Stepan; her mother; even Lucas himself, until finally she blinks away these spectres, blocks her ears to their voices and, for a few charged seconds, has no memory at all.

CHAPTER 26

T HE FIRST TIME Rachel kissed a boy, she felt the strangeness within her – her lips felt different, her tongue was not her own. She was changed by it, she thought. It wasn't like kissing a doll, or the mirror, or the back of her hand, even when she'd licked it. The first time she slept with Lucas, she felt different again. His stubble chafed her skin and he made her insides burn.

How many times can that happen, Rachel wonders. Once, or twice, or hundreds and thousands of times? You feel something, you remember the feeling and it becomes a story. Yet the story changes; all the time, it changes. The end, as it approaches, is never really the end.

$$\approx$$

Once Lucas is sober, once the wound of Vee's betrayal is found not to be fatal, he tells Rachel it makes sense to stay in Kiev until they have used up the year's rental on the apartment. It takes him a few days to recover his equilibrium, but money must be earned, there are news bulletins to file, political in-fighting to comment on and a spike in interest from British news desks about a burgeoning doomsday cult that is rumoured to be brainwashing children in the oblasts south of the city. Enough to keep a freelance journalist busy through the dog days of July and August.

Zoya no longer translates for Lucas, though she still drives them occasionally, when the mood takes her, when she's not working on her own stories or poking at the margins of Mykola Sirko's business affairs, trying to find a weak link or a disgruntled official who might slip her a lead. At night Zoya stays with Elena in the flat on the second floor and Rachel rarely sees the old caretaker any more. Indeed, Rachel has concluded that Elena is avoiding her. The thought troubles her as she does her laundry in the basement by herself, though she doesn't go looking for Elena. No more *Simplemente Maria*, no more biscuits or extravagantly mimed enquiries about whether Ivan is eating properly or sleeping well. Of course she would ask Elena in if she came knocking on the door, but Elena doesn't.

Lucas notices a change in his wife. When he brings up the subject of what they will do when they go back to London she doesn't give him the cold shoulder, but talks of playgroups and getting in touch with a couple of estate agents. He can barely recall the girl he once knew, or what he once saw within her – something hidden that stirred him and made him wonder. Motherhood has changed her, he decides. She seems more practical now that the difficult post-birth months are over. She tries new recipes – cooks proper meals rather than chewy pasta added to whatever she can find at the market. She visits Suzie to drink coffee and hear the latest about the house along the lane in Tsarskoye Selo, including how Rob wants to buy it outright from Elena before the refurbishment is complete.

At the end of July Lucas suggests they fly down to Yalta for a weekend. To the seaside, as he puts it – their first holiday as a family. It is easy to arrange. They stay in a sanatorium built for communist party chiefs. Beneath the modernist chandeliers white-uniformed staff trained in balneotherapy and calisthenics feed Ivan soupy *kasha* flavoured with cherries and guide his limbs into geometrical shapes. The sea reminds Lucas of Brighton, while the tunnel down to the beach is like a set-piece from *Dr No*. One night he and Rachel make love on the unforgiving mattress of the big walnut bed and it occurs to him that if his wife keeps her eyes closed it must be because she is taking pleasure for herself. He can give her that, he thinks. They can work on that. He pushes Vee out of his mind – it isn't hard, now that she's been offered a job in DC and has flown over to meet her new boss. Despite his set-backs, he feels lighter, more optimistic. He has applied for a job in Alma-Ata. Another starter post, but this one comes with a house and the prospect of some TV work at last. He won't tell Rachel just yet. The interview is at Bush House on the fifth of September. They'll leave for London three days before.

When Lucas takes Ivan and wades into the Black Sea Rachel picks up a pebble, smooth and grey: a souvenir for their son of a place he will never remember.

'Take a photograph!' Lucas shouts, exultant, as he dips Ivan's legs into the lapping waves.

Rachel clicks the shutter on her little Instamatic. She won't tell her husband that she has already blessed their son's feet in the stream at Zoya's grandfather's hut. She lets the foam splash over her bare toes and scrunches them into the shingle.

Back at the apartment block on Staronavodnitksa Street, Elena steps out of the lift. The doors clank shut behind her as she shuffles across the thirteenth floor landing, one hand gripping a brown Jiffy envelope, the other hand fumbling in her pocket. Her joints are stiff this evening. Her fingers won't respond as they should, but she manages to grasp the key Lucas gave her and push it into the lock.

As the door swings open, she pauses, catching her breath. No one is at home. Light from the living room window floods the hallway and she feels its warmth on her face. She should have made this journey before, but she couldn't face the young mother, Rachel. She couldn't face her own shame.

She slips off her shoes before making her way to the bedroom. The curtains are drawn; there is no air in the flat, but she won't stay for long. As she bends down, wincing, and rolls the drawer out from beneath the bed, a light brown cockroach flees beneath the wardrobe. The padded envelope looks odd amongst the nappies. It can't be helped. The drawer is the only place where that husband of Rachel's won't rummage.

As Elena leaves the flat, closing the door firmly behind her, a shadow passes in front of the window by the rubbish chute and blocks out the light. She peers, and flinches. A man stands in front of her. She knows this man, or thinks she does. This is the gangster who drives the silver car, the man who has threatened her, the man she would have stabbed if she could on the way back from Zoya's hut.

'Zdravstvuy, Mama.'

Sacred, dreadful words. Finally, everything she has hidden, everything she has buried is laid bare.

'Oleksandr?'

Her heart is absorbing every atom of her son. She lost him forty years ago, and now he is here. He has been here all along.

Her shoulders drop. She breathes out. She waits.

When Rachel was ten, her parents took her to Poppit Sands, at the mouth of the Teifi Estuary. Not for a holiday or anything – just a picnic and a swim. Her mother packed Shippam's beef paste sandwiches and a thermos of tea, both of which she stowed in a string bag along with Rachel's vest and knickers rolled up in an old bath towel. Rachel's father drove; it wasn't sunny, exactly, but watery shafts of light pointed down towards the bay like God's fingers and the beach swept round in a picture postcard curve, so that was all right.

The nearer you got to the water, the greyer it became. Rachel faced the sand dunes and inched in to the sea backwards. The wind whipped up the spray and she screamed when a wave crashed without warning across her shoulders. She could see her mother, sitting on Rachel's coat, watching her, lips pursed against the salt. Her father was busy in the hollows behind. She could only make out his top half, but she knew he was wriggling into his trunks in that special way beneath the towel.

Rachel's father dived clumsily through the surf. He wanted to teach her backstroke, but his touch was unfamiliar and she didn't like the way the waves broke over her face, so after a few minutes he left her to jump through the waves on her own. The water lifted her, pounded her, pushed her off her feet. She stayed in the sea for longer than was good for her. Her legs became numb. Her fingers turned blue. At lunchtime she ate her sandwich with chattering teeth.

Later, while her mother thumbed through her copy of *Good Housekeeping* and batted away the sandhoppers, Rachel followed her father up into the dunes. He hadn't changed out of his swimming trunks and he wore an aertex shirt that barely covered his thin haunches. His collar flopped open and his wet hair flopped down, which made him look different, like someone else's dad. He seemed different, too. He pointed and named things, he squatted and peered. She tried not to think about the bald patches on the bulge of his white calves and instead placed her feet in the hollows and landslides left by his salt-marked sandals.

Then, in a muffled incline, downwind of the beach, Rachel's father turned and said, 'Let's make a fire.' When he stooped to pick up a curved rib of driftwood and produced a box of matches from his breast pocket, she felt a tingle low down in her stomach. The smoke made her cough, the crackle of the dried marram grass made her jump but soon she was running about, searching for anything that would burn and feed the flames.

When Rachel's mother discovered them she put an end to the nascent conspiracy. Rachel was marched to a public toilet to shake the sand out of her knickers while her father kicked over the embers and jangled his keys. In the car park her feet were checked for tar. They didn't stop for ice creams; the traffic into Cardigan was already building.

All the way home, Rachel leaned her forehead against the window to cool her burning skin. She remembered the way her father lay down in the sand, frowning with concentration as he cupped his hands, then smiling at her as the fire took hold, his body shielding it from the wind's worst excesses. She remembered the way the flames licked and leaned, and she tried not to blink.

Six months later, Rachel's father was gone. This didn't surprise her. At Poppit Sands she'd learned that people could be more than one thing.

⁂

On their last morning in Yalta, while Rachel and Lucas are eating breakfast in the sanatorium's cavernous circular restaurant, Lucas is asked to take a call at the central reception desk.

It is Zoya.

'Elena is dead,' she says down the crackling, popping line. 'Please tell Rachel. This morning. Stepan found her.'

'Christ,' says Lucas. Then, 'What happened?' He readjusts his voice, aware that the young woman behind the desk is listening. He thinks Zoya might have waited until they got back to Kiev.

'A leak of some type in the apartment building. Down in the basement.'

'Was it gas?'

'It would seem so. The police have been there.'

'Christ.'

'Please tell Rachel. She will want to know.'

'Sure – leave it with me.'

It is only when Lucas has replaced the receiver that he thinks of all the things he should have said, like how sorry he is, and will the apartment block be safe, and who the hell is Stepan.

⁂

'That was Zoya,' says Lucas, when he rejoins Rachel at their table. 'Some bad news, I'm afraid.' He frowns, unsure how his wife will react. 'The old *dezhornaya* – Elena – has died.'

Rachel turns her head and looks out of the window, down past the tops of the ornamental yuccas and the oleander bushes of the formal courtyard gardens to the white marble paving below.

'Rachel?'

'How did it happen?' She turns her head back to her husband, her thoughts separating, re-grouping. 'Where was she found?'

'Basement,' says Lucas. 'Do you think she did it herself? Someone called Stepan discovered her.' He checks his watch. 'It's shocking news – I'm sorry. I know you'd become fond of her. Did she have any relatives?'

'I don't know,' replies Rachel, her voice far off, like an echo. Then she changes her mind. 'I heard she had a baby, but she lost it.'

❧

When Rachel and Lucas return to Staronavodnitska Street there is nothing to show that a death has occurred. The basement door is shut, as is the door to the flat where Elena had been staying. All that time, thinks Rachel, she'd been so fearful of a fall or a push or a chance letting go from the balcony on the thirteenth floor until Elena had shown her how foolish she'd been. Perhaps Elena had always known the threat came from somewhere else.

She doesn't find the package until the evening, as she puts Ivan to bed. It is tucked in the drawer between the nappies – a brown padded Jiffy bag, addressed to her in her mother's insistent scrawl. When she looks inside she finds a circular pot of face cream. The silver lid gleams as she takes it out.

Her mother has sent her a jar of Visibly Different. She sits down on the bed, rubs her thumb across the raised EA for Elizabeth Arden, then twists off the lid. It has been opened already; the surface bears the mark of someone else's finger, but it doesn't matter. The scent of her mother's skin rises until once again Rachel is a nine-year-old girl, standing in the bathroom doorway of the bungalow, watching her mother dab small dots along her cheekbones, pulling at the slack folds beneath her jawline, her lips drawn tight to keep the cream out of her mouth, those fierce eyes in the mirror, angry with ageing, with her daughter, with herself.

Rachel puts the jar down and studies the package's post-mark – the fifth of December. Her mother sent it in time for Christmas. There is no card to accompany the gift, nothing for Ivan or Lucas. While the three of them have been in Yalta it has arrived here amongst the nappies.

'Only for grown-ups,' Rachel's mother had scolded her.

Elena had a key. Lucas gave her a spare when Rachel was ill.

Truth flashes and shimmers like a fish in the reeds. Sometimes, if you're lucky, you may grasp it.

৵৫

'Mum,' says Rachel, when her mother answers the telephone.

'Rachel – is that you?'

Rachel catches the notes of an advert's upbeat jingle before her mother turns off the television. 'Yes Mum. It's Rachel. I'm coming home. On the third of September.'

'I see. You are sure, this time.' A pause. 'I'll have to make up the spare room . . .' Her mother's voice wavers with questions.

'I got the face cream, Mum. It was delayed – in the post. But I've got it now.'

The line pops softly like a bronchial chest.

'Well, it was meant for Christmas. The cold weather never did your skin any favours.'

'Thanks Mum.' Rachel, pressing the receiver to her ear, waits, and at last she hears the sigh that is not an ending, though it is a release.

'I'll make the bed up. And the cot – it's still up in the attic. For Ivan. We can put him in your old cot.'

⊰⊱

The next day Rachel carries Ivan downstairs on her hip and goes outside in search of Stepan. She can't find him at first, but eventually she spots him squatting in the long grass near the fence by the military academy. He is red-eyed, still dressed in the football shorts and grubby plastic flip flops he'd been wearing the last time she saw him. He doesn't move when she approaches.

'You found Elena in the basement,' she says, at a loss for a better way to begin.

Stepan looks down. He is scratching in the dirt with his finger.

'That must have been awful for you,' she adds.

Silence.

'Can you tell me what happened?' Ivan wriggles in Rachel's arms. She sets him down, feet on the ground and grips his hand to keep him steady. 'Stepan?'

Now she sees that Stepan's shoulders are heaving. He makes a high-pitched sound through clenched lips; he buries his head between his knees and his child-sized t-shirt rides up to reveal an inflamed patch of eczema across his ribs. His distress is so pitiful, so raw, that for the first time she aches to put her arms around him, this troubled youth who has no one to comfort him.

'Where is your – uncle?' she asks. 'That man you live with?' She reaches forward and rests her free hand lightly on his wrist.

'Not uncle,' he mutters, pulling back his arm and wiping the snot from his nostrils. 'You not my mum. Go leave. I don't know why Mykola think you special.'

'What?' Rachel has been worrying about how to raise the subject of Mykola. She isn't expecting Stepan to do it first.

Stepan makes a strange sound like a hiccup or a bark. 'Elena, she give me money, then Mykola, he give me more. But I tell you, Elena is better.' He rocks backwards, then knocks his head against his knees. 'She say you not special.'

Rachel squats down, still holding Ivan's hand. Stepan's words are muffled, difficult to hear, though she feels them like a stone thrown at her face. All the same, she knows what she must ask.

'Stepan, tell me, does Mykola know Elena has died? Was he there when it happened? I think he's got something to do with it. You heard them that day in the car . . .'

'You not my mum. Go your mum. Go away.'

Ivan, sensing an opportunity, lurches towards the boy, who has curled up like a woodlouse. There is dog mess everywhere, so Rachel reaches forward and scoops him onto her knee. Ivan arches his back, not wanting to be held. Rachel must rise to her feet if she is to keep her balance. She wills Stepan to look at her, but he won't move his head because there is a river between them, one she has never attempted to cross until now, when it is too late. After a minute of standing there with her son amongst the ragweed she retreats across the waste ground and returns to the apartment.

When she peers out of the kitchen window she thinks she can see him: a dot by the chain-link fence.

Half an hour later he is gone.

❧

'You have been sitting in the sun,' says Zoya, scrutinising Rachel across the little table in the café along Lesi Ukrainky where they meet. 'You should wear a hat, like Ivan. You will have brown spots. Skin cancer.'

Rachel rubs her nose and fishes the camomile teabag out of her waxed paper cup. Ivan is sitting on her lap testing his teeth on the cap of the plastic bottle of mineral water he is clutching. She called Zoya to see her one last time on her own – to say goodbye – but as always there is so much that remains unspoken.

'I like your sunglasses,' she says. 'Very Marilyn Monroe.'

Zoya, poker-faced, touches the shades perched on top of her head. 'So, will you stay with Lucas, or divorce? I think you will divorce.'

'Zoya!' Rachel tries to sound outraged, but what comes out is an uneasy laugh. 'Don't you ever hold back? Bite your tongue?'

'Often,' says Zoya. 'More than you know.'

Rachel sips her tea. It tastes of sticks. 'Well, you don't know everything. I can't think about the future in Kiev. I need to go home, let things settle. Then we will see.'

264

Zoya snorts. 'Oh yes. You will see. Already you know what you will see.'

'He needs me, I think. He wants to make plans. I never expected—'

'He needs you to know when to go.'

Rachel wonders if anyone else in the café can hear them. She glances around, but the café is nearly empty apart from a young woman sitting by herself at a table near the door, her arms folded, legs crossed, one foot pushing against the base of the table as if she has been waiting just a little too long. Rachel lowers her voice. 'Well, I didn't come to talk about Lucas and me. I want to ask you something. Will you keep an eye on Stepan? Look out for him, I mean.'

Now Zoya leans back and stares out of the window. 'That boy? He knows how to look out for himself, don't you think?'

Rachel follows her gaze, half expecting to see Stepan's face pressed against the glass, peering in from the pavement. Instead she sees a *kvas* truck with one wheel stuck in a pothole. It is blocking a lorry that is trying to turn left across the boulevard. A horn blares but the *kvas* truck won't shift. Cars are backing up.

'Elena really cared about him,' she says. 'And he cared about her. He's just a child. He needs someone to protect him. I should have helped—'

'So!' Zoya taps her packet of cigarettes on the table for emphasis. 'You feel guilty. Well, I don't. Stepan betrayed Elena. He will do anything for five dollars, or ten. He spied for Mykola Sirko, and,' she barely hesitates, 'I will tell you something now - something you need to know. Mykola was telling a lie when he told us what Elena had done - a very big lie. She was not a mother when the Germans invaded.

But later she did have a son – Oleksandr – born in 1952. She couldn't keep him – the father was a local Party boss who caused a problem for the high-ups in Moscow. Well, he was removed. Shot on the street one day not far from here. Probably Elena thought she would be next. Her family did not survive the famine and she had no one else. So Oleksandr grew up in a home for children whose parents are dead.'

'An orphanage.' Rachel, as if nodding might help her absorb what she is hearing.

'An orphanage, yes – across the river. They gave him a new name.'

'Mykola Sirko . . .'

'And when he was a young man Mykola traced his mother. He must have paid a bribe for the information or blackmailed an official, but he never told her who he was. Instead he taunted her. He left cruel messages and rented empty flats for his businesses right under her nose. Then you moved in to the apartment block. Well, Elena did not know what he was saying when he stopped us in the car, but I think he told you that lie to make you hate her.

'She didn't guess who he was?'

'I don't think so. He was registered at the orphanage when he was six weeks old.'

'That's terrible.' Rachel whispers the words. 'Do – do you think she killed herself?'

Zoya shrugs.

Rachel presses her free hand across her eyes, shutting off the tears that are forming beneath her lids. Elena's child did not die in those Nazi murder pits on the edge of the city. Mykola's lie had been unspeakably cruel.

'How did you find out?'

'Elena told me she had a child,' says Zoya. 'One afternoon while we were folding sheets. I think the burden was too much. So I started looking. It was difficult, but I know who to ask. And this man was following her. I made the connection that Elena could not. He left horrible things on her doorstep. He tied dogs together to make them bark all night, or paid Stepan to do it for him.'

'Stepan?'

'Stop repeating. Yes, Stepan. He does anything for money. He is spy!' Zoya makes a sour face. 'Well, I have Elena's rent money, she left it in a box under her bed, five thousand dollars, and you know what I am going to do with it? I am going to buy a lawyer who will dig up the crimes that Mykola Sirko has done. He does not deserve your pity, you understand?'

'Shh, Zoya, please . . .' Rachel sees a baby in her mind's eye, falling, falling. Maybe it is Mykola, or maybe another. She blinks. 'It is Stepan I wanted to talk to you about. Look after him. Elena loved him, like a grandson. We can't abandon him.'

Now there is a glint of triumph in Zoya's eye. 'But you can – you are disappearing! Poor little Snegurochka!'

Rachel's heart is thumping. She fights back the urge to count the cars, count the passers-by. In three days she will be on a plane. In four days she will visit her own mother, still the same daughter, now with different knowledge inside her. She takes a breath. 'Sometimes you say I have no business being here; then you say I am wrong to leave. Well, I didn't ask for things to happen, but there are consequences, they pile up even when I do nothing. And if I ask for your help, that's something, isn't it? It's not everything. I am leaving. But it's something.'

267

Zoya turns her head and looks out of the window. She is frowning, as usual, and in the glare of sunlight Rachel sees a woman who might be thirty, or fifty, with dark roots showing through her bleached yellow hair.

'I won't give him Elena's money,' says Zoya.

'That's not what I meant—'

'So you might as well know. Stepan is already sleeping at my flat. In my grandfather's bed.' Zoya covers her mouth with her hand, but her glistening eyes betray her. 'The little rat tells me it smells of piss. Ha! I tell him it is better than the other.'

CHAPTER 27

THE DAY BEFORE Lucas and Rachel are due to leave Kiev, Rachel goes for a walk. It is the first day of September, a Sunday. The summer has been hot and dry since the early rain in June; already the horse chestnut leaves are starting to curl at the edges. There is a tang in the air, almost acidic – a whisper of coolness. Ivan doesn't want to be in the pushchair, but it is after lunch and he will sleep soon – precious time she ought to use for packing. She isn't ready to leave, though. Not until she has taken one last stroll. The pavements and footpaths are woven through her now, their circuitous routes bound to her nerve-endings.

Rachel pauses at one of the new craft stalls outside the monastery. The table is laden with wooden toys, some brightly painted and gleaming in the afternoon sunshine. Others are plain, cheaper, the do-it-yourself variety of stacking dolls – one for papa, one for mama, one for baby, or two or three. She is tempted by a bell-shaped figure with intricate gold and blue patterns on its skirt that tinkles when she lifts it.

Ivan reaches forward, his sunhat tipping back from his head as he strains at the belt of his pushchair. His clothes are summer-thin and he isn't wearing shoes, so the woman behind the table scowls disapprovingly, but Rachel doesn't care. She asks the price of the toy, counts out the right money and when it is handed over she pops it into her bag. Another souvenir for her son, she thinks. He is too young to remember their walks, the things they've seen. It will keep him entertained on the plane.

She turns the corner and heads along Lavrska Street towards the top end of Tsarskoye Selo.

⁂

Mykola crosses himself three times as he emerges from the little church in the Lower Lavra and exits the monastery via a gate in the wall. His car is parked a short distance away near the bus stop; he prefers to approach and leave the monastery on foot, to spend a few minutes alone to consider his petitions to Our Lady of the Dormition. His bodyguard, loitering in the trees, flicks away his cigarette when he sees him, and Mykola tries not to show his irritation as he climbs the steps at the edge of the park. The practicalities are distasteful to him, but security has become a necessary evil. These days paying the hospital bills of the local police chief's daughter won't keep the snakes in the sewers. He knows someone has opened a file on him down at the Justice Ministry.

Today he has business to attend to, an appointment in town. The thought distracts him from more recent preoc-cupations: a certain breathlessness, an inability to sleep. His doctors tell him his heart is healthy, but in the church just now he had to put his hand on the wall to steady himself. He's a businessman, yet he also sees ghosts.

At the top of the hill, Lavrska Street is full of trucks and trolleybuses. It takes him a few seconds to adjust to the traffic, though he doesn't resent the pollution or the sense of organ-ised chaos around him: it is always good for cash-flow, for progress.

Then, just as his bodyguard opens the door of his silver Lexus, he notices a woman with a pushchair on the opposite side of the street.

He gestures to his man to wait for him at the car and walks south-east, in the direction of the river.

⚜

Ivan starts wailing as soon as Rachel turns into Panfilovstev Street. He wants to walk, his new obsession, but he likes to touch everything and there is broken glass amongst the weeds along the fences.

'Let's go to Elena's house,' Rachel murmurs, unwilling to return to the apartment just yet, and as she pushes her son down the rutted lane that dwindles between the cottages and the noise from the main road fades and the stones beneath the buggy's wheels crunch and pop, he sits up. Eyes wide, he grips the sides of his buggy like an infant prince to whom all things – the insects, the overhanging branches, the weeds in the potholes before him – are both fascinating and unworthy.

The house, when they stop in front of it, has been transformed. A triple-glazed veranda runs along the front, with white wicker furniture just visible beyond the toughened glass. The path to the front door is paved with marble and security lights stare, blankly, from their steel mountings beneath the eaves. To the right sits a brand-new garage, its door open, empty, a dark maw. Beyond it Rachel can see the tiled roof of the sauna. The workmen haven't quite finished yet; their tools and some bags of sand or cement lie beneath a tarpaulin.

The house itself is quiet. Deserted, even. The upstairs

271

shutters are closed. If Suzie were here, Rachel would be embarrassed to be found outside, uninvited, but the stillness convinces her that no one is home. Turning left, she pushes Ivan slowly alongside the old blue-painted picket fence that marks out the property's perimeter. The fence seems out of place now. Rachel recalls talk of a wall or something more secure, more private. She peers at the once-neat vegetable beds, already a tangle of bolting carrots and leeks, and wonders when these, too, will be concreted over.

Her gaze shifts towards the five or six fruit trees that huddle a few yards away in the lower part of the garden.

'Pears!' she says, unbuckling Ivan, lifting him up to her hip. Each fruit hangs from its branch like a gift, yellow and speckled, now waiting to be plucked and either gorged fresh from the tree or steamed, preserved or pickled. 'Apa!' repeats her son, kicking his legs and beaming. All that hoeing and weeding, pruning and thinning out, all those pots on the windowsill, those tiny black seeds. Elena would laugh at Ivan shouting at her fruit, but she never wasted food. She would want him to eat some.

A pear drops to the ground with a soft thump. Wasps bob and dip around the disturbance; the long, thin grass in the shade beneath the trees is littered with windfalls. Some of them are rotting already, the skin covered in brown circles and bruises, puckered and concave, with a dusting of velvety spores. Others look perfect, almost as if a careful hand has placed them there. They won't last long. The worms and the ants are already advancing.

Rachel hoists Ivan into the air and sets him down on the other side of the fence. Then, hitching up her gathered denim skirt and holding on to a post, she stands on the seat of the pushchair and swings a leg over. The seat slips from under her and she scrapes the inside of her knee before landing awkwardly next to Ivan. Now the pushchair lies on its side on the path, one wheel slowly spinning. She frowns, anxious for a moment, then remembers that of course they can leave by the gate. She turns and ducks beneath the branches of the nearest tree.

The first two windfalls she slips into the pockets of her skirt. Their warm weight knocks awkwardly against her thighs, yet the urge to take more is too great and with no bag to hand, Rachel tugs off her old cardigan and spreads it on the ground. Soon she has collected a small pile. The scent from the fruit is heady – not sharp and cidery, but dense and honeyish. Insects crawl over her hands – ants, mainly, and the odd wasp, though she isn't stung. When she shakes off the wasps they swoop drunkenly or lie on their backs and wave their antennae in the grass. She glances towards her son, who has grasped a fence post with one hand and is tugging at plantain heads with the other. No pear for him until they get back to the flat. The wasps will go straight for the sugar.

It is hot work, but Rachel gathers more than she needs. She ties the cardigan arms to make a bundle, then reemerges from the trees brushing a twig from her hair and looks up towards the house.

Still quiet.

No, not quiet.

A yelp to her right – a shriek of protest. Rachel turns to see a figure straightening up on the other side of the fence. A man in a suit is standing there; he is grasping Ivan beneath the armpits. Bare legs dangle in the sunshine. Mykola Sirko is taking her son.

'What are you doing?' she asks, bewildered. 'Give him to me.'

Mykola regards her with his dark, sad eyes. 'You should not be here. I will hold him. He knows me.'

A cry catches in Rachel's throat. She has dreamt about this man, she has looked for his face on a crowded street, she has recoiled from his inferences and his stories about Elena, and now Elena is dead.

Ivan isn't crying, though she sees how clumsily Mykola is clutching him. This Mykola seems different from the man she last saw on the road in the birch woods. His eyes flicker about. He is less steady on his feet.

'Give him to me,' she repeats. Ivan stops wriggling and stares at her, seeking clues. She steps towards the fence without taking her eyes off her son. *Stay calm*, she tells herself. *Don't frighten him.*

Mykola moves backwards, keeping two arms' lengths between them. He leans sideways and grasps the overturned pushchair with his spare hand, setting it upright.

'Be careful. There are wasps.' His voice is low, soft. He looks at Ivan as if wondering what to do with him.

Rachel's ribs press against the pickets. 'Ivan's thirsty. And hungry. I need to take him home.'

Mykola inclines his head. 'This is natural. But I cannot let you feed him anything the old whore has grown. You must leave the fruit.'

The old whore – he means his own mother. Rachel's heart is pounding. Ivan is wearing the little socks with the hens – the ones Elena bought him. She wants to feel her child's hot damp feet in her palms. She is breathless with the pull of him, the longing to draw him close. She remembers the cardigan she is gripping in her hand and drops it to the ground. Pears spill and tumble across the grass.

'I won't take them. I don't want them.'

Mykola doesn't react.

'Elena was kind to me,' she goes on, rushing her words. 'Whatever she did before, I know she regretted it. She helped me. To give you up like that – she must have been desperate. She must have thought she was keeping you safe – giving you the best chance.'

Mykola raises his free hand and rubs at the skin between his eyebrows. 'You are mistaken,' he murmurs, his gaze switching to the house. 'Your friends have told you some things. The past, you should know, holds many stories. I told you one myself. Nevertheless, a mother should never break her bond with her child.'

Ivan keeps twisting his head. A wasp buzzes near his shoulder.

'You're right,' says Rachel, willing it to stay away from her son. 'But when you have no choice, like Elena—'

'No!' Mykola's voice rises at the end of the word as if he is instructing a child. 'She had a choice. Always! Elena Vasilyevna's lover, my father, worked for the Kiev Regional Committee. His barren wife wanted a baby, so Elena agreed to exchange me for this.' He waves towards the house, then the fruit trees. 'Problem – the wife did not like me. Other problem – the NKVD did not like my father. Some minor disagreement, someone else after his position . . . He was shot in the head on Lavrska Street, where you walk. Outside the monastery! Well the monks took me in, but they could not keep me. Elena Vasilyevna knew, yet she chose to compound her crime. She did not take me back. Instead she locked her gate and tended her garden. Potatoes, onions, pears!' He is shaking his head, as if he still can't believe it. 'No one took her name off the papers, you see. So now it is mine and I will destroy it and burn all the trees.'

He starts walking towards the gate that leads to the house. He is pressing Ivan against his shoulder with one hand, while with the other he drags the pushchair behind him. Rachel follows, walking parallel with the fence: steady, steady, not shifting her gaze.

When they both reach the gate Ivan strains against Mykola's grasp and starts shouting in short, staccato bursts: '*Apa! Apa!*'

Rachel can't bear it any longer.

'*Please . . .*' She breathes the word out, willing it to touch this man; for him to show mercy.

Mykola parks the pushchair in the long grass and turns to observe her, his head tilting slightly.

'You are afraid, Rachel.'

'I want my baby.'

'Like a good mother. The mother I know you to be.' He rests his free hand on the latch and frowns. Then, with a soft, slow '*tak*' of resignation, he opens the gate and gives up the child.

Rachel, her body shaking, pulls Ivan into her arms, greedy for his weight as he wriggles, pressing her lips against his neck. She brushes past Mykola and takes a few hurried steps towards the lane before she sees the wasp on her son's thigh, but when she flicks it away it stings the back of her hand. The pain is instant and intense, like the anger that unexpectedly grips her.

She stops, looks back.

Mykola is still gazing towards the house, arms loose at his sides.

'She might have loved you,' she says. 'If she'd known who you were. You should have told her!'

'She did know – at the end.'

'How?' Rachel is almost shouting. 'Were you with her when she died?'

'She was leaving your flat.'

'And you followed her? You should have left her alone! So what if she visited? We gave her a key! She was returning something that belonged to me!'

'You did not listen to my warning. I have struggled to forgive you.'

In the silence that follows, in no more than a moment, the truth rises, clear and cold.

'You killed her,' murmurs Rachel.

Mykola's head drops; he won't look at her now. He is shrinking back into the depths of his abandonment.

'At the end she did not need me. Even for that.'

This is how Rachel will remember Mykola, his head turned away, his gaze fixed on the things she cannot see. But first she must make her way home.

As shock takes hold she stumbles as she half-runs along the lane. She still hasn't reached the turn in the road when a horn blares, short and sharp. Ivan's nails dig into her arm as he starts to wail. A black jeep sweeps in from Panfilovstev Street. The stones beneath its tyres make a cracking sound like cap guns.

The jeep fills the narrow lane. As it slows to a crawl and its chrome bumper inches level with her thigh the wing mirror snags an overhanging branch. Rachel shields Ivan's head with her stung hand and presses herself against the hedge that pokes through the fence to her left. The vehicle's windows are tinted; she can't see the driver, but the passenger window glides down and a woman removes her sunglasses.

'Hello! Where are you going?'

It is Suzie. Her eyes have a pinkish tinge; the skin beneath them is puffy and grey. Rachel shakes her head, too overcome to explain about her throbbing knuckles, about Mykola, about Ivan's distress.

'I came to pick windfalls. From your garden.'

'Oh – you should have called . . .'

Now Rachel sees Rob in the driving seat. His broad shoulders and square head fill the space beyond his wife.

'Sounds like trespassing,' he mutters sourly, his shades mirroring the sun's glare. He flicks off the air conditioning and leans forward over the steering wheel. 'Who the fuck is that on my driveway?'

Rachel looks at Suzie, at her strained face, at the elastic band peeping out from her sleeve. 'I'm sorry,' she says, apologising for the trouble that will come; trouble that it is too late to halt now. She must concentrate on the narrow gap that leads round the back of the jeep towards Panfilovstev Street beyond.

'Who *is* that?' persists Rob, thick thumbs pushing on the horn so that Rachel jumps and Ivan stiffens.

'Mykola Sirko,' she says, yanking her skirt free of the hedge

'Mykola Sirko – that cunt. I told him to stay out of my way . . .'

Ivan is struggling to get down. Rachel realises she has left the pushchair by the gate, but there's no going back. 'He's

Elena's son. Your new landlord!' she shouts, her hand pressing against the rear window as she clambers round the bumper. The street ahead curves away to the right. Its trajectory pulls her forward – her tired feet, her arms that ache and throb, but which now she knows are strong.

I *am leaving*, she thinks, and the two windfalls in her pockets bump like soft fists against her thighs.

⁂

Once Rachel has passed the old houses, once she has crossed the tramlines at the bend on Staronavodnitska Street and avoided the dogs idling beneath the rowans, she slows down and takes several deep breaths. The smell of warm concrete fills her nostrils, along with exhaust fumes and a hint of dry leaves. There is the apartment block ahead of her, its shadow stretching past the dump bins. Ivan has stopped crying, so she sets him on the pavement and lets him walk a little. His fingers grip hers as he struts and goose-steps across the car park. With every stride he seems more confident of the ground beneath his feet.

When they reach the entrance, she lifts him up and carries him through the heavy doors, nods quickly at the new *dezhornaya* peering out of her cubicle, then directs her son's hand so that he can summon the lift.

'Adeen, *dva, tre, chitirye*,' she counts, right up to thirteen, in a funny voice that makes him giggle.

Upstairs on the landing, in the open doorway of the apartment, she pauses. Lucas is out, packing up his equipment at the office, shredding old files. The rooms are silent; the ceiling is silent above her head. She closes the front door behind her and settles Ivan on the parquet before moving to the kitchen to bathe her hand. Only then does she slide the stolen pears from her skirt pockets, sniff their musty sweetness and take a knife out of the drawer to cut away the bruised flesh. She saves the pips in a saucer, thinking she might plant them by the fence on the waste ground or leave them on the windowsill for the birds. The rest she slices into slivers, pale and glistening with juice.

'Tea time, Ivan,' she murmurs as she carries the plate through to the living room and sets it on the sofa for her son.

The afternoons are growing shorter already. Soon the women spilling from the trams will dig out their winter hats, but for now the warmth lingers. Rachel stands at the balcony window long after the fruit has been eaten, listening to the slap of Ivan's bare feet as he cruises down the hallway. He will want his milk soon, she thinks, as she gazes at the trees and roofs of Tsarskoye Selo, as the sun draws itself over the back of the apartment blocks, as the silver ribbon of the river, the gold domes of the monastery and, finally, the glinting sword tip of the Motherland statue lose their lustre and sink into shadow.

ACKNOWLEDGEMENTS

I AM HUGELY indebted to many friends, colleagues, students and fellow writers.

My thanks to the Hyde Writers, whose early enthusiasm gave me the confidence to continue. I owe particular thanks to Richard Stillman and Paul Davies. Thanks also to the St James Taverners – I came late but you didn't mind. It is a privilege to share work with such fine novelists and poets.

I am eternally grateful to Carole Burns and to Claire Fuller for reading entire drafts, for constant encouragement and for pointing out the things I could not see. Thanks to Paul Ayling and Ruth Cruickshank, to Anne Booth and Virginia Moffatt and many other kind and brilliant friends.

My creative writing colleagues at the University of Winchester are the best – all of them. Thanks Julian Stannard, Nick Joseph, Mick Jardine, Stephen Thompson, Vanessa Harbour, Judy Waite, Mark Rutter, Glenn Fosbraey and Kass Boucher for wine and irreverent writing talk. Special thanks must go to Andrew Melrose and Amanda Boulter for their steadfast support via the Doctor of Creative Arts programme.

Without Paul Anderson, who has generously read the manuscript and made suggestions, I would never have travelled to Kiev. Heather Griffiths dug out her copy of Tim Burford's *Hiking Guide to Poland & Ukraine* and recalled sights I had nearly forgotten. Thank you both. My thanks also to Irina

Oxley and to Floradarya Rustamova who helped with some Russian vocabulary. Any errors are mine alone.

My most particular thanks go to wonderful Chris and Jen Hamilton-Emery at Salt and of course to Linda Bennett, my visionary editor. Linda not only took me on as a Salt author, she supplied me with Sour Cherry Patches at the exact moment I needed them.

Final thanks and huge love to my family: Patrick and Erica, Sarah and Jon and Jonathan and Anne along with my nieces and nephews; my dear mother Gill Heneghan, who travelled out to Kiev to make sure I was all right; my late father Michael Heneghan; and most especially my children Rory, Nellie, Jeremy and Meriel. Francesca too. Ice creams all round.

NEW FICTION FROM SALT

ELEANOR ANSTRUTHER
A Perfect Explanation (978-1-78463-164-2)

NEIL CAMPBELL
Lanyards (978-1-78463-170-3)

MARK CAREW
Magnus (978-1-78463-204-5)

ANDREW COWAN
Your Fault (978-1-78463-180-2)

AMANTHI HARRIS
Beautiful Place (978-1-78463-193-2)

S. A. HARRIS
Haverscroft (978-1-78463-200-7)

CHRISTINA JAMES
Chasing Hares (978-1-78463-189-5)

NEW FICTION FROM SALT

VESNA MAIN
Good Day? (978-1-78463-191-8)

SIMON OKOTIE
After Absalon (978-1-78463-166-6)

TREVOR MARK THOMAS
The Bothy (978-1-78463-160-4)

TIM VINE
The Electric Dwarf (978-1-78463-172-7)

MICHAEL WALTERS
The Complex (978-1-78463-162-8)

GUY WARE
The Faculty of Indifference (978-1-78463-176-5)

MEIKE ZIERVOGEL
Flotsam (978-1-78463-178-9)

This book has been typeset by
SALT PUBLISHING LIMITED
using Neacademia, a font designed by Sergei Egorov
for the Rosetta Type Foundry in the Czech Republic. It
is manufactured using Holmen Book Cream 70gsm, a
Forest Stewardship Council™ certified paper from the
Hallsta Paper Mill in Sweden. It was printed and bound
by Clays Limited in Bungay, Suffolk, Great Britain.

LONDON
GREAT BRITAIN
MMXIX